Shim

Dyllon L. Foster

About the author

Dyllon L Foster has always had a passion for writing. She spent the majority of her childhood reading as many books as she could, feeding her desire to write. Sadly, after losing her mother at a young age, she was forced to put her passion for reading aside and began working instead. Ten years later, she picked up her laptop and hasn't stopped typing since.

Contents

1. Eleven Years Old — 6
2. Helen — 20
3. Paul — 35
4. The Kiss — 47
5. Opening Up — 70
6. Progress — 95
7. Truth's out — 117
8. Betrayal — 141
9. The Stranger — 159
10. Confused — 172
11. Unexpected — 195
12. Wow — 215
13. Crush — 231
14. Lost — 248
15. Heartbreak — 265
16. Grief — 279
17. Moving On — 296
18. Looking Back — 309

One

Eleven Years Old

"I'm bleeding!" I scream frantically, ripping the last square of tissue off to try and somehow stop myself from bleeding to death. My vision is blurred from tears, and my shaking hands are making it difficult to actually see where the blood is coming from. I hunch over and peer down through my legs and into the toilet to find drops of bright, red, blood, dripping back into the water; staining it more with every drop. The tiny square of tissue that I have left instantly soaks through, leaving me with no choice, but to use my hand to try and apply pressure to it. What is happening to me?

The bleeding isn't what I'm used to; it's not pouring out of me like it usually does when I hurt myself. Instead, it's become slow and light; controlled almost. When I initially tried to wipe it off, it disappeared. Or at least I thought it did, but when I went back to check again, there was more light blood.

I managed to leave three gouts of it on mum's brand, new, grey tiled floor when I got out of the shower, before I realised that I was bleeding. It's only the bathroom floor, but mum is like a sniffer dog when it comes to these things; She is so fanatical about cleanliness, that she notices every, single speck of dirt or dust that isn't meant to be there. Even if I do try and wipe it off, she'll still probably be able to figure out that I'm bleeding and start to panic. The last thing I want to see before I die, is my mother crying and panicking over it.

"Open the door, sweetie," she says calmly from behind it. I didn't realise she had been listening the whole time. She pushes against the door slightly, causing me to sprint towards it to slam it shut again, while holding the towel up against my breasts. As if she hasn't seen me butt naked a million times before. If the bleeding doesn't stop, I'll have to consider using the towel, but that would have to be a very last minute decision. Funnily enough, the one day that I 'borrow' mum's white, expensive 'spa only' towel, is the one day that I end up randomly bleeding from my vagina.

"I can't," I sob back. The thought of her seeing me naked is embarrassing in itself, let alone showing her where the blood is coming from.

"Darling," she replies, lowering her voice. She seems less panicked than I thought she would have been. Perhaps, she didn't hear me when I screamed 'I'm bleeding'. "Let me in, so that I don't have to shout it out and have the whole house hear. I'm sure that's the last thing you want." With the entire family downstairs, she does have a point, but how is she so calm about all of this?

"But, can you just promise not to look?" I reply, sniffing. I don't really want to let her in, but if I want to give myself a chance of surviving, I guess I do need some help. I wrap the towel around my body tightly, and begin to unlock the door; peeping through the gap behind her to make sure that no one else is with her. Especially not my dad. The smell of Uncle Toby's cigarette smoke flows in through the bathroom window, making me feel a little nauseous. My senses feel heightened, especially my sense of smell; Uncle Toby has smoked my whole life, and it's never bothered me before. The bass from dad's new sound system, blaring house music out, feels like it's vibrating through my entire body, and the sound of everyone talking over it is deafening.

"Promise not to look where?" she says, bursting through the door the second she gets the chance. "Where is the blood coming from?" So, she did hear me. She locks the door behind her and stands in front of it protectively, as if anyone is going to be able to get through it once it's locked. Her mouth is slightly curved, almost as if she is trying to conceal a smile.

"From-" I can't even get the words out. I'm so embarrassed.

"It's okay, Wendy. I have a feeling I know what you are going to say, and if it is your period, it's nothing to be ashamed about, at all," she replies, smiling at me reassuringly. Except it's not reassuring me at all. "Point to it, if it makes you feel more comfortable." I begrudgingly point towards my vagina, squeezing my legs tightly together before looking down at the floor. I can't look at her. In fact, I'll probably never be able to look at her again after this.

"Please, don't tell dad."

"Oh, Wendy." Her beaming smile is becoming slightly disturbing, and if I'm honest, is making my blood boil. How can she still be so calm when her child feels like they're going to die? "It's natural, and something that all of us women have to go through," she says proudly, walking over to the bathroom cabinet. She takes out a small, duck egg coloured, box-shaped, package with an image of a very uncomfortable, skinny looking nappy on the front, and hands it to me. "Put one of these sanitary pads on and come downstairs to join the rest of us." She begins to make her way back towards the bathroom door.

"Pardon?" I shriek back in total shock. "Is that it? Mum!"

"Well," she replies frankly, standing by the doorway. "I have been telling you about your period for months, if not years. In fact, I've been mentioning it your whole life." She walks over to join me on the side of the bathtub. "You are bleeding because you've come on your first period, Wendy. It's all completely normal and nothing to worry about, at all. Put the pad on and come downstairs, okay?" Well no, actually. It's not okay. I thought I would have been given some notice that I was going to start my period. Surely, it can't be normal for it to just start like this?

"Will I bleed on my period forever?"

"No, darling. You have your period once a month. Remember, it's a natural part of womanhood."

"But, I don't want to be a woman, mum." My voice trembles as I try not to burst into tears at the thought of my body turning into a woman's, and giving me no control over it whatsoever. "I want to be a boy. A man, like dad." My chest tightens as my breathing becomes quick, sharp and more shallow. Pins and needles tingle across my forehead, hands and feet, causing me to feel dizzy and nauseous. The house feels like it has gone completely silent, aside from the dull ringing noise in my ears, and I've found myself fighting back tears, as the thought of turning into a real woman goes around and around in my head. I want to run away and never come back. I need to get away from this, I don't want to have a period. I think I would much rather have bled to death than have the bleeding be a result of my worst nightmare coming true.

Mum looks at me and smiles lovingly, as I struggle to catch my breath and stop myself from hyperventilating. She kneels down in front of me and grabs hold of both of my hands tightly. Her soft hands squeeze mine as she starts making large O's with her mouth, breathing unnecessarily loud, and encouraging me to copy her. "Wendy, listen to me. Take one deep breath in, let it out and then tell me five things you can see." She created a routine to help deal with my anxiety attacks, seeing as I'm unable to control when I have them. Apparently it's called 'grounding'. It's meant to be a very helpful technique to get you 'back in the room' and focused on what's going on around you. Dad thinks it's pathetic, but it does work.

"You," I reply, taking a deep breath in an effort to get the words out and get it over with. "Um. The sink, the bath. Err, a towel, m-m-my toothbrush." My voice fragile and quiet.

"Four things you can hear?"

"Dad. Err, Uncle Toby, Max and you."

"Three things you can smell?"

"Okay, mum. I'm fine now." I reply, forcing a crooked smile. I don't feel like smiling. I've tried to tell them a thousand times that I don't want to be a girl, but they just seem to ignore it every time I do. I even heard them whispering one time and mum said it's just a 'phase' that I'll grow out of. Surely, it can't be a phase if I still feel this way, can it?

"Wendy," mum says, getting up off her knees. "I really hate it when you say that you don't want to be a girl. Being a woman is the best thing in the world. We're so powerful." I hate it when she does this. I'm not denying that girls are great, what I'm saying is that I don't want to be one. "Are you going to be okay to come downstairs? Mr Robinson has brought his daughter with him today, so you guys can get to know each other. She's the same age as you."

My anxiety attacks have become so common that we all just carry on as normal once I've had one. Sometimes mum likes to have a talk afterwards, but with us having our family barbeque, she'll probably want to have the talk later on. The sanitary pad is uncomfortable and really feels as if it's not meant to be there. It is no different to an awkward nappy, wedged in between my legs. I've never felt more like a girl than I have in this moment. It's disgusting! I can hear dad's deep, adenoidal voice laughing and joking around as I make my way downstairs. Mum says he's like a big child when we have family get-togethers, and she normally ends up having to tell him off by the end of the day; she says he's had too much 'adult juice'.

"There she is!" dad yells proudly as I head out into the garden. "My pride and joy! I was just telling Mr Robinson about you being accepted into Hither Green Academy. One of the best secondary schools in London I might add." He rests one hand on my shoulder and stands next to me, smiling profusely. Dad and Mr Robinson have been in competition with each other for as long as I can remember. They work together and when they aren't working, they spend a lot of their time on What's App, talking about crap. Mr Robinson owns an estate agency chain and sells properties for and to some of the richest people in the country. Every month, our family or the Robinsons will host a get together, normally in one of the empty mansions the company have up for sale. It gives them the opportunity to invite potential clients over and have them look around the property. Well, that's what Mr Robinson says, whereas dad says it's all about pretending they're rich and potentially reaching more clients that way. Dad fought his way into Mr Robinson's good books, and now spends the majority of his life trying to be better than him in everything he does, including the family dinners we have. I mean, of course I can understand why dad wants to impress him, but to do it every waking minute of the day is a little cringing if you ask me.

"That's great news, Wendy," Mr Robinson replies with a snarky look on his face. "You'll be joining Tianna. She was accepted last year, based on her grades back then. She was the only student to be accepted at such a young age," he gloats, scanning the room behind dad. "You haven't met Tianna yet, have you?"

"No, Mr Robinson. I haven't met her yet," I reply politely.

"Tianna!" he yells. He lets out a loud sigh, as he rolls his eyes and signals for her to come over from the couch. "Come and say hello to Wendy. She will be joining you in Hither Green Academy in September," he says, as what looks like a ginger bush on legs makes its way over from the living room. Her pale, tired looking face is covered in freckles, while her frizzy, fiery, red hair makes her body look petite underneath it. She pulls the sleeves of her hoodie over her pasty, bony knuckles and stares at the ground blankly. She looks so timid, I reckon all it would take is a 'BOO!' to make her burst into tears. "Well, say something then!" he demands. His eyes firmly fixed on her and his top lip rolled up in disgust.

"Hi," she mumbles. Her voice quiet and brittle. I feel sorry for her, and I don't even know why.

"Hey," I reply.

"That's great, now you two can be best buddies, eh, Wendy?" dad giggles, winking at me. "Why don't you two go and chill out? Wendy, you can show Tianna all the girly bits you have upstairs." Neither of us respond to that. All of the girly bits I have upstairs have all either been thrown in the bin, or hidden so far under my bed that no one will be able to find them. Mr Robinson gently pushes Tianna in my direction, giving me no choice, but to lead off away from the adults while they have 'their time'. She keeps her head faced downwards as I lead her through groups of people and towards the back of the garden, where we have a table and chairs cornered off. There's no way in hell I am bringing her upstairs to sit and pretend that I'm a girly girl.

"So, you're going to Hither Green, then?" I say shyly, looking around the garden in an effort to avoid eye contact with her.

No reply.

"Dad says it's a really good school. Should be good to make some new friends and stuff."

No reply. If this isn't awkward, I don't know what is.

"So, what grades did you get last year, then?"

Still no reply. I'm trying here.

She speed walks ahead of me and rushes over to sit down on a chair behind the hedge that separates the two halves of our garden, making me stop and consider turning back. She doesn't have to talk to me if she doesn't want to, besides, I didn't particularly want to talk to her in the first place, anyway. I'd rather sit in my room on my own, than chill out in my garden in silence, with a total stranger, that has quite literally sped as far away from me as she can. I'm sure I heard her say "come" from ahead of me, but I can't be certain whether I imagined it with how quiet it was, especially against the sound of dad's music and everyone talking over one another. She disappears behind the hedge and leaves me standing there, staring at it, uncertain on whether it's a good idea to actually be left alone with her.

"Can you help me?" she yells from behind the hedge. "I need to find some sticks."

"Huh?" I reply, walking around to join her in the sectioned off area. "Why do you need to find sticks?" She falls to her hands and knees and starts searching through the freshly cut grass with her bare hands. I wouldn't say you have to get on your hands and knees to find a stick in our garden. Anyone would be able to see one just standing up, normally. "Tianna, what are you doing?" Now I can see why her dad rolled his eyes like that. She's weird.

"I need to get away," she says, waving her hands around, sweating from her forehead. Her long, curly, red hair hanging over her face as she works herself up into a state. Her cheeks blush red as she fixes her wide, pleading eyes on mine. "If I can just build a tunnel of some sort, I'll be able to get away without them being able to see where I'm going. CCTV cameras won't be able to pick me up and the police won't find me. No one will, for that matter." She briefly smiles at the thought. "I really need to dig a hole that will get me out of here as fast as possible." It's hard to tell whether she is being serious. Her parents are super rich, she gets everything she wants and more, and her gran recently bought her a pony! What more could an eleven year old girl want in life? If they're not like me, that is. "Help me, please," she begs. I think she's being serious.

"I don't understand? I thought you were really happy." I quickly scan the garden behind me, to make sure there are no listening ears, and then make my way over to sit next to her. "You won't be able to make a tunnel, you know."

"I will, if you just help me," she replies, seemingly agitated. "You've only just met me, so you can't assume I'm happy, just because my parents are." True, but she still gets everything she wants in life.

"But, why are you so unhappy that you want to escape?"

"Because, every time I want to do something my dad says no, and I hate him!" She clenches her jaw and begins to grit her teeth, narrowing her eyebrows. "And my mum doesn't do anything about it, because she prefers 'the easy life'," she continues, holding two fingers up and doing bunny ear impressions with the top them.

"So, let me get this straight. You're running away because your dad said no?" Jeez, she is definitely a spoilt brat. If I ran away every time my dad said no, there would be no point in me coming home at all.

"No, you don't understand. He never lets me do anything I want to do, and he's mean!" she sobs back. "He's so mean."

"Okay, well if you dig a hole you're not going to get far and your parents will probably tell you off. Why don't you just come inside and create a plan that you can carry out some other time?" I'd also be grateful if she would carry out the plan somewhere else.

"No!" she yells, picking up a stick and viciously pointing it out towards my direction. "I am sick and tired of people telling me what I can and cannot do. If you're going to be one of them, just go away and leave me to plan my escape!" She edges closer to me, holding the stick out as if she plans on harming me with it. Her wide, lime-green eyes, cold and hard.

"Woah, look, I don't want any trouble," I reply, holding my hands up in the air to show her that I don't mean any harm. "I don't know what is going on with you, but I think I should go and call your mum, at least." I slowly begin to back away, keeping my arms held as far out as I can, so that if she runs up to attack me, I won't be as close as she thinks I am. My mind is screaming out for someone to come and interrupt before she does something dangerous with the stick. She's crazy.

"Tianna!" Mr Robinson whistles from the patio doorway. He must have been able to sense my distress or something, but whatever it is, he's probably just saved me from being murdered and buried in my own garden. Her body loosens up as she drops the stick and brushes her clothes down.

"Don't mention this to anyone, please," she whispers, her eyes now soft and weak.

Seven years later

Two

Helen

Jessie has made plans for the boys (and me) to spend the day at this giant arcade in the city. I've heard people talking about it, and I've seen photos online, but have never been lucky enough to go. We've spent months organising everything and strategically planning how we were going to impress our parents, so they all say yes to giving us money at the same time. I've spent the entire week remembering my p's and q's, bothering to tidy up after myself and bringing plates down from my room. All in the hope that it would have earned me enough money to be able to enjoy the day properly, without any restrictions. It paid off, as I was able to earn a whopping £30!

I met the boys in year eight in school, and as such, they know me as Wendy. None of them have ever questioned why I act and dress like a boy, or why I enjoy playing football so much, they all seem to just accept me as one of them. My time spent with them are the best times of my life. I don't have to pretend to be a completely different person, or remember to respond to my boy name – I can just be me. They don't call me Wendy, though, it's always 'dude' or 'mate' which works perfectly for me, as every time someone does call me Wendy, I cringe at the thought of having to respond, especially in front of random people. The arcade is set over six floors and has bright flashing lights, signs and funfair music coming from all directions. It's impossible to figure out what direction to go in first, and being lucky enough to visit the busiest part of London on a hot Saturday afternoon, means I get the pleasure of looking at the back of people's heads, as opposed to everything else ahead of me.

Cameron unknowingly wanders off towards the escalator, causing the rest of us to follow his lead. We head up towards the second floor, looking back down at all the machines in the arcade. There are hundreds, if not thousands of people here, all in their own worlds and so engrossed in their games; some of them queuing up behind others so that they can have a go on a particular game. Some counting their coins by the money changing machines, while others are walking around with their mouths open wide like we are. The stuffy, 'too many people in one place' type feeling is quickly replaced with a nice, cool breeze from a large, overhead, air conditioning system, covering the entire building. The escalator leads up towards a 'sports floor.' On the right are four basketball games lined up next to each other, with five basketballs in. Jessie looks over at me with his game face on. Without saying a word, we both bolt towards it, quicker than the speed of light; inserting £1 into the coin slot, and pressing the 'GO!' button simultaneously, so that we start at the exact same time. Our eyes light up as the basketballs are released and the game begins. The aim is to get as many balls through the hoop as you can within one minute. Whoever scores the highest, wins. Jessie gets really competitive when it comes to things like this, and every time he loses a game he moans for the rest of the day, which really ruins the whole group's mood. He's normally very good at basketball, though. His six foot frame gives him an advantage against my scrawny five foot six body.

"How do you do that every single time?" he moans, as the score board surprisingly screams 'WINNER!' at me.

"I don't know, Jess, maybe you just need a bit more practice before you're able to get up to my level," I tease back, knowing full well that I have no idea how I just won that game.

"Okay, how about table hockey?" he replies confidently, inserting another of his £1 coins into the machine, before I've had the chance to answer. I've only played table hockey a few times, and they've all been against Jake, so I've always won as he's five years younger than I am. When we spent time in the mini arcade at the bowling alley, dad said: *'it doesn't matter whether someone thinks they're better than you. Your job is to make sure that you call their bluff, and make them think it's the opposite way around. The minute they lose confidence, is when you can take all of the glory back'*. He was playing table hockey against mum and Jake at the time and made it look so easy.

"Go on, then, but if you lose, don't take it out on me!" I reply, winking and poking my tongue out as I do. This is about to be a very tense game. For both of us.

After a few minutes of serious concentration, and a few strategic moves to distract him, I was able to beat Jessie, causing him to walk off in a strop. He wanders off to a money machine near the escalator, and starts inserting 10ps in the hope that he wins more money back. Dad warned me to stay away from those games. *'If you are going to an arcade the last thing you want to do is gamble all of your money on a machine that will take it all. You'll be lucky if you get any of it back'*, he told me before I left this morning. Dad has always been very smart with the advice he gives me, and nothing he's said has turned out to be untrue. So, every time he tells me something, I listen very carefully. It's a bit different for mum, as she always seems to nag at me for one thing or another, but dad's advice is golden.

Cameron, James and Josh are on makeshift motorbikes. The motorbikes move from side to side with their bodies, to give off the impression that they are really in the game. The virtual reality aspect of it is pretty impressive. Cameron screams excitedly as his motorbike crashes into the wall and blows up, meaning he is out of the game. Meanwhile, James and Josh continue to play on.

"James quickly goes in for the kill," Josh commentates, trying to distract James. "He's silent. No one knows what he's thinking. He's being tactical," he continues, putting on a deep, husky voice in an effort to make James lose concentration. It'll never work. James is quiet and calculated. He doesn't normally talk until he has thought long and hard about what he is going to say back, and generally keeps himself to himself. "It's a very close call between the two J's. Is it really possible for James to win? Do we really think that could happen? Hey, Cam." he says from over his shoulder. "Did you know that James sent a naked selfie to his gran by accident?" He relaxes his stance on the motorbike as he waits for James' reaction. Josh is the complete opposite to James, and suffers from what I like to call 'word vomit' the majority of the time. He's got a bad habit of speaking out loud before he actually thinks of what he is going to say, and tends to offend people sometimes.

"Ha! You absolute idiot," James replies, keeping his eyes focused on the game as his motorbike quickly slides passed Josh's. "He's lying, Cameron. He just can't stand the thought of losing, again." The pair of them are like two pee's in a pod. Anyone would think they were twins just by looking at them. Their personalities are so opposite, that they perfectly balance each other out and can usually always be found joined at the hip. Wherever James goes, Josh is not far behind. Whenever Josh makes a bad decision or does something that could land him in trouble, James is there to give him advice. "He knows he'll have to drop 0.5% of his shares in the business if he does." They sell sweets from James' dad's shop to pupils in college, at break times. It's a good business, but they normally just end up spending all of their money on crap. Josh's 'get along with everyone' personality makes it easy for him to attract customers, while James' smart thinking allows them both to make a hefty profit. It is, of course, all undercover, and I always get the best discounts.

"You guys bet on your business? That's the stupidest thing I've heard all day." Cameron interrupts, scowling at them. His mum died when he was little, leaving his dad with four children to raise by himself. He always has the least money out of all of us, and looks at the rest of us to 'lend' him some when he runs out. We all feel for his situation and, don't get me wrong, none of us shy away from sharing what we have with him, but it gets to a point where 'lending' someone money you have slaved away all week for gets difficult, especially when you know that you will never see it back again.

"So, who fancies getting a bottle of vodka and heading to the park?" He says loudly, directing his question at Jessie, who isn't paying any attention to the rest of us at all. "Or, we should just all book flights out to Magaluf and have a Hangover style weekend. Who's in?" One of the things I love most about Cameron, is his adventurous personality and his eagerness to experience as much as he can. He always says that life is too short to miss out on anything, which I totally agree with, although Magaluf might be taking the 'You Only Live Once' approach a bit too far for me. Not a day goes by where Cameron doesn't try and organise some sort of crazy get away for the group. We've all given up on even responding to his suggestions anymore.

"Did you win anything, then?" I ask Jessie cheekily as I sneak up to find him turning his pockets inside out, looking for more coins to throw away. The look of pure fury on his face is priceless. He tries not to, but his bottom lip pops out slightly when he is sulking, and every time he tries to act normal, he makes it more obvious that he is furious.

"No, but I don't care, I was only playing that because I was bored," he lies, trying to suck his bottom lip back in. "Should we go and get something to eat?"

"Sure thing, you're the boss!" I wink back at him, it's easier just to be on his side rather than allow him to be in a strop for the rest of the afternoon. "What should we get?" The strong smell of onions frying on the hot dog stand outside, smells appealing. I think my mind is already made up, despite the fact that mum actually made me a few before I left the house this afternoon. We take a slow stroll back towards the exit, all of us talking over one another and not listening to a word we're all saying. Most of the time I'm with these guys, it's impossible to hear myself think, let alone get a word in.

"Shh." James holds his index finger over his pouted lips, gesturing for us to keep the noise down, before taking out his phone to call his parents and lie about already being on the way home. With us being eighteen now, you'd think everyone's parents would loosen up with the strictness a little, but James' parents don't seem to have got that memo. He's normally only allowed out for a maximum of four hours, before he has to call his parents and let them know he is on his way home. We all know the drill when it gets to the four-hour mark and how to avoid mentioning his name when he is on the phone to them. The aim of the lie is to prove to his parents that he has already left us, so if they hear that we're still there, it kind of defeats the purpose of the call. Luckily for him, though, there are so many people here that even if we had carried on making loads of noise, his parents probably wouldn't have noticed anyway.

"Twelve o'clock, but don't make it obvious," Jessie whispers, tapping Josh on the shoulder, turning his head to an awkward forty-five degree angle, and facing the direction I'm in. I think that was his attempt at not making anything obvious? I don't know, but if you are going to try and do something sneaky, I'm certain the worst thing you can do, is walk forwards with your head fixed sideways. Cameron, Josh and I immediately look in the direction Jessie pointed out, as obvious as we could possibly make it. Even though we all tried not to. "I still think the one with brown hair is bloody fit," he whispers, as a group of four girls walk towards us, laughing amongst themselves.

One of them stands out like a cow in a tutu. I recognise the shoulder-length, brown, wavy hair and maroon brown eyes as Helen's. I could probably spot her from a mile away. I met Helen as Paul when I was at a tennis match not long ago. We spent the whole day together when we met, and were laughing and joking around about everything. When it started to get late, we sat on the grass and watched the sun set. Her eyes turned into a ball of golden rays, circling a dark sun. The thin, black line around the circle of her pupils, made them look 3D as she glared at me. The smell of argon oil infused the air as the wind blew against her hair, and her soft, warm hands delicately stroked mine. Jessie tried to grab her attention as we were all settling down, but after brushing him off and choosing to spend the majority of her time with me, it became clear that she was into me. We hit it off straight away, and it was then that I knew she's the one; I just wasn't brave enough to ask if she wanted to go out sometime. I beat myself up over the fact that I didn't even ask for her number, so that I could have spoken to her again. But then again, getting with someone that knows me as Paul, when they live so close to home, is risky. Very risky. Anyway, I bought her an ice cream with my last £2, and remember having to beg the ice-cream man to smother it in sprinkles without charging me extra. I then had to beg him not to make it obvious that I had no money in front of Helen. She shared the ice-cream with me and playfully dabbed some on my nose, which turned into a massive roll-around. The end result? Let's just say, ants were lucky enough to enjoy the ice-cream instead. When I got home that evening, I promised myself that if I was ever lucky enough to see her again, I would ask her out on a date and well, I guess now is my opportunity. I just need to make sure she doesn't call me Paul in front of the boys.

"I still can't believe she's into you," Jessie huffs, as he watches Helen's eyes glisten when she spots me. "I really didn't see that one coming, no offence." None taken, because neither did I, but what is this, jealousy? From Jessie the womaniser? He puffs up his chest as he walks over to her, giving it the macho look, which I try (and fail terribly) to mimic, making myself look like an eejit before I've been able to say anything to her.

"So, are you enjoying that hot dog, then?" he asks Helen, staring at her with what we all call the 'Jessie glare', and raising one side of his mouth to reveal an attractive, cheeky looking grin.

"Yes, thank you very much," she replies, winking back at him playfully. She giggles and takes a bite out of her sausage while gazing at me. Her eyes soften as she stares deep into mine and chews slowly on her hot dog, seductively licking ketchup off her lip with her tongue. As normal, my body's initial reaction to something good, is to become nervous and awkward. Starting with the giant lump in my throat that I can't gulp down. Wendy and sexy don't work well together, so if she is looking for me to do something remotely similar back, she'll be waiting for quite a while. Paul is a little more confident, but Wendy is a problem right now.

It's difficult not to feel self-conscious with Jessie standing so close. He just has everything. The looks, the height, the clothes. His hair is always neatly shaven into a skin fade with a 1.5 on top. I've written down the exact style he gets so that when I'm able to cut my hair, I'll be able to look as good as he does. The slits in his bushy eyebrows weirdly compliment his hazel/green eyes, and his voice has broken into what seems like a woman whistle. It's kind of surprising that Helen hasn't fallen at his feet already. Normally Jessie doesn't have to do much to have a girl interested in him, but Helen has hardly paid him any attention. "Want some?" she asks, holding the rest of her hot dog out towards me.

"No, thank you. I had a few hot dogs before I left my house earlier on. I couldn't eat anymore if I tried!" That was a lie. That was a total lie. I'm actually starving. Being able to smell the onions frying from outside, see the actual hot dog itself, and having to watch her eat it, is difficult in itself. To then say no when I'm offered some. That's a different level of shy.

"You remember my friends, don't you, Mya, Lily and Casey?" She points towards Lily, who is linking arms with Casey, actively trying to avoid Cameron's awful chat up lines

"Yeah," I reply shyly, looking at Jessie in an effort to get him to p**s off so that I can get into Paul mode. He must have sensed my awkwardness as he casually puts his hands in his pockets and gives Mya the glare.

The boys' confidence in getting girls is something I can't seem to get my head around. How they strike up a conversation with girls they haven't met before, make them laugh and then walk away with their numbers is beyond me. Jessie pushes past Cameron and Lily. He straightens up his trousers, brushes his top down and squints as he smiles at Mya. I wish I had his confidence, his charm and his ability to talk to anyone, not even just girls. He has this ability to be able to just know exactly what to say and when to say it, without having to plan or think about anything. With me, however, I've spent every day thinking about what I'll do if I am lucky enough to see Helen again. I fanaticised about the jokes I'll make, how I'll act and what I'll do if I accidentally slip up and mention anything about me really being Wendy. The only problem is that now the moment has arrived, I'm completely speechless. I mean, how do you strike up a conversation with the perfect girl, when you know that you are not the person she thinks you are, and are in actual fact the total opposite?

"Did you get home late after the Tennis game?" I ask, clearing my throat, while trying to make it look like I'm a confident conversation starter. Thing is, I chivalrously walked her right up to her door and clearly remember the time being eight o'clock, but the only other thing I could think of, was to mention the hot dog again.

"You walked me to my door, silly! I should be asking you that."

"Oh, yeah, right. I totally forgot about that." Lying isn't my strong point.

"What are you up to tonight?" she asks. Completely taking me by surprise as that was about to be my next line.

"Um, nothing. I'll probably just go home and chill out. What about you?" I reply with my 'cool' voice on, trying not to sound too eager.

"Well." She takes a quick look around her shoulder and leans in closer to me, lowering her voice. "My parents are away for the weekend, so the girls were going to come over and watch a movie. You can come too if you like?" Her playful grin just screams confidence at me and because of it, I don't have to face the awkwardness of struggling to find the words to ask her out.

"Yeah, sounds good," I reply back excitedly. "I'll just double check that I have nothing planned, but whatever it is, I can't seem to remember it anyway, so clearly wasn't that important." I don't have anything planned, other than to sit on my laptop and talk to people I've never met in real life. I never have anything planned if I'm not out with the boys.

It's only now in this very moment that I've realised how very boring my life actually is.

"Do you want to give me your number and I'll give you a shout later on?" she prompts, holding her unlocked phone out towards me. I'm sure she is now trying to hint that I literally need to grow a pair and take the lead here.

"Yes!" I yell back excitedly with this mortifying shout that I do every time I get shy, while typing my number into her phone. She doesn't seem phased by my inability to just be normal and play it cool. Either that or she just hasn't noticed.

"What's this?" Jessie interrupts inquisitively, barging his way in between me and Helen. "A movie at yours later? Yeah, we'll be up for coming," he continues, winking back at Cameron who is still really struggling to chat Lily up.

It can't happen. Jessie can't come to Helen's. Neither can Cameron, Josh or even James for that matter. The person that I am around them, is the total opposite to the one I was when I met Helen. And although they're my closest friends, I've got this burning feeling that they just won't understand when I do try and tell them the truth. The last thing I want is for everything to get awkward, not now while I'm so close to getting the girl of my dreams. Without the boys there later, I'll be able to confidently act like Paul, without fear of watchful eyes judging me. I'll be able to put my arm around her, romantically lean in for a kiss, and then I'd have done what Jessie does by playing hard to get afterwards. With them there, the risk of them calling me a girl or addressing me as Wendy for the first time, is high. I can't ask them to lie for me, especially with Josh's word vomit, and the way Jessie and Cameron love winding each other and everyone else up about everything. If I let them see me acting all manly, lowering my voice and changing my behaviour slightly, chances are they'll never let me live it down. I don't even know if Helen would still be into me if she knows that I'm technically not Paul yet.

She sniggers quietly, completely ignoring Jessie again, I hadn't even noticed she'd managed to finish her hot dog already. "Great, well, once I know what time the girls are getting to mine, I'll send you a text with my address and a time."

Three
Paul

We have a rule at home where I have to say hello to everyone before I go 'storming upstairs' into my room. According to mum, the rule applies to everyone, but when she doesn't do it, it's okay.

Squeezing through our narrow hallway is difficult with Max's buggy in the way. The photo frames pinned up on the wall stand out so far away from it, that I can guarantee I will knock at least one down every time I walk through the hall way.

"Jesus, mum," I moan, struggling to fight past Max's changing bag, that I've just somehow managed to kick in the wrong direction.

"Hello to you too," she yells back from the kitchen. "Rather than moan about it, how about you help me out by tidying it all up for me? That would help me more than you just complaining."

"Should I put it all in the cupboard?"

"No, I'm going out once I've fed Max." So, I could have just carried on moaning about it. "Your father and I are going to Mr and Mrs Robinson's house later on. Do you want me to invite Tianna over to keep you company?" I still haven't told my parents about what happened the last time I spoke to her. I kind of tried to ignore it all, and just keep my distance from her as much as I could. It's worked so far, as I've gone seven years without having to say a word to her. I just make sure that I volunteer to look after Max and watch Jake every time she's around. It leaves me no time to hang around and mingle. "It's okay," I reply, hurriedly making my way into the kitchen to make sure she isn't already on the phone to Mrs Robinson.

"I might go out to meet the boys later. I think Jessie is having a movie night." Every time I make a new female friend, mum gets excited. She thinks that by spending more time with girls, it will bring out the more feminine side to me, and will turn me into the daughter she desperately wants me to be. If I tell her I'm off to spend the evening with Helen and three other girls, she'll just go way over the top with the questions and will interfere way more than she needs to. I'd rather not have to remind her that I'm never going to be the girly girl she wants me to be. I can't have that discussion right before I go to Helen's. I've got to make sure my head is clear and I'm able to stop everything from coming out.

"But, Anne said that Jessie is off to watch a movie at someone else's house later?" She rests one of her hands on the kitchen side and squints as she scans every part of my face. She knows I'm lying.

"Okay, don't make a big fuss over it, but the movie is going to be at a friend's house."

"What friend?"

"A friend you don't know."

"Yeah, who?" "Helen."

"Helen? A girl?"

Here we go.

"Yes, mum. A girl."

"Wendy, that is fantas-"

"I know, mum," I interrupt, pathetically enthusiastic. "It's great, but I have to go and get in the shower, or I'm going to be late." The one thing I can count on with mum, is that the minute I mention female friends, she will do everything in her power to make sure nothing gets in the way of me spending time with them.

My laptop loads up as I flick my shoes off and kick them across my bedroom, before chucking my jumper into the pile of clothes next to the dirty laundry basket. The whole aim of the basket is for me to use it, but it makes it easier for mum to do the washing up if it is already in a pile waiting for her. It's a win-win situation for both of us.

My internet personality is the total opposite to how I am in real life. When I am online, I am able to be whoever I want, without fear of being judged or laughed at by anyone else. Everyone on our online group chat accepts me without asking any questions; I just fit in. I'm not confident enough to join in on group video chats, but with everything else, I feel free. I'm popular online. The freedom to be my true self means that I can just speak, knowing that I am just as normal as everyone else out there.

My friends are a small group of strangers from across the world. We've spoken about arranging a day where we all meet up somewhere in the middle – the only thing stopping us is of course, money, but the thought of it is exciting in itself. You hear stories of people finding their soul mates online. They end up getting married, having children and staying together for the rest of their lives, whereas with my group, we have all been able to find comfort in each other in some way or another. I do wonder if any of them are like me and what would happen if I told them about my situation, though. We've had deep, late night conversations where I have been tempted to own up to everything, but I have found so much comfort in my online identity, that I can't bear the thought of losing these guys.

My laptop slows down and crashes slightly as a result of the notifications popping up, one after another. Sometimes all I have to do is switch the laptop on and I come back to up to a hundred messages from them. There are thirty five today, but only three of them have been directed at me:

Olivia: Hey Paul! Haven't heard from you today. Did you get the chance to read through my blog? Let me know what you think! 4 hours ago

Henry: Hey man, how's your day going? Mine completely sucks being grounded. I've spent the day babysitting my sister. Kill me now! 2 hours ago

Stuart: Hello! Earth to Paul. Are you there?? 2 hours ago

We rarely talk privately, even if what we're saying relates to one person. I guess that's one thing I really like about our little group; we're all very open with our conversations and are very inclusive, once you're in on the group chat, you're in.

Me: 'Sorry guys, I've been out all day. Olivia, I haven't looked at your blog yet, but I will tomorrow – promise. Sorry to hear about your day, Henry, hope the rest of it wasn't as boring as the first part, and, yes, Stuart, I am alive! Been at an arcade with some of the boys from college all day. Hey, listen, can anyone help me out? I'm hooking up with this really hot girl tonight, and was wondering if anyone could give me advice on how to, you know, make a move on her.'

Asking a group of internet nerds for advice on how to successfully make a move on a hot girl probably isn't the best thing to do, but they must be able to help in some way.

Stuart: 'I can't really offer advice, as I'm no professional when it comes to women, but do a quick online search and have a scroll through some of the blogs, there are normally loads there.'

I begin typing 'How to kiss someone for the first time' into the search engine and the number of blogs and forums that pop up are mind-blowing. I've never thought about searching for random topics like this before, and am pleasantly surprised to know that people actually write about this stuff.

One that grabs my attention reads:

"The thought of kissing someone for the first time can be overwhelming, but it doesn't have to be; Here are a few tips for kissing that special someone for the very first time;

1 – Don't overthink it, normally when you kiss someone, you find a natural rhythm and there is nothing to worry about;

2 – Set the scene – you don't want anything to be rushed and you end up being rejected as a result. Try and wait until the right moment, when you know you are both ready;

3 – Once you have set the scene, lean in slowly, gently place your lips on theirs and find your rhythm;

4 – Give them a gentle kiss and then pull away a little, ensuring that they want to kiss you back. There is nothing worse than leaning in to kiss someone to end up facing rejection;

5 – Heat things up a little, by gently moving your tongue around their lips. You may even want to go so far as to gently run your tongue around the inside of their top lip;

6 -You'll find that you both develop a natural rhythm and do whatever works for you. Don't worry about not kissing the same way at first. Both parties naturally end up mimicking what the other does;

7 – Don't forget to NOT overthink and try not to get nervous if you don't find your rhythm straight away.

Good luck!

So, pretty much just lean in, kiss her and don't overthink. It seems way too straight forward to me, although the word 'rejected' has already made me start to overthink. I've always been nervous about asking her out, but that was more to do with not making a fool out of myself in the process. I haven't sat down and thought about what I would do if she turned around and told me she just wasn't interested, and I had been reading her signals the wrong way. Then again, surely she wouldn't have invited me over if she wasn't interested in me a little, right?

Me: 'Thanks Stuart. I've found a good blog that has advised on setting the scene etc, but does anyone know what I do with my hands? Sounds silly, but do I touch her, or keep my hands by my side and wait? Someone send help! I am seriously beginning to overthink this.'

Stuart: 'Ha! Just do what you feel is right. I'm sure you will know what to do when you are doing it. If you don't, she will. If she doesn't, then I guess you will have to explore the darker sides of the web for advice on what to do with your hands. If you know what I mean.'

Me: 'Eww, no thanks! I'll stick with doing what I feel is right. Anyway, I'll catch you later – going to get in the shower.

I don't even want to think about what Stuart does in his spare time after that comment, but it certainly isn't something I am interested in doing. Jessie would be able to give me a perfect answer, along with step-by-step instructions on that subject. It's a shame I can't just call him up and speak to him about it all.

I slump down on my bed and stare at the ceiling with my arms behind my head, thinking about what my future with Helen will be like. I can picture us with children and can see her walking down the aisle as she prepares to become my wife. My parents will adore her, and I can already see mum taking her out on shopping trips with Max, while I go to football matches with dad and Jake.

My mind begins to wander off into a world of its own, thinking about nothing but rainbows and sunshine, when my phone vibrates, bringing me back to earth again:

'Hey, it's Helen. This is my number. The girls are coming over at around 5pm. We're just going to do girly things until you guys come over. Should we say around 6/7? Can you let Jessie and the others know, as I don't have their numbers? X'

Me: 'Hey! Sure, I'll let them know. What's your address again? X' As if I'd forgotten. I know full well what her address is. I walked her right to her door.

Helen: '259 Rochester Wink Road. It's a ten-minute drive from Hither Green, near the woods.'

Me: 'That's it. See you later.'

Normally, when I have a shower, I analyse every part of me that I hate. The large gap in between my teeth, my bushy, afro hair and hideous looking genitals. The shower is the one place I can't seem to get away from looking at my disgusting excuse of a body. With mum's recent redecorating spree, she's replaced the grey tiles on the wall with fresh, white ones and propped a large mirror up next to the sink, directly opposite the shower. She has then polished them to such an overbearingly high standard that they instantly look like mini mirrors; meaning everywhere I turn there is something reflecting my image back to me.

My breasts began to grow rapidly when I was in primary school, and since I came on my period seven years ago, I've felt myself becoming more insecure every day. Whenever I had an anxiety attack about it, mum trying to reassure me by constantly reminding me that it's all a natural part of womanhood, really didn't help. That being said, being forced to stand in a mirrored room butt naked, does give me the chance to picture what I would look like with the body I'm meant to have. Holding the shower head up towards my vagina and picturing myself with a penis there instead, makes it feel realistic in a strange sort of way. I wouldn't know what to do with a penis, if I'm honest, but the one thing I've always wanted to do is stand up while urinating. The boys are able to just whack it out wherever and whenever if they are bursting, while I still have to hold it until I find somewhere I can pee in a 'lady-like' way.

This shower is a little different to all the others I've had. Instead of avoiding the sight of my naked body, I pay close attention to my flaws and everything I need to conceal before I get to Helen's. Through the steam of the shower I practice squinting my eyes, biting my bottom lip and then pouting them both forward in an effort to look sexy, before running my tongue around the perimeter of my top lip and holding my own gaze in the reflection. The thought of it is sexy, but I look like a freak and anyone would run a mile if they saw what I've just witnessed myself doing. Is that even what men do? Something about it seems like a woman thing. I won't do that. My big lips have a natural pout to them which I don't know if Helen will like or not, but I can't really do anything about that. Jessie does this thing with his eyes that makes girls instantly fall at his knees. He is able to glare at them, and gesture for them to come over and talk to him without having said a word, whereas the only thing I am good at is either yelling at Helen when I get shy, or going completely silent as I'm too afraid to say the wrong thing.

I've recently taught myself how to make my breasts appear non-existent, by wrapping cling film around them tightly. It works, but there have been a few times I have almost passed out through struggling to breathe properly. Cling film requires a lot of sitting upright or I risk causing burn marks on my skin from where it begins to stretch and rip off. Not to mention the fact that there have been days I've wrapped myself so tight, that I end up literally dripping wet with sweat. My dad has a bulge where his penis is, and I've learned that a pair of socks rolled up into a long sausage shaped roll, seems to give me the same look, especially when I am wearing skinny jeans. Mum gave me one of her old handbags thinking I would wear it out in public, but it's turned into my 'get ready' bag, and keeps all my cling film and 'willy socks' in. I normally have to hide it as far under my bed as possible, because if my mother found a bag full of cling film in my room, it'll be taken straight downstairs into the kitchen and I'll never see it again.

Four

The Kiss

Mya has obviously been in touch with Jessie and made him aware of the plan long before I was able to consider letting him come along. Of course, the womaniser was able to get her number. I don't know why I didn't automatically assume that would have been the first thing he did when he spoke to her. Josh hasn't been able to make it, so that's one down, but Cameron and Jessie together can be a lethal cocktail at the best of times.

"When was the last time we came around the Green bit?" Jessie asks, gazing out of the window as the bus approaches the woods, two stops away from Helen's house. The smell of burning, alongside the fresh, cold air and bright sun, brings back hundreds of memories of us growing up. Every summer, we'd go camping in the woods near Blackheath. Dad would normally want to take me and Jake there on a family trip before we went there for holiday camp.

"Together? Jeez, I have no idea, probably back in 2015, " I reply, following his eyes to a group of men, emptying their camping equipment out of a car.

"We should get everyone together and do it again soon, those days were the best, man," he says, infecting me with the over-excited grin on his face. We all fall into a calming silence, staring out the window at the view of the fields and the camping sites that had been set up.

"Hello," a soft, brittle voice whispers from behind me. It's Tianna.

"Hello," I reply back politely.

"So, I started my period since we last spoke." She smiles to reveal a set of crooked teeth. "It's so heavy."

Cameron lets out a loud cough, followed by sniggering laughter and whispering.

"Wow, that's great. Have a good day," I quickly stand up, nudging Jessie and forcing him up with me so that we can get off the bus and far away from her. Tianna watches me as I get off, hanging her head down low as if she is embarrassed that I've just got up and walked away. I mean, what was she expecting me to say to that? Do girls really sit there and talk about their period? Because I would rather never talk about mine again.

"Who the hell was that ginger girl?" Cameron asks, looking up at the top deck of the bus as it drives away. "She's creepy as hell."

"Believe it or not, but I've actually known her for ages. She's been in Hither Green Academy since we started, and now she's in the college part of it too." I pause and wait for them to think about it for a second. "She sits at the front in English." They look confused. None of them seem to have noticed her at all. "Anyway, forget her. Let's just focus on finding our way to Helen's without getting lost."

It's hard not to feel a little anxious as we approach Rochester Wink Road. I can't help, but feel like coming here was actually a really bad idea, and that not only will I regret it, I'll also lose Helen completely. I really should have stopped Jessie and Cameron from coming, but with Jessie having Mya's number, it would have been difficult to make up any excuses. The smart option would have been to just not go altogether, but if I leave them all there and fail to show up, the chances of them talking about me and my real identity coming out, are quite high. I need to be there to stop any of that happening, or at least to explain myself if it does.

"Are you okay?" Jessie asks curiously, as he pays close attention to the limp in my walk, as I prepare myself to make up an excuse for not being able to go anymore.

"Oh, yeah. I'm fine," I reply back hoarsely. "I just feel a little sick. I might leave tonight actually. Think I just need an early night." The realisation that tonight could be the night everything comes out is beginning to feel like it will be way too much for me to handle. I don't even think I want to explain myself anymore, I just don't want to be there.

"Dude, seriously?" Jessie barks. Standing still and grabbing hold of my arm to make me face him. "Three early nights this week, mate!" He holds three fingers up close to me, as if his point isn't already crystal clear. He changes his tone a little, forcing himself to be more casual, so that he can convince me to come. "Come on? Just see how it goes. If you still feel sick after a few hours, then leave." His eyes are pleading with me. "You're the only reason I've been able to get in there with Mya, I need you there." His puppy dog eyes force me into feeling like I have to go with him. It's now that I desperately want to pour my heart out to him and tell him everything, but I know that I can't, not right now anyway.

Helen's house is bigger than I remember it. The drive is large enough to fit two campervans and another house in. The double fronted brickwork is neatly decorated with plants that run around the doorway, giving off the impression that you are walking into an enchanted forest. Mr confident pushes past Cameron and I and takes the lead, embarrassingly holding his finger on the buzzer for four seconds. Part of me is glad that Jessie is here to take the lead on that front, but the other part wanted to man up and do it myself. My anxiety hits the roof over the most inconsequential things that small tasks such as ringing a doorbell can seem way too difficult at the best of times, so maybe Jessie taking the lead was a good thing after all.

  The first thing Helen lays eyes on when she opens the door is Jessie. I've already failed.

"Come on in!" she whispers, moving out of the doorway to allow us space to walk in. We all unintentionally stop in the hallway with our mouths wide open in awe, as we scan the house from top to bottom. The right ride side of the large hallway leads off into a huge dining room, with a table big enough to fit twelve people around. The left leads off into a cosy movie type room where Mya, Casey and Lily are slumped into bean bags on the floor. A spacious winding staircase separates the two. Both rooms are open plan which, although it looks great, will make it difficult to have some privacy with Helen.

She doesn't notice that I am the only one to have taken my shoes off and left them by the door, which is slightly disheartening, as I've never actually done that before. Jessie wades straight in, making space next to Mya and squeezing himself in between her and Casey, while Cameron makes himself comfy on the end next to Lily. Leaving me standing here like a wally, unsure on where to go. Helen doesn't seem to notice that I am waiting for her to sit down so that I can sit next to her. So, instead of making myself look as stupid as I feel, I take out my phone in an effort to pretend that I am quickly responding to an important text. After a few awkward seconds of typing out the alphabet and pretending to press send, Helen gets comfortable on the sofa, giving me the red light to go over and join her. The skill of pretending that I am doing something important on my phone, while actively avoiding people, is something I picked up from dad. *'Sometimes, I just can't be bothered to talk to everyone that I see. When you're older you'll understand that a bit better. It's easier to have your head in your phone, and pretend that you haven't seen them, than it is to strike up a conversation with someone you desperately want to avoid,'* he always says. Even though I actually do want to talk to Helen.

"How comes you two get to sit on the comfortable sofa and we're all on the floor?" Cameron moans. He better not comment on everything tonight, or I'll be in trouble.

"Because, this is my house, and these are my guests!" Helen giggles back, gently brushing her hand over my knee as she does, causing Cameron to look at me weirdly.

"What are we watching then?" Jessie interrupts, as he takes the remote out of Mya's hand with the naughty grin he always does. He is such a professional badass and has no idea that I am his biggest fan. "Something scary?"

"Yes, please!" everyone replies at once, all in sync with each other. Everyone but me. I'm not a fan of scary movies. I don't like them, and I can't help but feel like anyone that produces them should be locked away in a psychiatric hospital. I have seen around four scary movies in my entire life and every single one has traumatised me, to the point where I sleep with the light on for days afterwards, praying that nothing sneaks into my room to kill me.

"Do you want to turn the lights off?" Helen asks, looking directly at me.

"Yeah, sure," I reply shyly, standing up and doing what I've been told. The honest answer to that is no, I would rather not turn the lights off and watch a scary movie in total darkness, in a house large enough to hide thirty serial killers and their wives in, but if I am going to be a man, I guess I had better man up.

The room falls completely silent as everyone relaxes in their seats and passes popcorn around, but I seem to have lost my appetite. I can't focus on the film with my mind running through every single bad thing that could happen tonight. First there is the movie – I can never allow myself to get into scary movies due to my pathetic cowardly personality. Second is what, if anything, will happen with Helen and whether I will be able to just face my fears and make a move on her. Third is the thought of Jessie or Cameron calling me Wendy for the first time in front of Helen. Bad luck seems to happen to me during times where I desperately want everything to go perfectly, and this is one of those moments.

Jessie is holding hands with Mya, gently stroking her thumb with his before casually putting his arm around her. She cuddles in close to him, still holding onto his left hand as he begins to massage her shoulders with the tips of his fingers. I'll never understand how he makes it look so easy and it is beginning to make me seethe with jealousy. Cameron is stuffing popcorn into his mouth and looks over at Lily. He awkwardly attempts to put his arm around her too. She responds by peeling his arm off and dumping it back on his lap, refusing to engage in any eye contact with him whatsoever. I can feel my face blushing with embarrassment for him, as I remember the word 'rejection' on my useful article and imagine Helen's reaction if I have read the signals all wrong.

Cameron's cringe-worthy actions have made me realise that it is better to be safe than risk being rejected, especially in front of all of these people. It would be a different subject if it were just me and Helen. There isn't really anywhere we can go to get some privacy unless we went into her bedroom, but that would just be asking for Jessie and Cameron to ruin things. I can feel myself drifting off into a world of pessimistic thoughts again when BOOM! Everyone jumps. Helen tightly grabs hold of my hand, Mya clings onto Jessie and buries her head into his chest, Lily covers her face with the blanket she had wrapped around her and Casey buries her head into Lily's shoulder. Helen's strong grip on my hand gives me the perfect opportunity to put my arms around her, in an effort to provide her with some comfort. Her thick knuckles squeeze into mine a little tighter as she cuddles into me under my arm. If I could describe the perfect moment, it wouldn't be this. The sweat on my chest is causing the cling film to slowly slip off and shrivel up and makes it so that I have to sit in a really uncomfortable position. Anyone would think I didn't want Helen anywhere near me with the way I am sitting upright, but any movement in the wrong way can either cause the cling film to make that rustling sound, or come off completely and reveal my size 36D breasts. Maintaining a straight pose while cuddling someone on a very comfortable sofa is a lot harder than I thought it would be. My brain feels like it is on overload with different emotions; I'm proud of myself for taking the first step but deeply concerned about what my breasts are doing under the cling film I've tightly wrapped around them. Neither of us dare to look at each other and I can sense an awkwardness coming from both sides, although that could just be me.

As the movie finally comes to an end, the group begins to come back to life, shuffling around and readjusting their positioning after having sat down for so long. Lily uses this opportunity to create a barrier of cushions between her and Cameron and he responds by acting completely oblivious to it all. I must give it to him for acting like he's unaffected. Knowing me, I'd have burst into tears the minute she peeled my arm off her. Jessie doesn't know how to sit down for too long, so I'm not surprised when he gets up and starts wandering around the room, analysing all of the photos on the mantel piece.

"So, who's going to give me a tour around then? This place is massive," he indirectly asks Helen by looking directly at her, but making out like he is up for volunteers. Helen hasn't budged, though, giving off the impression that she doesn't want anyone snooping around her house. I can't help but feel envious every time Jessie talks to Helen, despite the fact that I am the one that she is interested in. I think it's just because I've seen Jessie get any girl he wants, and he's made it obvious that he fancies Helen. If it were a competition out of me and him, I wouldn't stand a chance.

"Come on, you nosey parker. I'll show you around," Mya giggles, picking her crisps up and bringing them with her as she guides Jessie out towards the winding staircase. Lily links arms with Casey and tugs at her to follow Jessie and Mya. She looks desperate to keep as far away from Cameron as possible, but he follows closely behind anyway. Poor guy, he can't seem to take the hint.

The room falls painfully quiet as it empties and the credits on the film end, making me feel apprehensive about my next move. I've spent the whole evening wishing I could have a moment alone with Helen, but now that I have it, I don't feel so confident. I'm struggling to even look at her. Whoever decorated her house would get on perfectly with my darling mother. The majority of the furniture is mirrored glass, including the impressively large chandelier centred in the middle of the two adjoining reception rooms. None of it has a single smudge or handprint, meaning we have another polish freak on our hands. Her parents must be loaded with money to be able to afford a place like this.

Helen's subtle elbow dig into my side brings my attention back to her, I hadn't noticed she was adjusting her positioning to face me full on; her wondrously lustrous eyes slightly squinted as she holds my gaze. Her confidence is terrifying, but bloody amazing all at the same time.

"What?" I ask with a cloggy throat, clearing it with an embarrassingly loud cough afterwards. I can't put my finger on the reason why I feel more shy than I ever have in my entire life. Normally, I'm able to at least have a conversation with people despite how I feel inside, but I can't help but feel like I've lost all confidence to say anything at the moment. It's almost as if I've had some sort of brain default.

"Oh, nothing." She looks down at her hands and begins to fiddle around with her fingers.

"Are you sure?" Normally I am quite bad at reading signs from women as I know nothing about dating them, but her sudden quietness and her not making eye contact doesn't seem like something she would do. She looks different to how I first remember her. Her lips are small and plump, and she has a small, faint birth mark in the middle of her chin. She has more freckles than I initially remember, with a few faint ones sitting on the bottom of her nose which makes her look cute.

"So, I take it you're not dating anyone then?" she asks rather forwardly. I don't know what to say. I could be honest and say no and tell her that I have never had a girlfriend in the eighteen years that I have been on this earth, but I run the risk of looking like a complete loser. Or I could lie and tell her that I've got loads of girls interested and make out like she's got some competition. "I mean, you don't have to tell me if you don't want to, it's none of my business really," she continues, looking at me fixedly and making me feel like I don't really have a choice.

"No, I'm not dating anyone. Are you?" That was a decent enough answer, it's not a lie, but it's as far away from the truth as it could have been.

"No, I haven't dated anyone in a while," she replies, smiling innocently. The fear of rejection has disappeared and the only thing I can hear, is the sound of my breathing as I feel myself longing for her. It feels like we've become the only two people in my world and I can already picture our future clearly. I can see us having children – two boys and one girl. They all have her big, chocolate brown eyes and mesmerising smile, as well as the cheeky, infectious laugh that she dos when she tells a not-so-funny joke. I can't seem to take my eyes of her. Point number three of my helpful article - '*lean in and just do the damn deed!*' My world feels like it has come to a standstill as I suddenly realise that this is THE moment.

There already is a hungry tension between us as I softly rest my hand against the side of her face, leaning in towards her, gently guiding her face towards mine and delicately pressing my lips onto hers. Her lips are softer than I could have imagined and her mouth is astoundingly warm. I can feel myself lusting for her as our passionate kiss becomes heavy and fast, causing us both to adjust our positioning so that we are directly facing each other. Her eyes are comfortably closed and her pointy nose makes it so that I have to turn my head at a slight angle. The tension between us feels like it is growing to an uncontrollable level, as I notice myself fighting the urge not to touch her in any inappropriate places. My helpful article was right in saying that I would naturally find a rhythm as I've now found myself kissing someone for the very first time, and somehow knowing exactly what to do. It feels like this was always meant to be, and I unknowingly find myself gripping onto her waist as the urge to touch her begins to overpower me. I don't recognise myself at the moment, but whoever this person is, I want to be him forever.

Helen responds by resting her hand on the side of my face and using her fingertips to gently make her way down to my neck. Her hands are soft, small and warm and the feeling of her touching me sends me into a trance. She uses the palm of her hand to rub up against my neck and then her nails to scratch back towards her. Something about the pain seems to drive my hormones crazy. If Paul were real, the evidence of this would be a lot more obvious to her, but I can feel exactly what is going on downstairs. She begins to slowly move her hands down towards my chest, causing me to snap back and abruptly pull away.

"Are you okay, Paul?" she can't call me that with Jessie and Cameron here.

"Yeah, I'm fine. I thought I was going to sneeze!" I lie to her, rubbing my nose in an effort to convince her that I still need to. I don't know what she was trying to do, but she can't touch me anywhere near my breasts, especially with the right one having slipped out of the cling film and flopping around on the loose.

Cameron must have telepathically heard my distress as I hear him stomping downstairs, still stuffing crisps into his mouth. The guy never stops eating. "You have got to come and see the house, it is massive!" he yells excitedly. "Wait until you see the size of the bathroom, it's unreal." Another bad habit that all of the boys seem to possess, is the inability to talk normally when someone is right next to them. Whenever one of them is excited, they yell loudly, when it's perfectly fine to talk at a normal level and still have everyone hear you. It must just be a boy thing as Jake does the same when he is excited, although I'm hardly one to talk with my nervous yell.

"Go on, then," I sigh, trying not to make it obvious that I will be eternally grateful for him saving my bacon the way he just did. Besides, I am quite interested in seeing the rest of the house. You know, just so that I can visualise what our future will look like in greater detail.

Cameron leads me up the winding staircase and on to what looks like a never ending landing with way too many closed doors on either side. How many people live in this place?

"She has like four spare rooms," he says, stopping in front of one of the doors. "I was thinking we could try and have a sleepover when her parents go away again." He gestures with his hands as if he is trying to explain something really complicated to me. He does that a lot when he talks, it's almost as if he can't stop moving his hands. I can't help but laugh under my breath at him thinking he will be coming back here. If Lily has anything to do with it, he won't be stepping another foot in the door again. He opens the door behind him and moves aside to allow me to walk into a giant room, bigger than anything I've seen. Just when I thought I couldn't be more impressed by Helen.

The bright pink walls in the room are a little overbearing, but what's on them is pretty impressive. A 'wall of trophies' sits over four shelves with various prizes, trophies and certificates on them. All with Helen's name and the position she completed each sport in. She has one for winning first prize in swimming 1000 meters when she was ten, another for winning a paintballing competition, and one from Hither Green Academy Girl's Football Club when they played against Hertsfield. I wouldn't have known she was so sporty if I hadn't seen her room. Her bed is an old fashioned, four poster bed with glittery curtains around the sides with a large plasma TV on the wall opposite. The wall behind it is decorated with impressive drawings, that I'm assuming she drew herself. All of them are drawings of a fairy, but they each seem to hold different meanings. In one of them, the fairy is sitting next to a waterfall on her own, smiling at herself; in one of the others, the fairy is situated amongst a crowd full of people, but has a sad looking expression on her face. One in particular that grabs my attention, is the only drawing where the main focus isn't the fairy. Instead, it's a drawing of a girl, crying and leaning against a wall. The tear drops increase in size as they reach the ground but in one of them is the fairy, and she looks like she has just been woken up. The drawings are so impressively detailed, yet I can barely draw a stick figure without making it look like an alien.

Helen pops her head around the door, probably in order to make sure we aren't up to no good. I'm certain Cameron has already had a snoop through her knicker drawer, but she doesn't need to worry about that where I am concerned.

"You guys okay?" She looks uncomfortable with us being in here.

"Did you draw all of these by yourself? They're amazing." I point towards the drawings of the fairy, trying to make her feel a little more comfortable with me being here, but also ready to leave if she asks me to. Unlike Cameron, I know when my presence isn't wanted.

"Yeah, I usually draw in my spare time," she smiles back proudly.

"What's this one about?" I can't help but ask about the drawing of the girl crying, despite the fact that it looks like I've probably touched on a sensitive subject.

"That's my favourite one. The girl is depressed and thinks that nothing in her life is going to change. The fairy with the light bulb symbolises the fact that there is usually light at the end of a dark tunnel. It is basically a reminder that whenever I feel sad, there are better days to come." She blushes, looking down at the floor and rolling her sleeves down past her hands. It's weird seeing Helen shy when I am so used to seeing her confident.

"I think it's really good. You're very talented." I'm not just saying that because I fancy her either, even though I most definitely would lie just to get in her good books.

"Where's the toilet?" Cameron asks. I completely forgot he was here, but without even giving Helen the chance to reply, he gets up and wanders out of the room, leaving me and Helen alone again.

The urge to grab her, hold her and kiss her is all too tempting, but I don't want to come across as too confident for my own good and subsequently scare her away. Then again, loads of girls seem to find Jessie's confidence attractive. Her cheeks are still red from blushing and I get the feeling that she has gone a little shy after discussing her drawing with me. I never thought Helen was the type to get shy easily. We have a lot more in common than I thought.

"I think you are beautiful, Helen." The words fall out of my mouth like Josh's word vomit, and I hadn't given myself a chance to put my manly voice on.

She looks away and smiles to herself. "I think you are pretty cool too, Paul. I like you." Still looking towards the window.

We both sit in silence, smiling to ourselves for a few moments. I find myself biting my bottom lip as I try and stop myself from smiling at her last comment. My heart is pounding with adrenaline and I can't stop myself from wanting to touch her. Before I know it, we are kissing intensely again. I run my hands through her hair as she holds onto my face, playfully scratching the sides of my cheeks with her short, sharp nails. Her hair is soft and smells like conditioner, weirdly making me lust for her even more. Without giving it a second thought, I pull her upwards to sit on my lap and rub my hands against her waist and up towards her breasts. I've surprised myself with my strength in doing so, but I guess adrenaline played a big part in that.

A million thoughts are running through my brain about what I want to do to her. Her small breasts sit perfectly in my hands and her nipples harden as I gently massage them from under her top. Her breathing has become heavier while her tongue wrestles with mine. I instantly feel like a completely different person to the one that walked in here. The shy, overthinker that I normally am, has disappeared and been replaced by a confident stallion, ready to explore everything right in this very moment. I slowly move my tongue from inside her mouth and start running it down her neck while gently sucking on it, causing her to moan quietly. Undoing her bra is easier than I thought it would be – probably because I have become used to it, but she helps by leaning forward and arching her back outwards.

Her perfect, small, mouth sized breasts are sat right in front of me making me feel hungrier with the urge to taste them. As my tongue wrestles with her nipples, her moaning becomes louder causing me to put one finger over her lips in an effort to get her to quieten down a bit. The last thing I want is for Jessie or Cameron to come bursting into the room and catch us. I feel like a professional badass. Just like Jessie. I want her completely naked and to make me do anything she wants me to do.

She moves backwards, aggressively lifting my head up to face her while she kisses down on me. Something about her asserting authority over me is wildly attractive.

"What's this?" she asks, pulling on my cling film. I hadn't even noticed what her hands were doing.

I pull back quicker than she has been able to finish her sentence. That's the second time I've allowed her to get close to me like that.

"Oh, that's just from an op I had a little while ago, nothing serious, and it's all good now." The guilt of lying to her is crushing as my hands heat up and the back of my neck sweats. I can't have her find out this way. When she does, it'll have to be a conversation we both have in private, with no one else around and when I can be certain that she won't hate me for it.

"An operation? What was that for? Are you okay?" She's so trusting that she hasn't even thought twice about probing me further. I feel awful.

"Yeah, I'm fine," I lie in response. "It was nothing big, just a small thing. We'll talk about that another day." I try and pull her in for a distraction kiss, but she pulls back and starts clipping her bra back on.

"Is everything okay?"

"Of course. I just don't want you to be hurt if you've just had surgery, that's all." She replies, as she kisses me on my forehead and stands up facing my direction.

A loud, unattractive, but recognisable car horn sounds from outside causing us both to sprint towards the window and peek through the blinds. I tried to race her to the window as I know exactly who it is. It is my mother, and she has had the cheek to turn up without letting me know she was on her way.

"That's my mum," I mutter through my teeth, completely humiliated. "I asked her to pick me up so I wouldn't have to get on the train late." It's best if I try and explain, before she gets the chance to ask me why my mother is picking me up like I am still a school-age child.

"That's really sweet that she has come to pick you up," Helen smiles back. "So, you have to go then?" Her prodigiously smooth skin reddens as her face blushes.

"I do. I'll text you?" I whisper back, gently kissing her on her forehead as I make my way towards the door.

"Hello, Mrs Cunningham!" Jessie shouts from one of the windows in the other room as I make my way out of the door and towards the car. I totally forgot he was here.

The gravel under my feet is making it difficult to walk off the way I'd want to, it's turned more into a hike than a cool, boyish stroll. For some reason, every time I smell that burning from the bonfires in the woods good things happen, and today was a bloody good day. I've bagged the girl of my dreams, haven't had to have the talk about me not being a real boy yet and left with more confidence than I've ever had.

"How was it, sweetie? Did you have a good time? What movie did you watch?" Mum asks enthusiastically as I get into the car and gently close the door.

"It was good, mum, thanks for picking me up. We watched a scary movie, but I didn't really pay too much attention to it."

"Well, I'm glad you still had a good evening. I left a plate of dinner in the oven for you if you're hungry. We had loads left today," I do love it when she leaves a plate of dinner out for me. Her cooking is something I find myself dreaming about sometimes.

"Thanks, mum."

"So, tell me about Helen then, what are her parents like? You never really told me what they do, sweetie?" Mum is a barrister, but her intrusive personality is something she was born with. She normally has to know every single detail about people I hang around with, especially their parents. She actually made a point of befriending Jessie's mum when she realised that we are best friends, just so that she could make sure he was suitable best friend material.

"I don't know what they do, mum. I only met Helen recently," I reply back bluntly, praying that she ends the conversation there. The last thing I want to do is give mum any information she doesn't need right now.

"I'm sure you'll get to know them soon enough," she replies, her freshly painted nails barely touching the steering wheel. "I'm just glad you are finally mingling with girls, Wendy, it's about time you started to make female friends." It's hard to get through to my darling mother sometimes. I mean, I don't have a problem with female friends, but I am closer with the boys. She knows this. "You spend all of your time with boys, but Helen should bring out the girly side of you soon enough."

Five

Opening up

Paul

I spent every waking moment thinking about Helen last night; the smell of the conditioner in her hair, the cute dimples on either side of her face and her soft hands as she stroked my face. I fought off the urge to text her until around three in the morning, when I just knew that sending her a text that early would definitely have made me look desperate. I've spent the best part of my young adult life watching Jessie and the way he confidently picks girls up, without having to put too much hard work in. I've analysed every single move he has made and how he behaves afterwards. My mental notepad and pen notes down the reactions he gets from it, in the hope that one day, I'll be able to use his skills, and have a girl fall in love with me, the way the rest of them do him. Every time I thought about contacting Helen last night, I thought 'what would Jessie do?' and reminded myself that it was best not to right away.

My laptop is beginning to take longer and longer to turn on than usual and it looks like I'll need another one sometime soon. I bought this one when I was in school, after saving all of my pocket money for six months. It is covered in stickers from where the previous owners let their three-year-old daughter decorate it. The bottom, right hand corner of the screen is slightly damaged as a result of her small fingers pressing against it, and it takes twenty minutes to load up and turn on, but it does the job perfectly once it's on. Downloading anything or updating the system normally takes around five hours, but I've gotten used to it all now. It works perfectly for me. It crashes slightly as it tries to keep up with all of the messages I have received overnight from my online gang. Which normally adds another ten minutes to the total time it takes for it to load. It doesn't seem to like my new online identity, but I don't care, because I love it.

Olivia: 'So, how did it go, buddy?' 23 hours ago

Henry: 'A hot date? How on earth did YOU manage to get a hot girl? And how did I manage to miss that conversation?! I need an update immediately!' 20 hours ago

Olivia: 'Hope your night went well. Have you read it yet?' 2 hours ago

Stuart: 'How did it go? You can message me privately if you don't want the others to know.' 10 minutes ago

Every time I promise to read through Olivia's blog, I have time to, but one thing comes up and it's like I don't have any time at all. I do want to read it, but I don't know if I will be able to commit to reading a new blog every week, I haven't even read last week's one.

Me: 'Sorry I haven't been online much guys. The past week has been pretty hectic. Last night was amazing. We kissed and a little bit more. We didn't go all of the way or anything, but things got very heated in a very short space of time and she told me she likes me. I'll aim to have a read through your blog today, Olivia.'

Henry: 'Okay, now I definitely need to know what happened. Tell me every, single detail. What do you mean you didn't go all the way, but "things got heated?" Spill.'

Me: 'A gentleman never tells Stuart. But I will say that I am 99.9% certain this is going somewhere. Hopefully, I'll be introducing her to you all soon!'

A gentleman never tells. How paradoxical is it of me to talk about how a gentleman behaves? I've never met nor seen one. My dad is more of a man's man than a gentleman and I don't see my uncles enough to be able to tell whether they have a gentleman's characteristics or not. Mum always talks about respecting people's privacy and I am a naturally private person anyway. Delving into the ins and outs of everything that happened isn't something I want to do, no matter how desperate I am to prove that I am as smooth as Jessie.

Henry: 'Wow, she must be something if you're refusing to tell us the gory details. Despite all of my teasing, I am happy for you, dude. It's about time one of us found a real-life relationship and stopped holding out for an online one!'

Stuart: 'Ha! You? A gentleman? Jeez, she has changed you already!! Happy for you though, mate.'

Wendy

Something feels different today. Thick, dark clouds have covered the country in dullness and my room shakes as thunder rumbles through the sky. Rain is on its way. The only difference to this one as opposed to all of the others, is that my life doesn't feel as gloomy as the weather when it's like this. I've woken up on such a high that anyone would think I had taken a cocktail of drugs. I guess in some ways you could say that the feeling of being in love is similar to that of being on drugs. The sound of pouring rain begins to slam against my bedroom window, making everything else sound quiet in comparison, and the house seem all the more cosy. It's always nice when you have a freshly cleaned room, fresh bed sheets and you can just chill out at home without having to worry about doing anything.

On the other hand, Jake's downstairs and it's raining – perfect recipe for some fun.

"Hi, big nose," I tease as I get downstairs, throwing a cushion at his head to get his attention away from his virtual world and back into the real one.

"I don't have a big nose, you do!" Jake teases back, pausing his game and taking off his headset. "Your head is so big that you have to step into your shirts in the morning!" He laughs to himself while diving off the sofa and swinging off my arm trying to start a fight. He knows full well that if he hurts himself I will get the blame for it, whether I actually have anything to do with it or not.

"Well, *your* head is so big that when it rains your shoulders stay dry," I reply, lifting him up and turning him upside down. He lets out a loud laugh causing me to quickly put him back down again before mum gives me a telling off for 'nearly killing the child.'

"Speaking of rain, do you want to go out for a bit? Get your wellies on," that was a sort of 'I'm not asking you I'm telling you' question, but he loves going out in the rain anyway.

Jake gets his crazy little personality from dad, who loves being outdoors and always has to be active. Dad used to set up camping sites in the front and back garden where we told each other ghost stories, toasted marshmallows on the barbeque and stayed up for hours. If we had been on our best behaviour, he would order a pizza and we would tuck into that and have the marshmallows for dessert. Summer times used to be fun. The sky was always clear, and we were able to faintly make out images from the stars if we really looked hard enough. Mum would pop out with hot chocolate and stay for a few minutes before going inside to enjoy her time in peace. The best times, however, were when it was pouring with rain. The sound of the rain hitting against our tent made it feel cosier inside. Dad had a battery powered lava lamp that he would bring out with us. He set everything up so that we were nice and warm for the night. He always somehow made it seem like we were a million miles away, when in reality, we were only a stone's throw away from the house.

"Yeah!" Jake screams back with excitement, shooting past me and running to the door to put his wellies and raincoat on. "Where are your wellies?" He looks disappointed.

"I don't have any wellies, Jake, my feet are too big for my old ones. I'll tell you what, though, when my feet get wet, I'll borrow yours. We can swap?" My attempts to cheer him up work and his smile beams from ear to ear at the thought of us swapping shoes for the day. It will never happen as his feet are half the size of mine, but the one thing I've learnt from having little brothers is never to ruin their imagination.

We burst straight out of the door and into the pouring rain with our matching yellow rain jackets on; Jake with his wellies and me with my trainers. Very bad idea, but they're all I have. The earthy smell coming from the wet soil on our front lawn makes it feel like we are back in the woods with dad. The road is completely empty, with the exception of the odd person running through it holding their jackets over their heads, while clinging onto an inside out umbrella for dear life. Everyone else is indoors, in the warmth and avoiding the rain, whereas Jake and I are out doing what we do best – getting messy! There is something about choosing to go out in the rain that makes me feel great. It's frustrating when I am on the way home from college, or trying to stay dry in other circumstances, but actually planning to go out and get wet always makes me feel oddly refreshed afterwards.

Jake jumps straight into the first puddle he sees without giving me any notice, drenching us both in rainwater before we've even reached the end of the road. His short curly hair has shrivelled up into a small afro while drops of water drip from it and onto his face. As we carry on through the park, Jake is somehow able to find some of the biggest puddles I've seen in a while. He's definitely done this recently with dad. The bigger the puddle, the more rainwater that goes into his wellies through the top, but he doesn't care. His adventurous personality makes him completely oblivious to it; he'll do anything that involves getting wet, or basically just coming home the complete opposite to how mum would want him to.

He looks a lot happier than I've seen him in a long while. His little face is glowing and he's more energised than normal. Saying that though, I haven't really spent much time with him recently, it could just be that he's excited to be spending some time with me.

"Can I ask you something, Wendy?" he asks. His firm grip on my hand tightens as his cheeks blush red.

"Sure you can, little man."

"Why do you dress like a boy?" He looks up at me with mildly curious eyes.

"What do you mean?" I know exactly what he means, but I would much rather not go into it and confuse the poor boy.

Asking someone to repeat the question does actually give you a few seconds to quickly think of something to say.

"Why don't you dress like mum?"

My mannerisms clearly haven't gone unnoticed and with Jake asking, mum and dad have also probably seen the difference too. I mean, I can't imagine him coming up with something like that by himself. He has me thinking for a few moments, about whether I should open up to him or not. Jake is innocent in the way he see's things and I can't imagine him reacting negatively. My only concern is whether he will tell his friends and they don't approve of my lifestyle choice. It would tear my heart in two if I knew that he was being bullied or teased as a direct result of what I am going through.

"I'll tell you what, I'll explain everything at dinner time when everyone is together. How does that sound?" I compromise.

My knee jerk reaction at Jake's question has me wondering whether now is the right time to sit them down and tell my family that what once thought was a 'phase', is actually my reality.

As we head back into the house and through the hallway, the smell of mum's mouth-watering chicken and mango curry fills the room, and makes our stomach's rumble simultaneously with hunger. Jake quickly kicks his shoes off any old way, before stripping down to his boxers in the hallway and dumping a pile of muddy, wet, clothes in my arms.

"Dirty whites straight in the washing machine and darks in the laundry basket please!" Mum says with her head practically inside the fridge. She forgets that we all already know the drill as we are reminded of it every day. Never try and help out by turning the washing machine on, even if it is full and the door won't close anymore. Just put the clothes in the machine, go upstairs to wash your hands and leave everything else to mum. For someone that wants me to be more independent and start preparing for adult life away from home, she really is making it difficult for me to actually grow up. Surely one step towards adulthood would be to do my own laundry? And that's just a small step. "Dinner will be ready in around fifteen minutes so both of you get changed and sort yourselves out."

Mum is a professional multitasker; she has Max perched on her hip, the hand she is using to hold him with is also shaking his bottle, and the other hand is preparing the rest of dinner. Three separate pots cooking on the stove, something in the oven, a baby on her hip and a phone resting in between her neck and shoulder. When we come back downstairs the table will be decorated to look all pretty, Max will be in his chair and everything on the stove will be off. She never looks like she is struggling, she just always gets on with it. If I was a real girl, I would be her biggest fan. She makes it look so easy.

My room feels warm and toasty after being outside in the cold rain. My fingers and toes have gone wrinkly and cold from where they were wet for so long, but the sound of hail stones smashing against my windowsill, and just knowing that I have somewhere warm to get out of the rain, makes it feel all the more perfect. I can't seem to stop myself from thinking about Helen every time I have a moment to myself, but I am so determined to get this right that rather than make myself look desperate by saying the wrong thing or texting her too much, I gain advice from my trusted friend that is the internet:

'If you are wondering how long you should wait before texting your crush after a date, here are a few pointers that we believe might help:

1) You like her. She likes you. You've already established that bit – what you don't want to do now is rush too much or leave it too long;
2) Don't worry about coming across as too forward, women love nothing more than a man that is confident enough to profess his undying love to his woman. However, bear in mind that if you are texting her constantly and not giving her enough time to breathe, she will most likely interpret your efforts as desperate;

> 3) *Don't text her if you've just left the date. Give it at least a day and let her know that you are thinking of her;*
> 4) *Don't talk about everything via text or a phone call – as tempting as it is to want to dive in and know everything about her straight away, it will make it hard for you to think of anything to talk about when you see each other. Meaning things could get awkward, and that's the last thing you want.*
> 5) *Try to get the conversation going slightly so that you don't have to worry about anything being awkward when you see each other. Remember, it's still very early days.*

So pretty much text her and don't talk about too much, but also don't talk about too little. Get the conversation flowing, but don't allow it to flow too much. That's not confusing at all.

"Wendy and Jake, dinner is ready!" Mum yells from downstairs.

The table is decorated to perfection, as usual. Mum normally likes to go for farmhouse style décor to match the rest of the kitchen, except on days where we have the extended family over. The cute little bouquet of Gypsophila sits next to a large, jam jar shaped pot with water and slices of lemon in. She's decorated the rim of the giant jam-jar water jug, with red and white laced ribbon. It all looks really lovely. I forget how much I used to love family time by the table. Mum always goes the extra mile and makes sure that dinner times are perfect for all of us. She used to always say that dinner time is where we talk about and forget any problems, so that we don't go to bed with anything on our minds. I used to think it was a waste of time, but it's now that I've grown up and have problems of my own, that I realise how important those moments were. I've hardly been around for dinner times lately and when I have, I've been in my room and not the slightest bit bothered about going downstairs. Dad flies through the door just before we all start to tuck in, his top button already undone and tie in his hand. He gently kisses mum on the cheek and heads straight to his seat.

"This looks amazing, honey, what is it all?" Dad's mouth literally watering as he eyes up the buffet style meal mum has laid out for us.

"I hope you're not putting dirty hands on my table darling," she replies, looking at him with that scary stare she normally gives me when she's about to go from zero to one hundred. "We have a mixture of everything today. Chicken and mango curry with rice, fried chicken and the oxtail left over from yesterday." She leans over and picks up a plate, handing it to him and reaching over for the curry.

"Well, it looks delicious," he replies, eyeing up the last bit of oxtail. "I'll be having all of it, do you want to order a take-away for yourself?" he teases, making them both burst into a silly laugh that only they do when one of them says something that really isn't funny.

Mum and dad are childhood sweethearts and have been together for twenty-five years. They were one of the first couples out of their friendship group to have a baby and became very young parents when mum accidentally fell pregnant with me. I was the product of a very happy, young relationship, where both parents were forced to grow up and enter into adulthood quicker than everyone else around them. Mum talks about having me sleep in a buggy while she worked throughout the day when I was very young. She went from working in a café, to a superstore and then onto waitressing while she was studying. She used to breast feed during breaks and would always get dirty looks from her male colleagues and an over exaggerated grin and thumbs up from her female colleagues. Both annoyed her just as much as the other, she hated the way the men in her office reacted to something that is just a natural part of life, but she hated that the women in the office felt it was necessary to go over board when they saw her breastfeeding. All she wanted was to have a normal conversation with someone and not feel like she was doing something unordinary.

Dad worked for Mr Robinson for what felt like forever, but put his law degree to good use and began teaching a couple of years ago. My parents shifts at the time meant that they didn't really see each other, and it was all out of their love for me, although mum reckons the distance is how they've been able to stay married for so long. They worked hard to put a roof over my head when I was a baby and worked even harder when they had Jake. We're all now living comfortably since Max joined us, and although the house is a tip and feels like it's not big enough, it works for us. Despite everything that they have been through, they have managed to stay stronger than ever, though. It could be dad's playful personality that refuses to take life too seriously, or mum's nurturing vibe that wants to look after everyone and everything that comes through the door. Whatever it is, they are the perfect pair.

"How was your day out with Wendy then, Jake?" Mum always asks him first as he suffered from an illness called 'lack of attention' when Max was born. He still occasionally struggles with it, but he's getting better. Lots of medicated 'attention' from both of my parents worked wonders. Not to mention the PlayStation 4.

"Good," Jake replies, slurping up his orange juice and using both hands to carefully put it back down again so that it doesn't spill in front of mum.

"How was yours, Wendy?" she asks, piling up a huge spoonful of vegetables onto my plate as she does.

"It was good, too," I reply, looking at her blankly in response to the vegetables.

Jake seems to have forgotten about our little deal, as he hasn't brought up the dressing like a boy conversation, meaning I can either forget about it and brush him off again until the next time he does ask, or I can just come out with it now while I have prepared myself for it. I like to think that they would understand and accept my choices, but I also remember when I had this conversation with them when I was little and they told me I was being ridiculous.

There have been mixed opinions on the forums I've read online. Some people say they wish they did it while they were younger, while others wish they had waited a little longer. Some have beautiful relationships with their families after opening up, and others don't talk to any of them at all. It is difficult to be able to tell what direction I will end up going down when I have spoken to my family about it, because they are normally confusing at the best of times. I'm certain that those who don't speak to their families anymore, probably expected them to accept it.

The lump in my throat makes it difficult to eat as I scan the room and watch everyone tucking into their dinner; Mum's funny faces as she feeds Max and dad's terrible table manners. Jake has a problem with drinking too much juice at the table and always "drops" his vegetables under the table without mum noticing.

"M-m-mum, dad," I say bravely, clearing my throat in an effort to look confident in what I am about to say.

"Yes," they both reply at the same time, making mum blush.

"I need to talk to you about something, but I need you to promise that you won't get mad?" I can't look at mum as I say that. Every time I ask her not to get mad, she gets angrier than she would have been if I hadn't said anything in the first place. Dad has a weak spot and normally tends to stay calm when I ask him not to get mad, but this is something far bigger than what he is imagining.

"What is it, sweetie?" Mum asks calmly, her cheeks blushing red and I can already tell she is preparing herself to hit the roof.

"Something is wrong that I need to talk to you about." I pause to look at both of their facial expressions. They're unreadable, but I suddenly feel like now isn't the right time. "Um. So, basically, I think I want to be a boy and I have done for ages." I pause again, waiting for one of them to get angry, but neither of them say a word. "I'm sure you have already realised, but I hate dressing like a girl, I have no interest in anything girly and I hate my body." Each word feels like a weight being lifted off my shoulders. "I've introduced myself as a boy to some people and it just feels so right, I feel like myself when I do. I know this might be hard to understand, but I think I am transgender." The weight has most definitely been lifted off my shoulders, but I don't feel any better for saying that. I suddenly feel really small and I can't bring myself to look my parents in their eyes.

Dad coughs, which turns into a slight choke and him having to turn away from the table to compose himself, while mum swallows her food and takes a sip of her water, before taking a deep breath and looking at me seriously. "What do you mean you want to be a boy, Wendy? You can't be a boy. You are a girl." She has the 'max voice' on and I can feel myself getting frustrated already with the patronising.

"Well, you know that time when I told you that I want to be a boy? It hasn't gone away, and it wasn't just a phase." I can feel my hands shaking and heart beat speed up, as the realisation that my parents probably aren't going to be able to accept it begins to sink in. "When I am Paul, I'm so happy it's almost like nothing else in the world matters," I plead with them, trying to get them to really understand what is going through my mind. "I don't feel insecure or uncomfortable. I don't look at myself and feel disgusted or anything, I'm just me, and I love being that person."

"Wait, Paul? Who is Paul?" Dad interrupts, I'd totally forgotten that I haven't really explained that I have already chosen my new name. He doesn't look happy at the thought of me mentioning a random boy's name.

"I'm Paul, Dad." I can feel my heart hammering against my chest and my hands begin to shake. I really haven't thought this through.

"What do you mean, you are Paul, Wendy? You're talking in riddles now just say what you are trying to say," he demands, his voice a little raised. The promise to keep calm beginning to wear off.

"Paul is who I think I was meant to be. I've spent years analysing why I feel the way I do and researching what is going on with me, and it is a lot more common than you might think. There is a term called transgender. That is what I think I am."

"Oh, for crying out loud." Dad sighs. "Wendy, you are not transgender. Don't be so ridiculous. You were born a girl, meaning you were always meant to be a girl. You can't just be a boy trapped inside a girl's body. It is impossible," he replies. He looks stern, cold and unwilling to open his mind to try and understand.

"No, guys, look. So, mum, when you were pregnant with my twin and I, you miscarried, right? I think the twin that died is the one who's body I am inside. It sounds completely crazy, but I strongly believe that is what happened. Did the hospital say anything about why you miscarried?" Their faces are so expressionless that it's hard to tell whether mum is about to punch me or hug me from across the table.

"That's enough, Wendy," Dad says loudly, making Jake stop slurping his juice and sit up straight. "You are a girl. You are eighteen years old and spend all of your time hanging out with boys, something which you have done for your whole life. It is clearly the reason you feel like you are meant to be a boy." He stops and glances over at mum, resting one hand on her shoulder supportively. "It is impossible for one of the twins to die and you end up as a transgender person as a result. That in itself is utter nonsense, so get that out of your head right now." Mum doesn't like to talk about the miscarriages and as much as it breaks my heart to see her hurt, I think it is something we all need to see as a potential reason for why I feel the way I do.

"Darling," mum says in a unexpectedly calm voice. "There is nothing wrong with being a woman." Oh, here we go, I wish I hadn't say anything now. "Women are so strong. We bring life into the world. We carry babies in our stomach for up to forty weeks, and then we nurture them until they are old enough to do so independently." Her voice changes from the patronising Max voice to a more persuading one. "We can cook, clean, work, listen to more than one person at a time and everything else we need to in one go. Can you imagine your dad being able to do half the things I do without having a mental breakdown?" She looks over at dad and cheekily grins and then quickly carries on before he gets a chance to speak. "We have hormones going wild and I totally understand that being a young adult is challenging at the least, but you don't want to be a boy, Wendy. You are just going through some changes." She doesn't understand at all – it has nothing to do with the 'challenges of being a young adult.'

"No, mum, you're not understanding," I snap back. Scratching the side of my hand with my nails as I try and fight my irritation at not being able to explain the way my mind is working. "I am meant to be a boy. I want my name to be Paul and I really want to go for surgery to change my gender. Something, somewhere has gone seriously wrong and I am trapped inside this disgusting body as a result. Everything online says that I am transgender and there are loads of people from around the world in the same situation as me. You wouldn't actually believe how many people there are." I can feel myself becoming excited as I quickly take my phone out of my pocket and begin scrolling through some of my saved forums, to show my parents everything I've learned about the LGBT+ community.

"I knew she shouldn't have been allowed a phone so early on, Nadia," dad hisses at mum. "What did I tell you? She was too young for it. All that rubbish on the internet has got to her head!" I've never seen him look at mum so angrily before.

"Don't blame me for this, Ben," mum growls back. "Maybe if you were around more often, she wouldn't be feeling like this. She probably feels like she needs to be a man to replace you and your absent backside! It's nothing to do with the internet, you don't see Charlotte's kids running around saying they want to be boys and they are on their phones every waking minute of the day!"

Oh boy, what have I caused?

"No, guys it's not-"

"But, this isn't about Charlotte's kids, though, Nadia. It's not about me either. If I didn't work, we wouldn't have half the stuff we have now. Wendy wouldn't even have that stupid phone if I didn't work because *you* wouldn't have been able to pay for it," he argues back bravely. Arguing with my mum is a very bold thing to do.

"Dad, it's nothing to do with the-"

"Oh, here we go! You can stuff your job because I would be fine without your money, Ben!"

"Mum, please."

"Yeah, let's see how many spa days you can treat yourself to without my money coming in." Dad laughs to himself. "It will suit me perfectly anyway, I'll stay at home with the kids and 'pretend to be rushed off my feet', while you go out and slave away for someone else all day, then come home to me moaning all the time." Wow. He really is brave today.

Seeing my parents argue for the first time feels kind of lonely, especially knowing that it is all my fault. I don't recognise either of them at the moment, they're normally so nice to each other. Jake has gone into his own world playing with Max, meaning if he is this comfortable with them arguing, this isn't the first time something like this has happened in front of him.

"Well, if neither of you want to listen, there is no point in me trying," I hiss at the pair of them. They're so engrossed in their argument that neither of them notice me storming out of the kitchen and slamming my bedroom door upstairs. If there's one thing mum hates most, it's slamming doors unnecessarily. If she had noticed me slamming my door, the whole house would know about it. My heart sinks at the thought of being trapped inside this body and stuck in a world when my family and friends don't understand. As I slouch down into my bed, with my legs hanging off the side, my phone vibrates from my pocket.

Helen: 'Hey. How are things with you?'

I feel a little guilty that I've left it so late and she has been forced to text me first instead.

Me: 'Hey. Sorry you haven't heard from me. I've been super busy. I've only just found the time to sit down.'

That's a lie.

Helen: 'Oh, it's fine. To be honest I've been really busy too. I probably wouldn't have been able to respond to you earlier. What have you been up to then?'

Well, I wasn't expecting her to ask me that.

Me: 'What haven't I been up to? It feels like I have done everything lately. What have you done?'

I'm praying she doesn't push the matter more. All I've done today is take Jake out in the rain and eat dinner with my family. It's the most I've actually done in years and I do technically feel quite exhausted from it, but I can hardly let her know I am as lazy as I am.

Helen: 'I don't think my day was as busy as yours. I've just helped my sister prepare for her baby shower, went shopping with my mum and then came home to cook dinner for the family. We always take turns cooking family meals.'

Me: 'What did you cook?'

Helen: 'Spaghetti Carbonara and apple pie with custard for dessert.'

Me: 'Sounds lovely. You'll have to teach me how to make the perfect apple pie sometime. Would you like to go on a date soon?'

I've done it! Slipped that in there like a pro!

Helen: 'Yeah, sure. I'm free most weekends. What should we do?'

Me: 'Should we say this weekend? I'll think of something and get back to you.'

Helen: 'Okay, can't wait x'

The 'x' drives my hormones wild again, remembering the way her real kisses made me feel.

Six

Progress

"What are your plans for tonight?" Jessie whispers, covering his mouth with the palm of his hands in an effort to not get caught talking. He's done that since we were in school, without realising that whispering in a room that is already dead silent, doesn't actually make him sound quiet. "We're going to the park for a bit of football later if you're up for it. Someone from the losing team has to host a games night at theirs." He grins. It's an unusually warm day and we normally do something when the weather's nice. Actually, we'd do something anyway, but it seems like things are more organised when the sun's out.

"Yeah, sounds good," I reply, with my head faced forwards. "Mum wanted me to babysit Max, but she didn't confirm anything before I left this morning, so I'll double check and let you know when she's gotten back to me."

"Wendy Samuels and Jessie Whitehall! Please do not talk in my class unless I ask you to," Miss Wortag loudly interrupts, screaming louder than normal to ensure that everyone in the building can hear her. Miss Wortag has been my English teacher since I was in year nine in secondary school. I should have realised that by choosing to study English in a sixth form within my school, I'd have a high chance of being stuck with her for another two years. We all started calling her the Warthog when we figured that she is the grumpiest teacher in college. She makes the class line up outside our classroom as if we are still a bunch of school kids. Once she arrives at the door, she unlocks it and stands with her body slightly in the doorway, forcing us all to have to squeeze past her on the way into the classroom, while she scrutinises each and every one us. If anyone is late handing in homework, they are instantly given detention. If anyone cough's without permission it's detention, heck if anyone breathes without having asked first, it's detention. She seems to make a point of calling me Wendy and emphasises every syllable that makes up my name. Which not only makes me cringe at the thought of having to reply, but burns as she deliberately reminds me that I am female in her eyes, when she can clearly see I want to be anything but that.

"Yes, ma'am," I reply back sarcastically, rolling my eyes and letting out a large sigh, knowing full well that I will most probably be given detention tonight after that. It's only since I started college that I've realised how much of an issue I have with authority, even if it has made the rest of the class glare around to look at the one who dared to speak back to the warthog. They all begin to chuckle and talk amongst themselves and I can feel my face heating up with through embarrassment. For someone that says they have no confidence, I sure as hell proved it there, didn't I?

"SIIIIIILENCE!" she screams, making everyone, including me, jump and instantly focus on nothing but her. I watch her as she scans the room with her stern and dark, evil eyes, analysing every single pupil across the room from row to row. Everyone keeps their heads forwards and avoids eye contact. No one dares make a sound. She gets onto me and I can feel my eyes watering and tingling slightly as I try and keep them focused on the board. I don't feel scared of the warthog like everyone else does. I almost feel sorry for her. Something about her face just says that she needs a hug. She looks sad every time she thinks no one is looking, but the minute she catches someone looking at her, she puts on an angry face and growls at them to look somewhere else.

Rumour has it, she used to be the friendliest teacher out there and then something happened one day that caused her to come in grumpy every day since. Other rumours have said that she had a twin sister who died in a car crash. The twin now haunts the girl's toilets near the lobby and has been haunting her for years, which puts her in a bad mood every time she is in college. I'm not really sure about that one, but there has to be a reason for her permanent bad mood.

When the bell rings to mark the end of each lesson, Miss Wortag is the only teacher that makes us stay seated for five minutes afterwards, knowing full well that we are desperate to leave. She watches us all start twitching wanting to leave as we get ready to engage in real life conversation like real humans do. It's almost like she enjoys watching us suffer.

"Your homework this week is on page 15 of your exercise books. Please have that in by next Wednesday," her high pitched voice screeches across the room. "If you need any help with it you know where I am, but after all of your hard work over the past three weeks, I expect you'll be able to do it unaided. Wendy, can you wait behind, please." She stops and grins at me as if she has just gotten one up on me. "The rest of you off you can go. I'll see you all next week."

Normally when I get detention, she yells it out in front of the class in an effort to embarrass me so it can't actually be anything too serious. Surely, she would get more pleasure out of humiliating me in front of the class as opposed to doing it in private? Jessie and I don't dare look at each other as the classroom empties. He hates being asked to stay behind after lessons, and would be moaning all week if I got him detention because Miss Wortag thought we were up to no good behind her back.

The warthog walks towards me once the classroom has emptied. She leans on the table in front of me, takes her glasses off, lays them on my table and then crosses her arms.

"Wendy, when you joined my class last year you were great. You completed all of your work on time and you were my top student for the whole year." It's weird hearing her say something to me that isn't rude. Her voice softens a little, but her face remains emotionless. "Everything seems to have changed lately. You don't appear to have any interest in getting your work done and spend the majority of your time talking to Jessie. Is everything ok?" I feel her cold, evil front leave and a warm side to her begin to show as she waits for my response.

"Yeah, everything is completely fine."

"Are you happy?" she prompts. The words pierce through me and causes my eyes to well up slightly. I don't remember the last time someone asked me if I was happy and the truth is, I don't know if I am. I'm lost and confused, but at the same time I have found some comfort in my two identities. I am very happy that I have met a girl and things are going well with her. I'm happy that I am lucky enough to have friends that care about me, both online and in person. I'm unhappy when I overthink about the worst that could happen if everyone finds out about my story and hates me for it. Or if they all decide that I can't be friends with any of them anymore. It scares me. I'm also unhappy at the thought of my friends only liking me because I act like Paul and wondering whether they would even want to be friends with Wendy.

I look back up to find Miss Wortag glaring at me with inward eyebrows as I try to figure out how to word what I am feeling. I desperately want to tell her that yes, there is something bothering me. Yes, I am unhappy. Yes, I have changed and I don't understand why. I want to tell her that I don't know who I am, where I am going and what I want to do. I don't like my body. I fantasise over what it would be like to be a boy and I am confused as to why I feel like that. I don't feel normal and I don't want to feel like this anymore. I want her to understand and tell me that everything will be okay and help me figure out why I feel like this. I need her to help take me out of this confusing place that I am in and encourage me to be whoever I want to be. As I drift off into a world of emotions and unsatisfying thoughts, Miss Wortag coughs which brings me back to the room. I look down at my exercise book, hold on tight to the edges with my shaking hands and take a deep breath. "Yeah, I guess so."

"Are you sure?" She doesn't sound convinced. Her puppy-dog eyes pleading with me to open up to her.

"Well." I opened up to my parents last night and they seemed to think it was ridiculous, but surely Miss Wortag has some sort of idea on what is going on. "I don't know what is wrong. I feel like I was born into the wrong body and I'm confused. No one seems to be taking it seriously, but I don't want to feel confused anymore. I think my parents thought the feeling would have disappeared after a while, but it hasn't and I'm not really sure how to deal with it anymore." I don't think any of that made sense, but opening up to another person gives me hope that something good will come out of this.

She takes a deep breath and then exhales slowly, before staring out of the window for a few seconds. "Well, I don't know what it is, but I would suggest you keep on top of your work before your grades fall. It will be difficult to pick yourself back up again afterwards. For your own benefit, I will sit you next to Tianna from now on." And just like that, the hard front comes back on. She picks her glasses up and adjusts them onto the end of her long nose, straightens up her back and walks towards her desk.

"Tianna?" I shriek back in horror. "Why do I have to be moved, I haven't done anything wrong." My voice trembles as I try and fight back emotional tears. Why do I have to be the one that gets moved? The woman clearly hates me.

"It's not about having done anything wrong. You are a very smart person and I think the company that you are keeping at the moment isn't great for your learning." She's completely ignored everything I just said and I find myself doubting whether I have actually said anything or just imagined it all. The woman confuses me, one minute she is sad, the next she is angry; one minute she is trying to get me to open up, the next she is walking back to her desk as if I hadn't said anything at all. Me being the only person to feel sorry for her was clearly a mistake on my part. "That will be all." She gestures for me to get out of the classroom while she pretends makes herself busy flicking through an empty exercise book. Everyone always says the warthog is cold, but I never once thought that she could be this cold. What is it with everyone brushing me off whenever I try and talk about this subject in particular? Any other subject is fine, but this one seems to make people go deaf and feel uncomfortable. How do they think I feel?

Football

Football is the one thing I can do that helps get everything off my chest and at the end of a tiring game I always feel like I've released the tension in my body. Dad constantly talks about the way exercise releases endorphins and makes you feel happier. He says it's important that we make sure we always have exercise in our routine. The best thing about this game is that we decided to play in the fields next to the woods and there is nothing I love more than the smell of burning from the bonfires and camp-sights nearby.

After the match we all collapse onto the grass in exhaustion, sipping our water and laying down spread eagle without a care in the world. Josh is the most unfit out of all of us and his panting causes everyone to burst into hysterical laughter. He pauses and looks at me strangely. "Can I ask you something?"

"Sure," I reply, nervous that he has picked me out of everyone.

"How come you don't hang out with girls?"

His question startles me.

"What do you mean?" I reply back apprehensively, while the rest of the group stops to listen in on our conversation.

"I mean, how come you like hanging out with us instead of girls from school, or whatever?" he clarifies, looking around for someone else's approval. Thing is, I knew exactly what he meant. I was just hoping he would change his mind and retract his awkward question.

"Um." Jeez, where do I start? "Well, I guess my story is a little complicated, but I've always felt comfortable being a boy, basically." I can already feel myself preparing for the backlash of telling them the truth.

"Sometimes, I do forget that you are a girl, to be honest. You even look like a boy. It's weird, but it's not, if you get what I mean?"

"Yeah, I know what you mean," I reassure him. Weird is definitely a good way to describe my situation.

"Why do you feel comfortable being a boy, though?" Cameron interrupts, sitting upright so he can get more involved in the conversation. "I don't get it." His confidence in asking anyone anything, always makes me feel uneasy, especially in these circumstances.

"I don't know, to be honest, Cam. I guess I've always felt this way and I haven't really known how to express myself. I hate being a girl it makes me feel sick. It's really hard to explain but I just have this burning feeling that I was meant to be a boy."

Home

The rest of the evening was all right. No one commented on the subject after that. In fact, they all carried on as normal. Looking back on it now, I'd probably have explained the situation a little more to them. That's if they wanted me to.

Paul

Me: 'Hey, so I thought that we could go to a theme park over the weekend? The weather is meant to be nice.'

Helen: 'Hey Paul. That sounds good. The weekend is a whole five days away, though.'

Me: 'Well, are you free tonight?'

Helen: 'I can be for you.'

Me: 'Do you want to meet up in Manor Park?'

Helen: 'Sure, what time?

Me: 'In about an hour? I can be there by eight?'

Helen: 'Okay. See you then x'

I hadn't looked at dates or places we could go on the weekend prior to sending Helen a text, but I had to say something so that she doesn't think my silence is me not being interested. The playing it cool game is a lot harder than I thought it would be. I mean, how cool is cool, if you know what I mean? I'm conscious of the amount of times I contact her as the last thing I want is for her to run a mile the minute she realises I am besotted with her.

My laptop carries on fighting on through and switches on, crashing every thirty seconds as a new pop-up literally pops up.

Me: 'Hey, is anyone online?'

Henry: 'Hello stranger. How goes?'

Me: 'All good man. Sorry I haven't been online much. What's new?'

Henry: 'Stuart video called us all and had a breakdown. He isn't happy about his new stepdad moving into his. Think that is what he wanted to talk to you about the other day.'

Olivia: 'OMG, Henry it wasn't your place to say that, you should have let Stuart explain it to Paul.'

Me: 'Ah, I'm sorry to hear that. I'll try and make some time to speak to him this week.'

Henry: 'How is your new lady friend? I'm assuming she is the reason you haven't been online much.'

Olivia: 'Yeah, he's definitely been having a fun time with her. One minute he's going on a hot date, the next things got 'heated' and before we know it, Paul has disappeared for days!'

Me: 'Ha! No, it's nothing like that. Promise, although I do have to go and jump in the shower as I'm meeting her tonight. Have a good evening guys.'

I've spent the majority of my teenage life online, talking to these guys. When I came home from school all I wanted to do was get on my laptop, so that I could talk to them about crap for hours until it was time to go to bed. Dad blames my situation on mum, for introducing me to the internet from such a young age, but they had no idea how much it helped me. My online identity is the person I wish I was able to be in real life and without it, I don't know what I would be like today. I feel bad for popping on and offline quickly without giving anyone the chance to actually have a conversation with me, but as mum always says, when you grow up, you don't have as much time for your friends as you used to.

Hot days are difficult to dress for. When I'm at college, everyone more or less knows me as Wendy so although I hate being her, if it gets way too hot I can at least walk around in a t-shirt until I've cooled down. I hate wearing things that make certain parts of my body more obvious, shorts for example. They bring attention to my knees and how girly my legs look. Vest tops or t-shirts make my breasts look overly large , so I've decided to go for a pair of tracksuit bottoms and one of dad's old t-shirts.

The park is quiet and with the drop in temperature, the walk through it feels more chilling than what I had prepared myself for. Helen meets me by the playground, wearing a tight vest top tucked into a short, high waisted skirt and ankle boots.

"Howdy!" I joke, pointing to her boots.

"Hey, you!" Her infectious smile instantly has me mimicking hers the second I see it. She wraps both of her arms over my shoulders and pulls me for a long, 'I've missed you' kiss, holding onto me closely. "How have you been?" she asks, gently grabbing hold of my hand and pulling me over to the swings.

"It was all right. I spent most of it with my family. Didn't really get up to much, if I'm honest." The sudden realisation that I've caught myself out after lying to her the other day, hits me as soon as the words come out of my mouth, giving me enough time to prepare myself to lie in an effort to protect the last lie.

"I thought you said you had been really busy?" Her confrontational approach is quite scary, but I was prepared for it.

"Oh, yeah. It was just family stuff. Nothing interesting. It felt like I was rushed off my feet, but looking back on it now it doesn't seem like I did much, if that makes any sense?" Technically that is not actually a lie.

"Ah. I get what you mean. That's how I feel on most days."

Helen doesn't seem like the type of girl to shy away from confrontation which has its pros and cons. Pros because her confidence is undeniably attractive, and she seems to be a girl who knows what she wants. Cons, because if she found out about me through anyone else but me, I can imagine her being furious about it, and not being as forgiving as I would want her to be. Cons, because she doesn't come across as one to give second chances; something about her confidence gives off the impression that she doesn't take any crap from anyone. Cons, because she is so darn hot that I can't imagine her waiting around for me to get my real bits, while she brushes off all of the guys that are ready and willing to give her the world right now. I can't seem to work her out. She doesn't give off the impression that she wouldn't be happy with it, but then again, she also hasn't done anything to make me think she would be fine with it either. Everyone I talk to seems to brush off the most important part of my situation, which normally frustrates me, but I would much rather Helen brushed it off than felt disgusted at it and walked away completely.

"So, what do you do in your spare time then, Mr Paul?" She interrupts my trail of thought, bringing me straight back into the moment to focus on her and only her.

That's a funny question, actually, because I spend my spare time being the total opposite to what she thinks I am.

"Nothing much, if I'm honest." I shrug my shoulders in an effort to act like I'm not bothered about how I come across, but secretly cringing at the thought of not being able to list any interesting hobbies. "I usually spend my spare time scrolling through the internet and talking to people online. What about you?" My ability to hide the truth without actually telling a lie is a skill I don't think I should be proud of. It's taken years of lying to my friends and family that has got me to this stage.

"Shopping with my mum and older sister, or nothing really." She replies, holding her hand outwards to get a good view of her nude coloured nails. "My dad likes to take us on expensive holidays during summer. He owns a yacht in Mallorca which he's going to give to me, and he's just ordered me my first car. I've already ordered pink eyelashes for it."

"Wow." I don't know whether I'll be able to keep up with the expensive gifts her dad buys her. That's for sure.

"Yeah, if there's one thing I hate about living in the UK. It's the rubbish weather. I'd be happy if I didn't have to see rain again. As soon as I get the yacht, I'm out of here."

"You've got to be kidding!" I reply, trying to hide the fact that I'm seriously disappointed that she hates one of my favourite things. "Going out in the rain is the most amazing feeling ever!"

"No, it's not!" she replies frankly. "Chilling by the pool, getting your tan on, wearing a nice bikini and getting loads of nice photos by the pool. That's the most amazing feeling ever. So, what do you look for in a relationship, then?" she asks with that confidence I find so attractive. Completely changing the entire subject and throwing me off key again. Come to think of it, I've never really thought about what I would want from a relationship. I've spent all of my life concentrating on what I want to do with my body instead.

"Me? Um. I guess I just want someone that stands by me through thick and thin and someone that supports me no matter what. Sometimes things happen that can challenge your relationship and put a strain on it, but I guess I just want someone that is willing to ride along through the hard times and enjoy the good times with me. What do you look for?" That is what I want. I want someone (Helen) to accept me for me, love me for me and wait for me until I transition. I want her to focus on my personality and what characteristics I have, as opposed to my body parts.

"That's really sweet," she replies, stroking the side of my head. "I don't think I've thought about it like that before, but I totally agree with you. Someone that doesn't run away when the going gets tough and will stick around for the sake of the good times would be perfect, but I just mainly look for loyalty and honesty." I don't think she meant for it to sound any different to the other words she used in that sentence, but for some reason, the word 'honesty' makes my heart sink into my stomach. "It's hard for me to forgive someone when they have lied to me or haven't been able to stay loyal. I want someone that respects me enough to just be brave and be honest about everything from the beginning, no matter how bad things are."

I can't tell whether she is indirectly talking about my situation and I can instantly feel myself becoming paranoid and nervous. I'm fully aware that now would be the perfect time to tell her the truth, especially while we're on the topic of honesty, but I'm so scared that I'll lose her. I never thought in a million years that she would be interested in me, so if I can just somehow hold out until I've had my surgery, she won't have to know anything. Besides, she said she wants someone that is honest from the start. By telling her my name was Paul and letting her believe I have always been a real boy, I've technically been dishonest from the get go. There is no way she will forgive me if I tell her anything now.

"I'll have to go shortly. I've got an early start tomorrow and I always struggle waking up on time. I couldn't stand it if I were to get bags under my eyes." She points towards her eyes as if I didn't know what she meant. "I need my beauty sleep and all that." I don't want her to go. We've been here for so long, but it feels like the time has flown by, I could stay out here with her forever. We walk over to sit on the grassed area and enjoy a goodbye cuddle. Helen rests her head on my arm, our hands tightly holding onto each other's and both of us silent, enjoying the moment.

The light strokes on the back of my hand with her fingertips send me into another meditative trance. The grass is either freezing cold or wet, and my back aches from holding her body weight up as well as my own, but despite the uncomfortableness, I don't want to move and potentially ruin a moment.

She adjusts her head so that she is looking at me, holding my gaze for a few seconds with her beautifully expressive eyes, before pulling me in for another heavy and passionate kiss. Pins and needles tingle my head and makes the world around me spin, as I focus on what her lips feel like pressed against mine. She playfully bites on my bottom lip before running her tongue around it, causing me to feel weak under her spell. I hardly noticed that I have started breathing a little deeper as our kiss becomes slow and heavy. Her smooth tongue gently wrestles with mine while her firm hold on me keeps me exactly where she wants me. I can't seem to stop myself from wanting to touch her. The uncontrollable urge to rip her clothes off and explore every, single part of her body has me clenching my fists in frustration. I move my attention from her lips and onto her neck. The faint smell of her perfume hypnotises me as I rub against her waist and run my tongue down her neck. This person that I am when I'm with Helen is amazing. I don't know if it's something I've seen or watched somewhere, but this person knows exactly what to do and is confident enough in being able to go through with it.

My heavy kissing on her neck makes her breathe harder and elongate her neck outwards to give me more to work with. I squeeze onto her tightly before leaning over and slowly pushing her down onto the grass with my forearm under her head. She looks even more mesmerising laying down and my appetite for her just keeps on growing. I don't think I can control the need to kiss her and she is making it clear that she feels the same. She doesn't seem to want to stop and holds her hand against the back of my head to stop me from moving away from her.

I work my way back down to her neck and in between her breasts where she holds them both up against either side of my face. I feel like I am going to explode as I slowly massage them and use my tongue to pull her nipples out from under her bra. My downstairs area is tingling with excitement and screaming with frustration all at the same time; the adrenaline from being outside where someone can catch us has every sense heightened and makes it feel all the more exciting. The cold wind against my hot, sweaty skin feels weirdly pleasurable. Her heavy breathing, gentle moaning and hands guiding my head from one breast to the next makes it clear that I am doing something right and that she is just as hungry as I am. I let her guide my head around her body before moving downwards, past her nun and onto her smooth, soft legs.

My appetite for her has reached an irrefutable level and I find myself craving every part of her. I want to see it, taste it and experience every part of her nun. I want to know what it feels like touching someone else's and just know that I have the manly skills to handle it properly. I don't know what I will do when I get there, but I'm sure as hell ready to do anything she wants me to. My hands shake as they reach the mouth of her arousal and the sudden realisation that I have reached it sinks in, causing a wave of emotions to flood my mind. It is a lot smaller than I had imagined it would be. My testosterone injections have made mine grow to a disgustingly large size, compared to hers and they're completely different. The warm, dampness from underneath makes it evident that despite not having a clue what I am doing, I am much better at it than I thought.

"Stop," she says loudly, sitting upright and adjusting her top back.

"Sorry," I reply shyly. I think I've taken it too far.

"No, it's not that I don't want to. I just don't want to rush anything. Besides, I really have to go. I was meant to be home twenty minutes ago," she reassures me while looking at the time on her phone. "Walk me to the gate?"

"Of course." I'm slightly embarrassed that she had to tell me to stop. Years of porn, internet searches and sexual frustration has clearly all started to come out on Helen, but I'm disappointed that I couldn't sense that she was uncomfortable. The whole 'not coming across as desperate' thing doesn't seem to be working at all.

The slow walk back to the gate is quiet, I'm completely mortified at what has happened and Helen is probably thinking about how she'll let me down gently. Her thumb is still stroking mine as our fingers are intertwined together, meaning she must still be interested a little bit at least, right?

"Text me?" She stops at the gate, holding both of my hands and facing me.

"I shall." I kiss her forehead and pull her in for a cuddle before watching her walk away. Her cuddles give me a sense of security and have made any negative thoughts about my performance disappear.

Seven

Truth's out

I haven't heard from any of the boys since yesterday, which is weird. Normally I'll hear from at least one of them before the bell goes at the start of college, but I didn't see any of them when I walked in this morning. They haven't responded to any of my texts and Jessie hasn't knocked on the classroom door to get my attention on his way to the toilets yet.

We have this thing when I'm in History and he's in Spanish, where whenever we're bored, we meet up somewhere and bunk for ten minutes. Whenever it's raining we hang out by the toilets and seeing as it's pouring, it would definitely be a toilet day. It's something we've done since school. He normally has his phone in his hand and replies to me within a matter of seconds, but two hours since I sent him a message without a reply, isn't normal.

James and Josh weren't setting up their mini stall behind the P.E. hall when I walked past and I haven't heard Cameron's loud voice all morning. None of them are in my history class, but I can't help but feel weird that I haven't heard from any of them yet. Rather than wallow in self-pity and allow myself to be an attention seeker, I surreptitiously take my phone out of my pocket, conceal it in between my legs and put my hand down in an effort to make it look like I am focusing hard on yet another essay. The trick is to let out a loud cough and simultaneously put your hand over your forehead while you do, so that it doesn't look too obvious.

I find my mind wandering off into another world, lusting over Helen and every inch of her perfect body while scrolling through the internet, searching for forums that might help with my burning desire to make things official: *'How do I tell my girlfriend that I am not really a boy?'*

The question itself brings up a number of unhelpful forums and blogs, none of them relating to my situation in any way. One of the blogs in particular reads:

'If you are lying to your partner about who you are, the best thing to do is to be honest if you want the relationship to go anywhere. Besides arguments about money, one of the main things couples fall out over is dishonesty. If you have found yourself wrapped up in a lie and unable to find a way out, the best thing to do is be honest. As soon as you can.'

I was kind of hoping to read an article that encouraged me to continue lying and gave me tips on how to hide my real identity. I guess this one does have some relevance as one of the things Helen said she wouldn't tolerate is dishonesty.

I'll tell her the next time I see her. If I don't do it then, I never will. Once I've told her, I'll face the boys and tell them too. Like mum says, there is no time like the present.

Lunch time

Still nothing from Jessie or any of the boys and no sight of them all, giving me no choice, but to sit next to the nerds at lunch. Tianna, Alice and Katie are honestly the weirdest group of people I have ever known. I knew Tianna was weird before I'd even started the school as I had the pleasure of meeting her when I was eleven, but Alice and Katie are too. They are all so quiet, it's hard to tell whether they actually talk to each other. They tend to stay close to one another the majority of the time and, to be honest, I don't think anyone would be interested in mingling with them anyway. Anytime I walk past them, they are either making plans for a home science project or staring into space, completely oblivious to the world. Tianna doesn't really talk when I sit next to her in English, despite the fact that when I really *don't* want her to talk to me, she finds the weirdest things to say, at the weirdest times, and she always seems to just pop up. Watching her dissect her burger with her muddy fingers, and rearrange all of its contents around, just to put it all back in the burger and eat it again, has quite literally just made my skin crawl.

"What do you think?" Alice interrupts my trail of thought and catches me giving Tianna a stink eye.

"About what?" I reply, bluntly, reluctant to engage in a pointless conversation with any of them.

"Mars. Do you think humans will be able to live there in the future? And do you believe in aliens?" she asks enthusiastically.

"Um. Yeah, sure. Sounds good," I reply, hurriedly eating my now cold burger so that I can get the hell away from here.

"Oh, hey, I didn't see you there," Tianna says proudly before I've had the chance to escape. "Can you smell something that smells like vanilla?"

"What?"

"I made a perfume using vanilla wax melts that I had at home," she continues, holding her wrist up towards me. I'm not putting my nose anywhere near her wrist, the girl freaks me out. I also cannot smell a single thing other than chips and burgers from the kitchen.

"I can smell it. It smells lovely," I reply, moving my head backwards to avoid her wrist being shoved in my face.

"There you are!" Josh's deep voice vibrates from behind me. I've been looking for you everywhere mate, where have you been?"

"I've been in class. Why didn't you just text me?"

"Oh, yeah. Didn't actually think of that. What are you doing with these lot?" he whispers, holding the side of his hand against his mouth and leaning in towards me.

"I didn't really have a choice," I whisper back, avoiding eye contact with Tianna, who I can see is staring at me by the corner of my eye. "Where's Jess?" I ask, scanning the hall behind him, still feeling kind of lost without my best friend. You never really know how much of an important role someone has in your life until they aren't there.

"He didn't come in today." He bends down to reach my level and leans in close so that no one hears him. "Don't let on to anyone, but his brother called in pretending to be his dad and said that he's ill. He'll be out later, though." He looks behind him to make sure no one heard.

"Wait. Did you say he said he'll be out later?"

"Yeah."

"How do you know that and what's happening later?" I'm more concerned with the fact that Jessie has confided in Josh and not me, it's normally the other way around.

"Because he sent me a text, dur," his voice slightly lowered. "I don't know where we're going, but we'll find somewhere."

Home

Still nothing from Jessie. I can't think of what I could have done to offend him and the thought of him not wanting to talk to me is horrible. I can't help but feel paranoid that my secret has come out, just before I've had the chance to tell everyone the truth. Something about his absence today has me feeling lonelier than I imagined it would have. I've never fallen out with him before and if I feel like this after not hearing from him for one day, I don't ever want to fall out with him. Mum has always said that my relationship with him isn't healthy. She reckons I'll struggle making new friends when we leave college and go our separate ways, but after spending every weekday with him in school and then college, I can't see myself being best friends with anyone but him. We've spent the past six years joint at the hip; when he isn't around, we text each other about crap all day. He's practically the other half of me. It's hard to accept such a huge change in habit with no notice whatsoever.

My bathroom is surprisingly messy today meaning one thing and one thing only; dad has been in charge of the tidying up. He'll never hear the end of mum's moaning if the house isn't spotless and exactly as she left it by the time she's home. Dad and Jake have left their wet towels and underwear from this morning on the floor, the lid for the toothpaste is missing, the toilet seat is up and Max's bath toys are still in the bath. I don't even want to imagine what the rest of the house is like, but it's safe to say that mum is going to hit the roof.

My phone vibrates from the bathroom cabinet as I try and find the right temperature in the shower, causing me to nearly slip and break my neck trying to run to it quick enough. As if the text was going to magically disappear if I didn't get to my phone on time.

It's not Jessie, though, it's Helen.

Helen: 'Hey. Are you free this evening? We need to talk.'

Oh boy. This doesn't sound good.

Me: 'Yeah I'm free. What do we need to talk about?'

Helen: 'Meet me in the park in an hour?'

Me: 'Okay. Is it something bad?'

Helen: 'I'll see you in an hour.'

I feel overwhelmingly crazy with paranoia, with Jessie ignoring me, Cameron and James being missing in action and Helen wanting to talk to me. Not to mention the fact that she wants to meet in the park when it is freezing cold and wet outside. Something just doesn't feel right, and I can't stop myself from thinking the worst. If any of them have found out about my secret without me having had the chance to explain, I don't think they'll forgive me, especially not Helen. Although I feel slightly more concerned with what Jessie's problem is and I think I'd rather sort that out first. Bros before, well, you know.

    The park is dark, cold and still wet from where it rained earlier. The hole Jessie and I dug in between the gates was uncovered when I arrived, which is weird because I didn't show Helen about our secret way to get in when the gates are locked. I didn't want her to know that I come here that often. It's creepier tonight than it normally is when we come here late. The rustle from the leaves as they hit against each other, has me sharply turning around every few seconds to make sure that if anyone is following me, they aren't too close. The deafening silence from the rest of the park, along with the faint howling of the wind as it pulls and pushes me in different directions, is terrifying, and I don't think I've known myself to walk so fast before. One of the tall park lights flicker from above me as it fights to turn on, making it seem like a scene from a horror movie. The wind forcefully pushes me in the direction of the playground, speeding my pace and making it less obvious that I am petrified to any murders that may be lurking in the bushes. I can faintly hear voices coming from the direction of the playground. It sounds like there is more than one person there, but I can't recognise any of them as anyone I know. Regardless, hearing voices it comforting in itself.

A dark figure stumbles towards me as I approach the playground, causing me to slow down and consider turning back and running away. "There you are! The one we've all been waiting for. Come on in." It's Jessie. He is unsteady on his feet and I can only assume him swaying backwards and forwards is his attempt at coming towards me. "Welcome to our humble abode," he yells, spraying spit towards me. The strong smell of cigarettes and alcohol chokes me slightly as I walk in the gate towards him.

"You smoke?" I ask, baffled.

"No, I do not smoke, but I am most definitely smokin', get it?" He lets out a loud roar of laughter. I do get it, but I'm just struggling to figure out what part of it was so funny.

"You stink, Jess." I gently push him backwards in an effort to encourage him to keep his distance. "How long have you been out here?"

"How long? I don't know. Maybe years." He's not making any sense and I doubt he knows what he is even saying at the moment. He slumps his heavy arm around my shoulders and starts leaning all of his body weight onto me, giving me no choice, but to hold onto his waist to try and keep him upright. He is an unrecognisable, drunken mess of a boy with a bottle of strong rum in one hand and a cigarette in the other – the hand that is right next to my face. His pupils are dilated and his jet black eyes appear large and emotionless. The hairs on his arms are standing up and his skin is covered in goose-bumps from the cold.

"Where's your coat?"

"You want some?" he replies, holding the bottle out towards me and completely ignoring what I asked.

"No, thanks," I reply bluntly, pushing it away.

Behind a little bend in the playground are Cameron, James, Mya, and Helen. Cameron and James are sitting on the back rest of a bench with their feet on the part people sit on. Cameron is playing music on his phone, rapping along with the lyrics and James is nodding his head in rhythm with the beat. There is a strong skunk mixed with urine smell coming from their direction. I recognise the distinct skunk smell from Cameron, as he always smells of it, except this time his eyes are bloodshot red and glazed over. He doesn't seem to have noticed that I am here, which is unlike him. He never misses a thing. Helen and Mya are sitting on the swings, talking between themselves. Helen is sitting on the swing I pushed her on the other day and once again, I have to fight the urge to grab her and kiss her romantically. Every time I see her, she looks more perfect than she did the last time, and I can feel my heart racing with excitement as she and gives me that infectious smile.

"Hey," I wave shyly.

"Hey, thanks for coming," she smiles back warmly. "Should we talk?"

She jumps off the swing and walks towards the grassed area that we got heated on the other night and stands facing me. I don't feel the warm, bubbly vibe from her that I am used to. She hasn't given me a cuddle and appears to be standing at quite a distance from me. It could just be that I am paranoid that her and Jessie have been acting weird on the same day, but there's also the fact that I had no idea we were going to be joined by everyone else.

"Just before I tell you anything, you should know that I don't believe a word of it. I just feel like it's something you need to know, and I don't feel comfortable keeping it from you." I know where this is going. She knows. I can feel myself focusing on my breathing and as such, making it difficult for myself to breathe. I let out a giant gulp sound as I try and swallow the lump that has now formed in my throat once again. She hasn't noticed my hands shaking yet, but when she does, she'll no doubt be able to tell that I am petrified to have this conversation.

"Go on," I prompt. Not really wanting her to carry on, but I don't really have a choice in the matter. My mind has gone blank and I can't think of any reasonable excuse as to why I would have lied to her in the first place. How do you explain to someone that withholding the truth and lying are two completely different things? And how, if even possible, do you explain to someone that you love that any lies that were told, were done with nothing, but the best intentions? Despite the fact that they made it very clear from the beginning that lying is their one pet hate. I can't look at her.

"So, two things. The first one is that Jessie told me that you are a girl pretending to be a boy," she says, pausing to stop and look at me with unsuspecting eyes. "I made it very clear that I don't believe it as you can't be, but I thought it was kind of nasty that he's saying that about you when you guys are meant to be best friends."

Oh boy.

"And the second thing?" I reply, nervously. Trying to buy myself some time to gather my thoughts and quickly think of something to say to her.

"He tried to make a pass at me yesterday, but I told him to back off."

"He did what?" I yell loudly, totally shocked by everything she's said, but secretly trying to make a bigger thing out of the second point so that we can forget the first. "Why would he do that?"

"I have no idea." She raises her shoulders and holds her arms outright. "You know him better than I do. It could be that he is jealous, but there isn't anything to be jealous about." She lowers her voice so that none of the others can hear what she is saying. "I told him I'm interested in you and you only and that's when he said that you're actually a girl. I thought it was because your voice is the only one that hasn't broken, but that's just harsh"

The thought of Jessie telling Helen the truth just to get in her knickers is making me feel sick and burn with anger at the same time. I've never asked him to keep quiet or pretend that I am a boy, but there is usually a bro code with these things. If one of us is unsure on something, rather than discussing it with anyone else, we'll keep it between us until we know what the deal is. Jessie has completely ignored those rules. Then again, I guess I'm technically not one of the bros. I'm just me.

"I don't know what to say," I reply.

I'm scared. I want to tell her the truth, but I can't. Her mannerism suggest that she has completely ignored it as a ridiculous statement. If she believes the statement itself is *that* ridiculous, what will she think if she knows it is the truth?

"Well, please don't hate me, but I do have to ask. Is it true? Remember, I don't believe a word of it, but Cameron and Josh said it was true as well, so it only makes sense for me to just ask you outright." She giggles. That's it, the thought of me really being a girl is funny. It's a joke.

"Did James say anything?" I reply cautiously. Still trying to buy myself some more time.

"No, James told them all to shut up, but he wouldn't tell me whether it was true or not. He's the only one I'd trust out of them guys, which is why I had to ask you." She looks puzzled. "He didn't actually say it wasn't true." Because he can't. "So, is it true? Just say no, so that I can go right on over there and tell them all to stick their rumours where the sun doesn't shine."

I can't tell her the truth, but I most definitely cannot tell her a lie. If I make out like Jessie is lying, I will lose my best friend, and not hearing from him all day has already given me a taster of what that will feel like. If I tell her the truth, I will most likely lose her and the thought of that hurts my heart too much. I desperately want to tell her that I am wholly and unconditionally in love with her and that no matter what parts I have on my body, I am a boy, and nothing will change between us. I want to explain what will happen in the future with my surgeries and the fact that one day I will be a real man. I can't stand the thought of losing her over something that is out of my control and I refuse to allow my genitals to ruin things for me. I look over my shoulder at Jessie as he sways back and forth drinking the last bits of alcohol from the bottle. The pain in my heart feels like real, physical pain as I prepare myself to call him a liar, hoping that with the amount of alcohol he has consumed, he won't remember in the morning. He looks so innocent and like he wouldn't do anything to spite me, but with Helen being stone cold sober and me practically being forced to choose between the pair of them, the best option would be to upset the one that's unlikely to remember tomorrow. Although I don't know how I am going to live with myself for calling my best friend a liar.

"No, Helen. It's not true," I reply bravely. I can feel my whole body shaking as I blurt the words out quicker than I can register them. "Please don't say anything to Jessie – just leave me to talk to him about it." There's definitely no going back now, I grab hold of her hand in an effort to gently persuade her to stay put and not say anything.

"Absolutely not!" She yanks her hand back, pulling away from me. "That's a horrible thing to lie about, Paul. They are your closest friends and they have been making up rumours like that behind your back. It is borderline bullying and I won't have someone I care about be bullied by their closest friends." She storms off towards the direction that the rest of the gang are in.

I haven't thought this through at all.

"Helen, please!" I whisper loudly, running after her trying to grab hold of her hand again, but she's using them to intensify her march over to confront Jessie. She isn't listening.

"What are you two arguing about?" Jessie shouts across the playground, walking towards us. He has some nerve; he knows exactly why we are arguing.

"Nothing, Jess, we'll talk about it later," I reply to Jessie while looking directly at Helen.

"Tell me! Or should I take one big, fat guess?" he teases drunkenly.

"No, Jessie, just drop it." I growl back, hoping that the emphasis on his full name gives him a hint to back off.

"Actually, I'll tell you," Helen says, pushing past me and walking over to stand in front of Jessie. "There is something you need to hear. People like you are horrible, and I've seen them my whole life. Why would you make up lies about someone that is meant to be your best friend?" she asks. She has so much passion in her eyes. She really cares about me. Watching her fight for me, stand up against someone so popular and not even think twice about the consequences is so hot. "Making up rumours that I'm a lesbian is horrible, because I'm not. Anyway, I told you that all I would do was ask Paul myself."

She's called me Paul in front of them. Oh my god.

"Paul? Who's Paul?" Cameron suddenly snaps back into reality. I assumed he was too zoned out to be able to register any of this conversation. "Is that the name you've been using?"

"Hold on. Why am I the horrible one?" Jessie interrupts loudly. "What have I done apart from tell the truth? I thought you might benefit from hearing it, but I apologise for doing the right thing. Next time I'll leave you to get humiliated," he sulks.

"Can we please just leave this subject and talk about it when everyone is sober?" Putting the blame on alcohol and drugs seems like the best option here.

"Because you made up a malicious rumour out of spite, and what's worse is that you did that to your best friend," Helen hisses back, sounding out every single word so that he understands what she is saying. I think everyone understands exactly what's going on here. No one is listening to me, it's almost as if I've gone invisible. The only difference here is that I don't get the benefit of running away unnoticed.

"I'm not lying, Helen. Ask her yourself." He adjusts his positioning to look at me. "Wendy, are you a girl or are you a boy?"

All of my worst fears have come at once and the playground has fallen into complete silence as everyone looks at me and waits for a response. I'm numb with shock and can't think of the words to say. Lying behind Jessie's back is one thing, but to lie to his face, in front of Cameron and James is another. I'm backed into a corner with nowhere to run and no way of getting out of it.

"Hello, is anyone in there?" Jessie asks, waving his hands in front of my face and snapping me out of a daydream. Or should I say nightmare.

"Helen, can I talk to you in private? Please." If she would just let me explain my situation properly, away from everyone else and in an environment where I can explain without anyone interrupting, I reckon she would understand. But if I just admit that I am a girl now, in front of everyone, it will make me look like I purposely tried to make a fool out of Helen, and that was never my intention.

"She's a girl, Helen. We've all told you already!" Cameron shouts from the bench, sighing as if he is bored of the subject already. This is my life, it's not just some stupid, boring topic. Helen's big, brown eyes stare at me and begin to water up. She's already read my mind. She knows what I'm going to say.

"Answer the question, Paul," she says calmly, fighting back tears and trying to control her wobbling voice.

"Okay." I can do this. If she cares as much as she says she does, she'll understand. Eventually. "I was born as a girl, yes." I almost choke on the words as I say them out loud. "But, I am a boy. I can't really explain it, but something happened when my mum was pregnant with me that caused me to be born into the wrong body. I am a boy. I just don't look like one underneath my clothes." I can barely get the sentence out properly. Every word hurts and feels like I am stabbing myself in the chest. I can't look at her. I can't look at any of them.

"So, you lied to me?" Tears flow down her beautiful, rosy cheeks.

"No, Helen you don't understand, I didn't lie, I just withheld the truth a little," I reply. Trying to put everything I've thought of into words, but with the way it's been sprung up on me, I have no idea where to start.

"Wow." She laughs. "You are good. So withholding the truth and lying are different things? Withholding the truth is okay, that's what you're saying?"

I'm really not helping myself here.

"No, of course not. Look, I'm sorry," the lump in my throat has grown to a suffocating size. "It's not that I'm just a random girl pretending to be a boy. I am actually a boy trapped inside a girl's body. It's so hard to explain, and I know you won't understand, but I'm going to have surgery to change my body back into a boy's. I'm transgender."

"You're right," she replies, tears streaming down her face. "I don't understand and I don't want to. You lied to me and even when you had the chance to tell me the truth you lied again. I am not into girls and I liked you because I thought you were a boy. You were bang out of order for tricking me like that. I feel sick," she shouts loathingly.

"Wait," Jessie interjects again. "Did you just say the doctors are going to change you into a boy?"

"Argh, Jessie for the love of Christ, can you just drop it. Yes, they are going to change me into a boy." I yell at him, blaming him for putting me in this situation, when really it is no one else's fault but my own.

"Don't yell at me!" Jessie barks back. "You are the one that got yourself into this situation, don't take it out on me now that it's all out in the open."

"No, Jessie. You are the one that went behind my back. You made a move on my girl and then told her about my situation so that you could spite me when she said she wasn't interested. All you had to do was talk to me first and if you ever didn't understand anything, I would have explained it all to you." I want to cry, but that'll definitely be seen as a girl thing. "Why would you talk about it behind my back with the girl you know that I am dating, you know my situation." I'm not angry at Jessie, but I'm so overwhelmed with emotion that I don't know how else to react.

Jessie puffs his chest out and stares at me intimidatingly with his dilated eyes. "You are the one that is a shim, not me. None of this is my fault. If you weren't so messed up, none of this would be happening. You lied, not me. Helen deserves to know the truth."

"What's a shim?" James asks innocently.

"A shim is a she and a him," Jessie replies, causing Mya and Cameron to burst into tears of laughter. Cameron takes his phone out of his pocket and starts video recording, walking closer to me while holding the phone close to my face.

"So, the operation that you had. Was that all a lie too?" Helen asks, wiping the tears from under her eyes. I feel like I can actually feel my heart breaking in two watching her crying, especially knowing that I can't comfort her. "You know what," she continues, before I've had the chance to reply. "I don't even want to know. I never want to see or talk to you again and if you do try and talk to me, I'm going to report you for harassment."

"Helen, I'm so-"

"I said, I don't want to hear it. Go home before I say something I won't regret," she hisses, walking over to stand next to Jessie.

Walking away from the group feels like I am fleeing from a group of strangers. What initially scared me walking through the park, has now become my comfort as it means I am closer to the exit. The flickering park light ahead of me doesn't seem as terrifying as it did to begin with, and I've found myself staring at it, counting steps in my head and using it as a milestone; if I can reach the light without completely breaking down, I'll be five minutes away from the gates.

"Oi!" someone yells from behind me, it sounded like Cameron followed by a stampede of horses.

I can't turn around, my body just won't move in that direction. The only thing it knows how to do is run when I'm scared. The footsteps behind me sound like they're getting closer. I can't tell whether I've driven myself crazy with paranoia, or whether someone *is* running towards me. I quickly dash around to see who it is, trying to avoid making myself look like even more of a coward if there isn't anyone there. However this time is different. Instead of turning around to find myself being ridiculous over nothing, I am met with a heavy, blunt force against the side of my face that is quickly followed by another on the other side. The punches knock me straight down onto the cold, wet grass and within seconds I can feel more punches on every part of my body. Someone hits me hard on the side of my head, while someone else boots me in my back, causing my hips to thrust forward in agony. I want to run, but my body just won't let me get up. I can't move. All I can do is curl up into a ball, with my arms over my head and knees tucked firmly in towards my body.

I feel numb and paralysed at the thought of my friends hurting me like this.

"I'm not used to not getting my own way, Wendy," Jessie says breathlessly, standing over my petrified ball of a body as everyone else stops hitting me. "Don't go near Helen again, she's mine." He leans in closer and spits on the grass next to me, before walking off towards the gates. My vision is blurry, but I can faintly make out three figures walking away from me. It's the three boys.

I'm panting like an over excited dog, but this time I can't seem to calm myself down. The sound of Jessie openly mocking me and calling me a Shim replay over and over in my mind. Helen's sorrowful eyes and Cameron's horrible, cackling laugh, as he took pleasure in seeing me being humiliated is something I won't be able to forget easily. The thought of never seeing Helen again instantly feels like a giant hole has pummelled into my chest. Petrified, I begin to back away slowly, trying not to make a sound and encourage anyone else over to beat me up. My heart is drumming against my chest so hard, that I can hear and feel every beat of it against my trembling body. My chest hurts. It feels like I can only breathe in so far before it stops me, causing me to pant quickly to try and catch my breath. I can't breathe. I think I am having a heart attack, but the more I focus on it and try to calm myself down, the more I feel like I can't breathe.

'A panic or anxiety attack is nothing to be ashamed of, Wendy. You just need to learn to control your mind, so that you can deal with it when I'm not there.'

Mum's advice on dealing with panic attacks quickly runs through my mind as I take in a short, deep breath and hold it for two seconds, before letting it go. I try it again and hold my breath for three seconds and then let it go. The third time loosens up my chest and makes it easier to breathe again.

'Five things I can see – a tree, grass, the sky, clouds, my hands.' I tell myself, scanning the grassy field as quickly as I can.

' Four things I can hear – distant cars, wind, a dog, leaves hitting against each other.

Three things I can feel – My heart, the grass, my body.

Two things I can smell – fresh air, my fear.

One thing I can say – I can do this.'

Eight

Betrayal

"Wendy!" Mum shouts from behind the bathroom door. "You've been hibernating for a week. What could you possibly be doing in there that's taking so long?"

I didn't sleep well last night. In fact, I've barely slept all week. I woke up at around 3am to the loud, rolling boom of thunder. Followed by light rain, gently tapping on my window. Before I knew it, that light rain that I was beginning to fall back asleep listening to, turned into what sounded like a giant waterfall directly outside my house. Every so often my room would briefly light up with the instant flash from lightening; before falling into complete darkness, and I was certain that I saw Helen's face at one point. I normally love thunderstorms, especially during the night when I'm able to watch it from my window, but I didn't feel safe last night. Every time I closed my eyes, I saw Jessie staring at me hatefully. Although I had my eyes squeezed shut, I felt like I could see him so clearly when he knelt down to warm me away from Helen. I replayed the incident over and over again in my mind, reliving every feeling, every thought and every word that was said. Every time I thought about Helen, my stomach tied itself up in knots. I watched the golf ball sized lump on my eye turn into a purple/green bruise throughout the night and every time I went to the bathroom, it had gotten a little darker.

"Jesus Christ, Wendy. What happened?" Mum shrieks as she bursts through the door and catches me nursing my black eye.

"Someone tried to mug me, mum. That's all," I reply calmly, rubbing my stomach and swallowing spit in an effort not to throw up.

"I'm calling the police." She rushes over and takes the cold flannel from me, gently pressing it against my eye. "This isn't cold enough. You need frozen peas."

"No. No police, mum. I fought them off, they didn't get anything. It looks worse than it actually is," I try and reassure her, knowing full well that things are as bad as they can get. "I've held peas on it all week, I'll do it again in a bit, but it gets a bit too cold after a while."

"What happened? Did you get a good look at their face? I need to call your father. What were they trying to take?" Here comes the million and one questions from mum.

"They came up from behind me and one of them knocked me out. They were trying to take my phone and no, I didn't get a good look at their faces." I struggle trying lie to her because every time I do, she somehow catches me out. I'd much rather be grilled by the police than my own mother.

"Who punched you on the eye if they came up behind you?"

See what I mean?

"Mum, I don't know," I groan. My neck sweaty from the pressure of having to think of something to say that will get her off my back. "Please, just drop it. I'll explain it all to you later. I just need to get my head straight." I can't handle anymore lies, but I definitely wouldn't be able to deal with the backlash from telling her the truth. I just want to forget about everything that happened last week. I was hoping that by the time anyone noticed I'd been hiding, my black eye would have gone down, but it hasn't. Despite the fact that I've spent every night holding frozen vegetables against it.

"Okay, well, I'll leave breakfast in your room. Eat what you can and then I'll drive you to college," she replies warmly.

"Thanks, mum," I whisper, trying to fake a grin and hold myself together.

I hadn't thought about going into college.

"Actually, mum," I sob with my brave face on. "I'm taking the day off today. I don't think I can go in there with a black eye." I also don't think I'll be able to face Jessie, Cameron and James, but she doesn't need to know that bit.

She walks over to the side of the bath to sit next to me. "Darling," her smooth, manicured hands holding onto mine tightly. "A very close friend of mine was mugged just after you were born. She went through a phase where she refused to go anywhere through fear of it happening again and was really shaken up." Her inquisitive eyes wait for my reaction as she talks to me with her 'Jake' voice on. The Jake voice is basically mum's way of saying 'you're a big boy, but you're still a child'. I think she still thinks I am ten years old. "She ended up being diagnosed with post-traumatic stress disorder and it took her a long time to get back on her feet again. I won't let that happen to you."

"Mum, I'm completely fine. I just need to spend one last day in bed and get my head together," I reply with that cheesy, non-convincing smile that I keep trying to do.

"No, you'll be fine when you get to college and see your friends. It all starts with 'just a few days in bed'," she says, holding her index and middle finger out as if she is imitating quote marks. "Besides, you've got your exams in just over four months. You can't miss out on vital learning because of those low lives. "

Her workaholic attitude isn't something I've inherited.

The journey into college is a quiet one, with mum focusing on the road ahead and me staring aimlessly out of the window.

"I've passed a message on to your teachers. They're going to make sure that no other pupil treats you any different today, and will carry on with the day as normal. Anne has said that Jessie will look out for you too, although I'm sure that goes without saying."

"Who said what?!" I hiss, causing mum's cheeks to blush pink. I hadn't even noticed that she had pulled up outside college. It felt like we were only in the car for a second. "Why the hell did you call Jessie's mum? What has it got to do with her?"

"I thought I was doing the right thing?" she replies back defensively, raising the tone of her voice in an effort to somehow prove her innocence. "Jessie always looks out for you, he's your best friend. I just thought that you might find it difficult to tell him and that it would be easier for Anne to do it, instead." She pauses and looks out of the window, sighing and slumping her body into her seat. She looks tired. Her sunken eyes fixed firmly on the road ahead. "Sweetie, I want to help you, but you won't let me do anything. The worst thing you can do is deal with this on your own."

"You had no right, though, mum!" I moan back, trying to fight back tears. She had no right. Jessie had no right. Neither did James, or Cameron. "I don't want *this* discussed with anyone. I don't want people to look at *this* and laugh or feel sorry for it," I howl back, pointing towards my face. My swollen eye reminding me that it's still there with a light pulse every time I move. "I just want to be normal! Why can't anyone just let me be normal?!" I'm exhausted. I don't know who or what I am, my friends have turned into animals and I've lost the girl of my dreams.

"Oh, Wendy, don't be like that," mum replies, resting her hand on my knee. "Do you know why you can't be normal? Because you're my daughter and you're absolutely amazing. You'll never just be normal or average, because you're a superstar."

"Thanks, mum. I'll see you later."

She looked disappointed as I got out of the car and walked into college. I know she means well, but reminding me that I'm her daughter is the last thing I want to hear right now. Besides, the superstar speech doesn't work on me as I'm not a child anymore, which I think mum forgets sometimes.

Rather than go into English at the same time as everyone else (including Jessie and Cameron), I wait until the class have all gone in before slipping in behind Tianna. She walks over to our double desk on the far left and sits down, emptying out the contents of her pencil case, and sorting them into shapes on the table in front of her. She always finds a new way to be weird.

"Arnica," she says proudly, as I go and make myself comfortable as far away from her as I can. Her eyes focused on her pencils as she straightens them up next to each other.

"What?"

"Arnica. You can buy it in a gel form, or you can take it orally. It helps reduce inflammation." She hasn't even looked at me. How the hell does she know that I have a bruise?

"Oh, thanks."

"You're welcome," she replies, raising her top lip to reveal her teeth, which I'm assuming is her way of attempting a smile? "Do you like perfume?"

"Yes."

"Do you want to buy some?"

"No. Thanks."

"Oh, that's too bad. I brought one in for you anyway." She reaches for her bag and brings out a small, clear, travel sized tube. What's inside it, I don't know, but it certainly doesn't look like perfume to me. "You can have it for free instead."

For crying out loud. Now I *have* to buy it.

"No, I didn't realise you had one on you. I'd love to buy it," I lie. "How much are you selling them for?" There's a bit of change in my pocket which should be enough.

"£30," she replies proudly, causing me to choke on my own spit.

"Are you having a laugh?" I accidentally yell back, causing the rest of the class to look over. It's hard to tell whether she is being serious or not, but I don't think she has a sense of humour, so she must be.

"Technically not, but I am joking. It's free," she replies, her cackling laugh rings right through my ears.

"SILENCE!" Miss Wortag shouts across the silent room. Sometimes it's clear that she loves the sound of her own voice. The quiet she naturally instils on the class feels calming today, and her strictness doesn't seem like such a bad thing. I feel like I can finally gather my thoughts a little.

"You have sixty minutes to complete the exam," she continues, scanning the room with squinted eyes. "Take your time and don't rush. Remember, this is only a mock so don't worry if you don't finish it on time. My advice is to spend fifteen minutes planning and forty-five writing it out." She stops to cough at someone sitting in the back row. I don't even want to know what Jessie and Cameron are doing back there. "Don't spend too much time on one paragraph. The time now is 09:05. You have until 10:05. Go!" She continues to scan the room from row to row whilst we all get to work.

The question reads:

> Describe one thing you think should change in today's society. Explain your reasons for wanting that change as well as the impact it will have.

I don't need fifteen minutes to plan what I'm going to write for this one. I know *exactly* what I would like to change about the world. I want everyone to understand that each person on this planet is different and it is not up to anyone to make them feel unimportant for it. I want people to be able to live their life, without prejudice or hatred, and identify how they want to without feeling like a freak. It doesn't matter where people come from, what sex they are, their skin colour or what they believe in; all that matters is that we are all human and we are all different. Tianna is scribbling away; probably about increasing the national minimum wage or finding useful ways to abolish poverty, recycle properly and stop using plastic. The majority of the class are probably doing the same, but if people don't change who they are *inside* and how they treat others, how is the world meant to change at all?

I begin to write everything without giving it a second thought; my mind so engrossed in my imaginary world where everything is happy, and everyone is accepted for who they are. I'm writing from my heart; sending vibes out into the universe that this is something that *can* happen; letting everything from the past few weeks out and basically using my essay as a personal diary entry. I can't see or hear anyone else around me, I've drifted off into this perfect world where I am who I am, and everyone loves me for it. I picture mum and dad calling me their son, Jake and Max looking up to me as their big brother. I see myself with a wife and children. My children; going out to work in a suit to have everyone address me as 'sir' or 'Mr Samuels', finishing work and going to the pub with the boys, before coming home to catch up on the football, where my very own family are waiting for me. It's such a beautiful thought and makes my heart feel warm just from thinking about it:

'Everyone should respect everyone. There should be no rules on what you can and can't achieve or who you can be. If someone is born a female and wants to identify as a male, they should be allowed to without prejudice. My perfect world would be a happy one, with everyone getting along, parents would take more time out to understand what their children are going through and figure out ways to help them. Friends wouldn't turn their backs on each other and be mean to them over silly things. Everyone would just be happy. When someone is trying to figure out who they are and what they want from life, why do people have to be mean and cause them pain and anguish for NO reason? Why do they have to be humiliated and mocked? Why can't everyone just be happy?'

Tears block my vision and drop onto my work, causing some of the ink to run, ruining my perfect piece of work. *'Man up and stop crying,'* I think to myself as I wipe the tears away. The last thing I want is for Jessie to see me crying and know that he's contributed towards it. I want to text Helen. I have to speak to her and explain, but I don't know how to deal with the situation. She asked me not to contact her and threatened to report me for harassment, so as much as I want to, I can't. I mean, surely if she wanted to talk to me she would contact me, right?

"You should really try and take advantage of the time," Tianna whispers loudly, pointing to her blank lined paper on the table.

"Yes, thanks," I whisper back, trying to force a polite smile.

"Do you like green? Green's my favourite colour."

I thought we were meant to be taking advantage of the time?

"Yes, I like green."

"What's your favourite colour?"

"Green," I reply politely, without realising that by letting her know that we have something in common, the likelihood of her leaving me alone is rapidly decreasing.

Miss Wortag stands up impetuously, almost knocking the table over as she does. "Right, time's up. We still have another twenty-five minutes of the lesson, but luckily for you, I'm in a good mood and will let you go early today." Wow, Miss Wortag in a good mood. That's something I didn't think I'd ever hear. "Clip your essays together and leave them in a neat pile on my desk as you walk out. Oh, and also, make sure you are quiet as there are still lessons ongoing."

Normally in these situations, Jessie, Cameron and I would go and hang out on the benches in the picnic area. I feel lost. I don't know where to go or what to do without them, and once again, all I want to do is curl up into a ball and disappear.

"Come, join us in the tennis courts, we're going to eat lunch out there," Tianna says, catching her breath after having ran to catch up with me.

"I think I'll just go and check my emails or something, but thank you for the kind offer." Don't get me wrong, I do appreciate her trying, but we're so different that I'd probably enjoy my own company a lot more.

"Okay," she replies with a sour look on her face.

I didn't really want to check my emails, but I do want to be alone. The area behind the PE hall is what me and the boys used to call 'the hideout'. The only way to get to it is down the 'Teacher's Only Path' and literally fighting through vines and overgrown bushes. I don't know how Jessie and I found it. Since we went to school here too, we must have just decided to bunk one day and came across it. Cameron 'borrowed' the lawnmower when we were in year eight and cut the grass down. Josh and James built a seating area out of old wood pallets, as well as a fenced area to mark our territory. Meanwhile, I bought solar lights (that I'd taken from my garden) in and hung them up on trees. We never got to see them during spring/summer months, but it looked pretty cool during winter months. From the outside, it looks like an overgrown bush, but from the inside, it's a little retreat, secluded away from the rest of the world. Well, it *was* anyway. It's the only part of the entire school that no one goes near and seems like the perfect place to clear my head.

"I knew you'd come here," a deep, recognisable voice mutters from behind the bushes, as I fight my way through them and into the hideout. It sounds like Jessie. "Go away."

"Jessie?"

"You're not welcome here anymore," he says seethingly, as if I was the one that beat him up.

"How dare you!" I scream back at him. My heart thumping, hands shaking and voice already trembling as I fight back tears. "Is it not enough that you just turned against me like that? Now you want to stop me from going where I want to go?" I feel like I am burning with rage. I want to punch him, so hard. And then kick him, and slap him. I want him to feel scared, hurt and angry, just like I did. I'll never forgive him for this, ever.

"Look," he replies. His expression soft as he puts out a cigarette and moves in closer to me. "You can't be here, okay? Just go, now, before anyone see's you."

"What are you talking about, Jess? Go where, before who sees me?" Something is telling me to run, but something is also telling me to stay and confront him, while I feel brave enough to do so. "What the hell happened last week?" His wide eyes stare deep into mine and for the first time since meeting him, I feel like I'm looking into the eyes of a stranger. His hands are shaking as he stands there staring at me, with his fingers tapping against the side of his jeans. "Well?" I yell again, so proud of my confidence.

"I," he stops. Now I can read him, he is thinking long and hard about what he is going to say. "I can't, I don't. I don't want to be friends with you anymore," he stutters.

"Oh, great. You don't want to be friends with me anymore. So rather than just tell me that, you beat me up and tell me to stay away from my girl instead?" What is wrong with this guy? He hangs his head down like a child being told off by their parents.

"People have been saying things, and I - I can't-"

"I knew it!" A voice yelled from behind the bushes, followed by a laugh, causing Jessie to jump backwards and puff his chest outwards. Through the gap in between the two bushes, I can make out a scruffy beard and messy hair – Cameron. "What are you two up to in there, eh?"

"I told you to leave me alone!" Jessie yells at me, turning to face me. His fists tightly clenched down by his side and head held high. I don't recognise him. "Stop following me everywhere, I don't like you."

"Say cheese, love birds," Cameron teases.

"Why are you both doing this?" I ask Cameron with a broken voice, as he fights through the bushes and comes towards us. Every ounce of my focus set on controlling myself so that I don't cry in front of them. My feet feel like they have been cemented to the ground, as I realise that I'm currently standing in between Cameron and Jessie - the two people that beat me up the last time I saw them. The confidence I somehow mustered up a few minutes ago has vanished into thin air, and I suddenly feel like I'm trapped.

"I'm not doing anything, I've asked you to leave me alone," Jessie replies. "Now, do it."

"Look, I'm sorry that I wasn't upfront with you guys in the beginning." It's hard not to blame myself, when none of this would have happened if I was honest with everyone from the start. "I just figured you knew, deep down, that I am meant to be a boy. If I could go back in time and change the way I handled everything, I would."

"Yeah, yeah. Well you'll be pleased to know that Jessie and Helen are doing just fine. Isn't that right, Jess?" Cameron winks at Jessie, his mischievous smile sending waves of anger through my body.

"What do you mean?" I ask, directing my question at Jessie.

His body weakens slightly and the tight ball he'd rolled his fists into loosens. "Yes, we're fine." He cuts a dirty look over at Cameron and then takes a deep breath and turns to face me, straightening his stance back up as he does. "Actually, we're more than fine. We're dating."

"What the hell, man?!" I scream at him with vehemence. I can't believe what I'm hearing, I've been gone for a week and they are already dating. How does that even happen? She's moved on that quickly. He's completely fine with dating someone that I was madly in love with? I feel sick.

Jessie doesn't reply.

"Why are you doing this to me? Please, can one of you just tell me what I've done to deserve all of this? I thought we were best friends, Jessie."

"Well, let's face it, she was never really interested in *you* in the first place, now, was she?" Cameron interjects. "I reckon if she had to choose out of the *real* you and Jessie, we definitely wouldn't have been in this situation in the first place, if you know what I mean."

"But I loved her," I sob back. "You're not meant to do that to one of your friends." I don't know what's breaking my heart more; Jessie being able to do that to me, Helen moving on so quickly or Jessie and Helen kissing and doing everything that we did (and more). Or it could even be the fact that this just confirms that there is no going back for any of us. I've lost my best friend and the love of my life in one week.

"She didn't love *you* though, Wendy," Cameron says slowly, pronouncing every syllable of my name the way Miss Wortag does. "She never loved Wendy, and you are Wendy."

I can't breathe.

My forehead, nose and the back of my neck feel hot and itchy, and the open space that we are in suddenly feels like a small, warm and suffocating box. My heart is slamming against the walls of my chest so hard that I can feel my body vibrating with it. The urge to run has my legs twitching with adrenaline, but the fear of making myself look like an idiot glues my feet to the ground. I can feel my mind begin to wander off, imagining Jessie and Helen holding hands, cuddling up and laughing together. The thought of her walking down the aisle to me, quickly turns into her and Jessie walking out of the church after their wedding;

everyone cheering on the happy couple, everyone so happy to see them together.

Pins and needles tingle my feet as I find myself running as far away from Jessie and Cameron as possible. My tight chest hurts with a sharp pain, as I try and stop myself from having what feels like a heart attack. All I can hear is my breathing, everything else sounds like I am under water. Drops of puddle water splash up on my ankles as my feet move faster than they ever have, and everything around me seems like a blur. The cold air that I felt earlier suddenly feels hot and humid.

The overpowering sewage smell from the girls toilets has turned into the most comforting thing I have ever smelt as I burst through the door and slam a toilet door shut. The thought of Helen and Jessie keeps circulating around and around in my head. So much, that I have a pounding headache from it all. I'm so angry at myself for allowing this to happen. I mean, it's just common sense that if you lie to someone about who you are, they're going to end up hating you.

"ARGHHHHHHHHHHHHHHHHHHHHHHHHH!" I find myself screaming out in pain, as I curl up into a ball on the cold floor, repeatedly punch myself in the head, and pull my hair until I see clumps of it coming off in my hand. I've lost the strength to want to carry on trying and the thought of sticking with the norm and just being a 'normal girl' is beginning to sound like a good idea.

Nine

The stranger

The toilet door lets out a large creak as it opens and then slowly closes, followed by four very quick footsteps. They've come after me. As I take one deep breath in, the toilet remains in total silence and it is impossible to tell whether I imagined it or if someone is actually there. The sound of my breath trembling as I cautiously exhale is loud enough for anyone in the toilets to hear. There are no sounds of any toilet doors closing or anyone using the toilet, I can't hear anyone talking and I can't tell how many people are there.

A faint shadow slowly makes an appearance from under the doorway. It gets closer to me as the person behind the door creeps up towards it. The rumours that Miss Wortag's dead sister haunts these toilets doesn't sound so bad anymore; I would much rather have a ghost keep me company than a bully. The shadow gets close enough for it to stop right before my feet. It stands still and a strong vanilla scent radiates from behind the cubicle door. The smell is calming, and isn't one I recognise from anyone that I know, although the majority of mum's hand lotions are vanilla scented. Three loud knocks on the door make the hairs on my neck stand to attention. The shadow stands still. Frozen with fear, I find myself staring at it while counting every beat of my pulsing heart in an effort to stop myself from having another panic attack. The shadow knocks another three times, sending cold, sharp shivers down my spine. What initially seemed like a good idea, running into the cubicle is probably the worst thing I could have done. I am trapped.

"Just leave me alone! What else do you want from me? I can't take this anymore. Please, just leave me alone!" My body starts hyperventilating as I scream at the figure to go away. I can't take any more of it. As if I didn't hate myself enough to begin with, this whole situation has made me hate myself even more.

"Hey." A soft, muffled voice replies from behind the door. It's a girl.

"I saw what happened and I wanted to see if you are okay. Stupid thing to say really, because I know you are not. I just wanted to say I understand. You don't have to be scared," she continues. It sounds like she's covering her mouth with something. The shadow moves closer and turns into a ball like figure. She's coming closer. Gripping onto the cold, hard base of the toilet seat with one hand, and leaning against the wall with the other, I find myself trying to back away as far as the toilet will let me. I've become a paranoid, emotional mess.

"Look, I'm not with anyone," the voice whispers. "I know you probably don't trust me after everything you have been through, but I just wanted to let you know that you're not alone. I'm kind of going through a similar thing and I could really do with a friend. I'm guessing you need a friend too?"

Well, she is spot on. I do need a friend. I need someone that gets me and won't judge me. I'm desperate for someone that I can be myself around, without fear of them turning on me or hurting me. I need someone that I can trust and someone that trusts me. I need a Jessie that won't turn their back on me, despite our differences. Her calming presence has me feeling torn between trusting her, or sticking with my instincts and just staying alone for the rest of my life. "If you don't want to come out, you don't have to. I know trusting someone again is going to be hard after everything you've been through. I don't want you to feel pressured or uneasy with me being here so I will leave, but if you do change your mind, I'm always here for you." She waits for a moment, and then starts rustling something around, before holding a piece of paper under the door.

"Here's my number." She frantically waves the piece of paper in my direction. "Send me a text if you do want to chat." Her voice clearer than it was a moment ago, but still slightly muffled, she sounds fragile. "Take it then, my hand is going to go numb."

"Oh, yeah, okay. Thanks" I stutter back shyly, taking the paper from her strikingly hot hand.

"No, Thank *you*, Mr."

Mr.

No one's called me that before. I listen attentively as the sounds of her footsteps move further and further away, the squeaky creak of the door as it opens and closes again, and then the toilets falling into the impenetrable silence that I wanted when I ran in here.

Home

My bedroom has become my safe space, and with everything that has gone on recently, I'm grateful that I had somewhere to get away from it all, at least. No one can get to me while I am locked away in my bedroom. It doesn't stop them from being alive in my mind, though. I can't stop myself from thinking about Helen and her shock at everything coming out, Jessie and Cameron beating me up and not feeling any remorse for it, and the news that Jessie and Helen are now dating. Not to mention the fact that Cameron seems to be inexplicably amused by it all. And then there are my parents and the way they brushed it off, as well as Miss Wortag for completely ignoring it. My thoughts have turned into what seems like a never-ending nightmare, and I feel like I'm constantly falling further and further into the deep hole that I've managed to dig myself into.

"Wendy!" Mum yells from downstairs. I didn't even realise she was in.

Piling three glasses on top of two plates and holding a mug with my little finger, I carefully make my way downstairs. A strong smell of lavender heating up on the oil burner permeates the stairway, but other than that, the dead silence from the house is strange. She isn't waiting at the bottom of the stairs, making noise in the kitchen or talking to Jake, but I couldn't have imagined her calling me. Surely, I can't be going mad as well as everything else. Max's buggy isn't in the hallway, neither is mum's hand bag, or her shoes. I hadn't noticed the oil burner when I came home, but I think I would have if it had been lit. What kind of intruder comes into someone's house and lights the oil burner? I silently creep up towards the kitchen, holding onto the plates firmly with one hand and a butter knife with the other hand. I wonder how threatening I'll look to an intruder, holding up a butter knife, that is literally still covered with butter and breadcrumbs. The door creaks slightly as I open it. I hadn't realised there was a creak in our door before.

"What are you doing out there?" Mum moans from behind the door, followed by a loud tut. So, she is home.

"Nothing, coming. Just trying to open the door." I sigh, trying to give off some sort of hint that she could have at least offered to help if she knew I was out there.

Both mum *and* dad are sitting side by side, by the table, in dead silence. Neither of them look at me as I walk in, despite the fact that I've done something I rarely do – bring things down from my room, without being told to do so. I thought that was a miracle in itself, but what really is a miracle, is the fact that neither of them have acknowledged me. Mum lightly taps her red nails on the table as I make my way over to the sink. The pressure of her watchful eyes makes it difficult to concentrate, and I can already tell that she is in a bad mood.

Neither of them say a word.

"Where are Jake and Max?" I asked curiously, after finally realising that the reason the house feels silent is because they're not here.

"They're with aunt Trina for the night, they'll be home tomorrow. Sit down," dad replies. His blunt, dull, and quiet voice muttering out the words, while he points towards the chair opposite him. He doesn't sound happy at all. "What is going on, Wendy ?" He stares at me with narrowed eyebrows. He definitely isn't happy.

"With what?" I'm clueless.

"Well, one day you are a girl that thinks you are a boy. Another day you go out late and return home with a coconut of a bruise on your face, but no recollection of who hurt you. Mum then speaks to Anne who says that you're not talking to Jessie anymore. What is going on?" he asks again.

His voice slightly softer so that he can encourage me to open up to him.

"One day I'm a girl that thinks I'm a boy?" I shriek out in utter shock. "What the hell is that supposed to mean?" He didn't understand a single word I said last week. Either that or he didn't listen. I don't know what he is expecting me to respond to that. I don't *think* I want to be anything; I know what I am and what I am *meant* to be. I can't tell either of them how I got the bruise on my face because if I do, mum will march me over to Jessie's house and have us both kiss, make up and promise never to do it again. Things don't work like that in the real world. Not where Jessie is concerned anyway. I know him far too well.

"You know what I mean," he replies sternly.

No, I don't know what he means and quite frankly, I wish he would just shut up and think before he says things sometimes. I'm so exhausted from feeling like I can't get through to anyone anymore and in all honesty, I don't know how much more of it I can take. My whole world has fallen apart in the past week and just to make sure we end it with a bang, my parents have decided to argue with me. Today.

Mum coughs, "well?"

"I don't know what you want me to say, mum!" I reply, yelling. That lump in my throat that I've become all too familiar with making a suffocating re-appearance. "I'm lost and no one is helping me. All you guys do is ignore me and everyone else? Well that's a whole different story. I don't know who I am, what I want or where I'm going. I'm so confused." I sob, uncontrollably. My anger quickly turning into heartbreak as images of Helen and Jessie flood my mind. Snot, rapidly drips from my nose and my chest tightens as I take quick, sharp breaths. I can't fight back the tears anymore. "Nothing has changed since we last spoke about this subject." The words sound like a load of gibberish, but if it made sense to me, it must have made a little sense to them.

"But, I thought we cleared all of that up, Wendy?" mum replies, she reaches her hand over and grabs mine in an effort to comfort me. Dad's eyebrows are narrowed upwards and eyes wide, he hates seeing me sad.

"Cleared what up? What do you think this is?" I reply, pulling my hand away quicker than she was able to stop me. "I'm still in this disgusting body. You still call me Wendy. What the hell has been cleared up? I'm a boy, mum." My tears quickly begin to dry up on my face as the words feel amazing. I've never actually sat here and said the words 'I am a boy' to my parents. I've never actually said those words to anyone. Dad straightens up his back and takes a deep breath inwards, while mum tightly squeezes onto his hand.

"No, Wendy, you're not."

"I'm a boy, mum." I feel great. I feel like I can be so unapologetically me. I don't care what anyone thinks anymore. I mean, the people I was closest with made their feelings clear, so why would anyone else's feelings matter.

"Stop it now, darling."

"I'm a boy."

"STOP IT, RIGHT NOW!" Dad screams, standing up and slamming his fists down on the table, causing mum and I to jump in our seats. "When your mother tells you to stop it, you stop. Do you understand me?" His voice lowered, but still unnecessarily loud.

I nod my head, yes. That powerful feeling I just felt is gone and the room falls into total silence, all I can hear is the sound of mum's vintage grandfather clock in the hallway. I can't look at either of my parents, especially not my dad. He's never shouted at me like that before. I didn't even know his voice could go so loud. He hates me.

"What's going on at college?" mum asks, breaking the silence. "Have you fallen out with Jessie?"

"No," I reply, playing with my fingers on my lap, under the table.

"Funnily enough," she replies with a sarcastic tone to her voice. "When I heard that you had fallen out with Jessie, I spoke with your English teacher about the possibility of you being bullied." Why wouldn't she just ask me that directly?

"It turns out that Cameron, the one I said I didn't like, he's actually one of the worst bullies there is." Oh, don't I know it. Now would be the perfect time to tell mum about everything that is going on, but I don't know if I can. I'm scared about the repercussions and I can't bear the thought of making things worse. Also, if mum dragged me round to Jessie's house and Helen was there, I don't know if I'd be able to live with that. The thought of it is bad enough, but seeing them together is different.

"I think you need to speak to a professional about what is going on," she blurts out quickly, before turning to look at dad and blushing. It's almost as if she wasn't meant to say that.

"A professional?" I ask. "Well, if you're talking about a doctor, yes. I'd need to speak with someone before I'm able to start my surgery."

"What surgery?"

"To have my bits changed into what they're meant to be," I reply, pointing towards my vagina. I'm horrified that I have just had to say that in front of my dad.

"Hold on, no. That's not what I meant, Wendy." Her sunken eyes focus on the fresh bouquet of gypsophila on the table, while dad itches his nose and looks around the room. "We would like you to speak to a professional, as we think you may be suffering from a mental health condition that you are not able to deal with on your own." She looks over at dad for support, but he's now fixed his eyes on the flowers. "We want to help you, but we don't know how to, and we think it would be best if you speak to someone that will be able to provide you with the guidance that we can't." She does that pause and stare thing again, waiting for my reaction. "We are on your side, darling. All we want is for our little girl to come back. We really miss our Wendy."

"Argh, mum!" She was doing so well. "Can you please stop calling me that!" Every time I hear the word it makes my skin crawl. "I hate it, it's not me and I don't need professional help! What I need is for you both to just try and understand what is going on." The frustration of having to go over the same thing without getting anywhere is becoming draining, I have a headache. "All you've both done is ignore me when I've tried to talk about it, but your little girl is dead, mum. She died when you had a miscarriage." I utter the words out quicker than I was able to process what I was about to say. I've never regretted anything as much as I have that, but she won't believe me if I tell her that I didn't mean for it to come out the way it did.

"You rude, disrespectful and horrible little girl!" mum hisses as her eyes well up and hands begin to shake. Watching my mother's eyes fill with tears as a result of something I've done is heart breaking. I've never seen her cry, not even during sad parts in films.

"Mum, I'm sorry. I wasn't trying to be ru-"

"Just go to your room, Wendy! Get out of my sight!" She screams, breaking down into a quiet cry as I scramble to my feet and run upstairs. I crossed a line just then, and I don't know whether I'll be able to put it right. I know she won't believe me when I tell her that I wanted to take it back the minute I said it, no one does seem to listen to anything I say these days.

The pain just keeps on growing as my mind flickers from one event to the next. Every part of it hurting a little more each time I think about it. I could have been honest with Helen from the start, been upfront with the boys and hard-headed with my parents. I could have put my foot down when I had a chat with Miss Wortag and stood up for myself when I was at the hideout with Jessie and Cameron. I'm old enough and wise enough not to sit here and think about what I could have or should have done, but I can't help myself. Each time I do, I realise there were so many opportunities for all of this to have been avoided. The mess I've made of my life so far, doesn't seem to be giving me much hope that things will get any easier when I do transition.

My body trembles as I let out another loud roar in heartache.

I cry and cry until I physically cannot cry any longer and it begins to hurt my chest. The thought of running away and leaving everyone and everything behind is something that has crossed my mind a lot, but where would I go and what would I do? I could hitch hike a ride on the motorway in the hope that the person I ride with is going as far away from here as possible, and settle down somewhere else where no one knows me. I could shave off my hair and introduce myself as Paul to everyone, find someone that makes dodgy passports and order one in my new name. I could work out and become a muscular hunk that has more game than Jessie does. The thought of that excites me, but at the same time, the thought of Jake and Max growing up without me is something I won't be able to live with. My parents, although we aren't seeing eye to eye right now, will be hurt and will probably spend the rest of their lives looking for me.

The scrunched up piece of paper that the stranger from the toilets gave me, falls out of my pockets as I change my trousers. That overpowering vanilla scent spreads through my room as I unravel it, re-read the note and begin typing the number into my phone.

Me: 'Do you know who this is?'

The stranger: 'Mr?'

Ten

Confused

Paul

Me: 'Hey guys. What's new?'

It's hard being the bubbly Paul that everyone online knows me as, with all the crap going around in my mind. I've found myself craving comfort from my online identity - the Paul that I really am. I don't know whether it's that I need reminding that people do see Paul as a real person, or if it's just that I need to take my mind off of it all. My head hurts from where I've allowed myself to lay up all night, every night, thinking about everything, again and again until I fall asleep. Whatever it is, I'd be lost without my laptop right now.

Olivia: 'Wow, so you haven't forgotten about us and moved on with your new woman!'

Stuart: 'Ha! Welcome back. Did she get bored already?'

Henry: 'I cannot believe you dropped us all like that. You need to do a dare to make up for it, and film yourself doing it.'

Nothing's changed. They are all carrying on as normal without a care in the world. They have no idea how much I appreciate and value our friendship, now more than ever. I wrap my duvet around my upper body and sit upright with my legs crossed. My laptop resting on my thighs.

Me: 'I've really missed you guys. What's the gossip?'

Stuart: 'We've missed you too, bud. Nothing interesting, apart from Henry losing his virginity to a married woman, old enough to be his mother.'

Me: 'No way!! That is hilarious. How did you manage that?!'

Henry: 'She was a M.I.L.F and yes, it is true. I met her at a bar and one thing lead to another. I'm sure she isn't proud of it, but I certainly am! Anyway, what's new in the world of Paul?'

Speaking to these guys kind of reminds me of the boys. Stuart's impenitent personality closely resembles Cameron and Josh, while Henry reminds me of Jessie in some way. Both of them spend the majority of their day boasting about women they've been able to pull. Olivia's a lot like James, she doesn't talk as much as the rest of us do, but she is there whenever you need her; we call her the mum of the group.

Me: 'Oh, nothing interesting, same old really. What about you guys?'

Stuart: 'Nothing interesting? Dude, it feels like you've been gone for ages. If nothing interesting was going on, you'd be online talking to us boring lot. How are things with the hot girl? Have you gone all the way yet?'

Damn, I was really hoping they would have forgotten about Helen. The thought of her alone makes my stomach churn, let alone actually saying the words out loud, as I explain the situation to them. I want to tell them everything, especially about my situation, but if they get upset that I've lied to them about who I am, they might not want to talk to me again. I don't know what I'll do without them. Being able to be Paul, even just for a few minutes a day, is amazing. It is *the* most exhilarating feeling I've ever felt.

Me: 'No, we stopped seeing each other a little while ago. Listen, guys. I need to tell you all something. Are you going to be online later?

I've got to tell them. I've got to start being honest about who I really am.

Olivia: 'Yes, I'll be online from around 6pm. Is everything okay?'

Henry: 'I'll be here.'

Stuart: 'Me too. All okay?'

Me: 'Yeah, nothing to worry about. I've got to get ready for college now anyway, I'll speak to you guys later.'

I don't think they'll judge me or react negatively to it, but I am worried that they just won't understand. Answering loads of questions and pretending that I'm okay with just being a topic of interest isn't something I want to do. In my ideal world, I'd tell them, they will say 'okay', and that will be the end of it. Everything will carry on as normal. It's possible, as they're a good bunch of people, but then again, how well do you know someone that you've never met in person?

The fresh, ice-cold air from outside, makes my room freezing cold the minute I open the window, while the warm sun brightens the whole room up. There's something refreshing about bright, freezing cold mornings. It kind of reminds me of waking up in our tent with dad during our school summer break. Waking up in the woods, we'd always have hot chocolate by the fire pit, and blow 'smoke' out of our mouths with how cold it was. Today feels like it might be an alright day, as long as I can avoid any interaction with the boys.

College - Wendy

Science is the one lesson that I can't get away from the foreigner that used to be my best friend – Jessie. It is also the one lesson I'd completely forgotten I had today. With the teachers completely oblivious to what is going on, and the thought of making matters worse if I ask for help, as well as every other seat being taken, there really is no escaping him here. I'd sold myself a dream thinking I could go a day without having to interact with any of the boys.

Mr Ringer waits at the front of the class while we all take our seats. Jessie hasn't batted an eyelid at me as I make my way over to the desk to sit next to him. A strong smell of cigarette butts, mixed with way too much perfume, comes from his direction.

"Hi," he says quietly, turning to face me with a goofy smile on his face as I pull my seat out. He looks awful. The slits in his eyebrows have grown out, making them look bushy and messy. His beard and hair are overgrown and his teeth look like they haven't been brushed in weeks.

"Leave me alone, Jessie."

"Fine. I was just being polite." He grits his teeth and clenches his fist on the table, one large vein popping out of his forearm as he does. His fingernails are long and dirty and from what I can see on the palm of his hand, the part that isn't covered by his tightly clenched fingers, is thick, black, dirt. So thick, that it looks like he has been digging a hole in the ground with his bare hands.

"Well, don't. I don't need you to be polite." I reply through my teeth so that Mr Ringer doesn't notice me talking.

"No, but you do need to get a life," he teases. It's not funny.

"Oh, shut up, Jessie."

"Okay, well, don't say I didn't try." He lets out a quiet sigh and then crosses his arms.

"Try? Have you lost your mind?" I reply, whisper shouting.

"Shh, I'm concentrating." He holds his index finger over his pouted lips, smiles for the hundredth time and then looks back at Mr Ringer. I want to wipe that cocky looking grin off his face so badly.

"So, if you use that to answer the questions on page eight of your text books," Mr Ringer says loudly across the classroom. "I'll give you fifteen minutes to answer as many as you can. Once you're done, you'll swap answer sheets and we'll spend the first part of the lesson going through the answers."

I didn't hear a single word he said, and in all honesty, I didn't even realise he had been talking the whole time. I was so absorbed with Jessie and the fact that he was winding me up, that I've now got to humiliate myself and ask for him to repeat everything he just said, or sit here in silence and do nothing.

Science is normally my favourite lesson. Neither me nor Jessie have an interest in perusing a career that has anything to do with science, but we enjoyed messing around so much in school, we decided to choose the subject, so that we could stay together throughout college too. I'm surprised we weren't separated and permanently excluded from our school class with the amount of crap we used to get up to, but no one really said a word. Maybe we weren't as bad as we thought we were. I'd usually have to re-teach everything to Jessie as his attention is clearly no different to that of a gold fish's. Choosing to study science has now turned into the worst decision I could have made, though. All we're going to do is sit in awkward silence during experiments. He'll wonder off towards Josh and James and I'll probably just end up browsing the internet on my phone.

"Great." I sigh, slouching back down in my seat, while sneakily taking my phone out of my pocket. I can already feel Jessie's eyes glaring over at me as I re-read the stranger's message.

I didn't reply to her text last night. I guess I panicked when she replied, I wasn't expecting her to respond so quickly. The calm from the class as everyone flips back and forth between different pages of their textbook, gives me a few moments to think. She did reach out to me. I mean, I doubt she would have hid if I'd have opened the toilet cubicle door, but something about it just seems a little odd.

Me: 'Who is this?'

My palms sweat as I look up to find Josh glaring back at Jessie with an evil grin on his face. The stranger could be one of them! Then again, neither of them have their phones on them and I doubt they'd be able to encourage someone to do all of that in an effort to humiliate me. They're far too lazy to go through that much trouble. They'd much rather just beat me up and be done with it.

The stranger: 'It's nice of you to finally reply. How are you?'

Me: 'Huh? I'm good, thanks. Who are you?

The stranger: 'I don't want to say. You won't want to talk to me if I tell you who I am.'

Me: 'Why do you think I won't want to talk to you? This is weird.'

The stranger: 'Sorry.'

The stranger: 'I just want a friend.'

Me: 'Friends kind of know who they are talking to.'

The stranger: 'Have I made you mad?'

Me: 'What? No. I don't even know who you are, why would I be mad at you?'

The stranger: 'I don't know. Everyone seems to be mad at me lately.'

Me: 'I just need to know who you are.'

Jessie tuts and rubs his forehead, flicking his pen around on the table. He turns one page of his exercise book, reads that and then switches back to the answer sheet, before repeating the process again. He's confused and currently regretting falling out with me, I bet my life on it. He's far too focused to be behind the texts from the stranger. Josh and James are at opposite ends of the table, as if they are in a real exam. Both of them are also concentrating hard, and neither of them are saying a thing. Everyone else in the class appears to be doing the same, unbothered by my presence. So who is this stranger and why won't she tell me who she is? If she's not plotting to hurt me with Jessie and Cameron, why wouldn't she just be upfront about who she is from the start? Then again, who am I to talk.

The frustration of not knowing who it is and whether it will be someone I can trust is beginning to make me feel uncomfortable, and my neck has started sweating again. It's itchy and making the tag of my t-shirt stick to me.

"Yes, Wendy." Mr Ringer responds as I raise my arm.

"May I be excused for a toilet break?" Jessie starts sniggering. I forget Mr Ringer isn't my school teacher anymore, he's my college teacher. Meaning I'm an adult and shouldn't be asking to use the toilet like a child.

"Yes," he replies. "Thank you for asking so politely." He scolds a look across at Jessie, pointing to his watch to encourage him to focus on his work.

The toilets are another one of my safe spaces and the only part of college that I can go to clear my head of everything that is going on. The sound of water running through drains amongst the reassuring silence of the empty room gives me some well needed peace and quiet. People rarely use these ones after the rumour about Miss Wortag's sister circulated, and, after another rumour outbreak that people were getting shivers down their spine when using the toilet, everyone is too cowardly to come in here alone. These particular toilets are the coldest part of the entire building. No matter how hot it is outside or whether the radiators are on, the room is always freezing cold. You'll never see anyone stay here longer than five minutes, it's always straight in and straight back out again. Anyone except me, that is. The creepy creak in the door quietens as it gently closes, still echoing across the entire room. Someone really needs to sort that door out. My cubicle, or should I say, the cubicle that I've made my own, is on the far end on the left-hand side. It's situated as far away from the entrance as possible, so that I can go unnoticed if anyone walks in. The only downside is that with it being so far from the entrance, it's also far from the exit. So, if anyone does come in looking for me, I won't be able to escape easily.

The sound of quick footsteps from behind me cause me to jump around quicker then I was able to process what it was I heard. It's Tianna, walking from one toilet to another. Her fiery red hair floating in and out of the cubicles opposite me, while she pretends not to have noticed I'm here. How can she not know I am standing directly opposite her? She pops her head inside one cubicle and looks around, before moving on to do the same thing with another.

"Ahem!" I cough loudly, mainly to distract myself from how nervous I was at the thought of being left alone in a room with her.

"Oh, hey," she replies softly, still walking in and out of toilets. Let me guess, she's going to try and escape through the toilets this time. "I've lost my phone, have you seen one?"

"No, sorry."

"I did know you were there by the way, I'm just pretty stressed out about my phone. I've searched these toilets twice already," she continues. Finally giving up on her search.

"Well, if you can't find it, I'm sure you'll be able to get a new one. Is it insured?" I reply reassuringly.

"Yes, but that's not what's important. It's the people that I talk to on it that are. I don't know if I've saved their number to my SIM or my phone either." Her cheeks blush red as she works herself up into a flustered mess.

"Ah, I see. Well, that's too bad, I hope you do find it. If I see anything, I'll let you know." I reply, sliding in through the toilet doors, locking them behind me. It's kind of awkward now. I didn't actually need to use the toilet, but I can't just sit here in silence. I don't know where else she expects to find her phone if she has already looked here, twice. It's not like there is much to look through. I mean, there are eight toilets, eight sinks and two hand-dryers. The room is so painfully quiet, you could hear a pin drop. I can't hear her quick, light footsteps walking across the room anymore, or the sound of her moving around.

As I squeeze for just a drizzle of pee to break the silence, Tianna starts humming. She sounds happy, which, in comparison to how stressed she was when I just spoke to her, is strange. Her calming, long notes echo across the room, and it is now in this exact moment that I have realised how utterly terrifying she is. Forget the ghost or my own thoughts. My worst fear has now become Tianna. For all I know, she could be humming happily while she sharpens a knife behind the door.

Her humming abruptly comes to an end after the loud 'CLICK!', from the bolt of a toilet door opening. The thought of her on all fours, crawling towards me with her head twisted in the wrong direction, is the only thing I can think of. I don't know why I always have to be so dramatic, but I guess it is possible.

"I'm going now," she says loudly. "Am I going to see you again?"

She's in my English class, I'm going to see her tomorrow, as a matter of fact. But never mind that, she always seems to just pop up, I'll probably see her the minute I walk out of here. *And* my dad always invites her family over to mine. Of course I'm going to see her again.

"Err, yeah, why wouldn't you see me again?"

The room falls into silence again. It's kind of embarrassing talking through the toilet door, but I don't want to come out. I shouldn't have given her a reason to keep the conversation going.

"Sorry, I meant I'll see you around." She lowers the tone of her voice, sounding disappointed.

"Okay, bye, then." I think my over enthusiastic politeness might have come across as happiness that she's leaving. It is, but she doesn't need to know that. The sound of her rapid footsteps, followed by the main door opening and closing, leaves the room in total silence, apart from the constant drip of water from the tap.

Home - Paul

Dad always says that social media is not real life, and it is best to imagine that the things people say and do are not real things. When I bought my first laptop and stopped using the family computer downstairs, he gave me a speech about the dangers of meeting people online, giving out bank details to people I don't know, and just the general internet safety stuff. He used my uncle Toby as an example. On the internet, Uncle Toby is very successful. He goes on holidays all the time, he has a flashy car and an enormous house. In reality, he is in the process of selling his house, and his car, in an effort to keep his business afloat. Dad drilled it into my head that the people I see on social media aren't actually revealing who they really are, they're revealing what they want the world to see. I thought it was rubbish and that I'd be able to tell the difference between a fraudster and a real person. I still think that I would, but when I look at my situation and how the internet makes me feel, I realise that not everyone is out to gain something that jeopardises another person's way of life. For me, it is more about making myself happy and having the freedom to be whoever I want to be. For others, though, it might look like I am pretending to be a boy so that I can get some sort of gain out of it.

Being Paul on the internet takes everything away. Paul is a very happy person. He is funny, charming, ambitious and confident. He speaks up and joins in on debates, he can make friends easily and even flirt with girls if he wanted to. Paul is perfect. Lonely days would be lonelier without my online identity. My relationship with my family has been replaced with nothing. I've gone from being a part of the most popular group in my year to being a lonely, sad and pathetic excuse of a human being. The freak of the college, and most importantly, the only one that isn't normal like the rest. The only place that I don't feel like a freak is online, with my friends.

My heart feels heavy and the back of my neck hot as my laptop boots up. I throw my hoodie over to the other side of my room, aiming (and obviously missing) for the laundry basket. I've been ignoring this thought all day, and at one point, I'm certain I actually forgot about it. I haven't had the time to think about how I'm going to say it, what I'm even going to say and whether I'm ready to tell them everything. I guess once you've started off with a lie, it's so much easier just to carry on with it and hope it doesn't come out, but I really don't want to risk losing these guys like I have the others. If they aren't happy that I've lied, at least I can say that I was honest eventually.

I like to think that I am a smart person; my parents raised me to make smart choices and express my feelings when I feel uneasy about something. They encourage me to work hard if I want something, and dad has spent a lot of time teaching me how to stand up to people when I strongly believe in something. Talking about standing up to people, it was interesting to see his reaction when I stood up for myself the other day. Contradiction much? I was always taught that if something is hurting me I shouldn't do it. Standing too close to a hot radiator, for example, or playing with the door knowing that my fingers could get caught in it. I am fully aware that admitting to people that I have lied about who I am, will most likely leave me lonelier than I was to begin with, and my mind is screaming at itself to just not say anything. But I have to.

Me: 'Hey guys, sorry I had to shoot off like that earlier. I'd only just seen the time and had to rush to get ready for college.'

I've found myself wanting to talk to them now more than ever. I think it's because I know that this might be the last time I actually speak to them. I wonder if they'll report my profile and have it removed, or spam it with malicious comments, letting everyone know that I'm a fraudster. My addiction to my online personality before all of the drama started, was mainly something that enabled me to be Paul, but now it is that and so much more. They have turned into the only people that haven't turned against me, yet. Even though they have no idea what is going on, every time I go online it's like my outside world just doesn't exist anymore and nothing else really matters.

Olivia: 'Is everyone else here?'

Stuart: 'Yep.'

Henry: 'Yes.'

Olivia: 'Okay, let's talk.'

My hands shake as I struggle to find the confidence to just stand up for myself and tell them who I am. Tears begin to flood my eyes at the thought of losing them. I don't think I'm brave enough to do this, despite the fact that I made myself believe that I was.

Olivia: 'Paul?'

Why did I even say anything?

Me: 'Yes, I'm here. Okay, guys. There is no easy way to say this, but before I do, I just want you to know that I'd never do anything intentionally to hurt any of you. I would love nothing more than to just carry on as normal, and not fall out with you, once I've told you, but obviously that depends on how you all feel about it.'

Olivia: 'Whatever it is, I'm sure there will be no falling out. You can tell us anything'

Just like everyone else, Olivia seems to be a fair minded, reasonable person. However, just like everyone else, I run the risk of being ignored or just downright humiliated if I do tell the truth. The heat from the radiator next to my bed, causes my legs and arms to feel sticky and uncomfortable, not to mention the sweat from the cling film that I am yet to take off. The sound of dad's car pulling up on the drive distracts me as I find myself thinking of reasons to go and talk to him and disappear from this conversation. I listen attentively as he walks in the front door, drops his keys on the side and makes his way straight into the kitchen. The sound of the car engine cooling down outside, as well as dad opening a bottle of Supermalt as he walks in, is off-putting. I'm not complaining, though.

Me: 'I've tried (and failed) to get people to understand. I was born into a girl's body. I have female parts and my birth name is a female one. I think I was meant to be a boy. Deep down I am a boy. When I am Paul I am at my happiest and when I am forced to be Wendy, I hate myself. I'm sorry for lying. You guys accepted me for Paul and became such a comfort to me, that I didn't want to lose any of it. I know what is going to happen now, but if you ever do find it in your hearts to forgive me I would be very grateful.'

Olivia immediately starts typing and then stops. As does Henry and Stuart.

I think the logical thing to do in a situation like this, would be to leave the group and save myself from having to answer loads of questions, or get kicked off. But I can't help but feel like I owe them an explanation. They are a good bunch of people, and deserve to know the truth and that I respect them enough to give it to them. Everything Helen said about honesty and loyalty will stick with me for the rest of my life. It is true when she said honesty is always the best policy.

Stuart: 'Well, good on you for being brave enough to be who you were truly meant to be.'

Me: 'What do you mean?'

It's hard to tell whether he is being sarcastic or not. I know what he meant, but Stuart was the one that I was expecting a negative reaction from the most.

Stuart: 'I mean, good on you, well done, congratulations and all that Jazz. You are a good person, you shouldn't feel bad about being who you are. Can I also just point out one thing, though?'

Me: 'Do you really mean that? And yes, of course you can.

Stuart: 'You've literally wasted so much time explaining something so simple, when you didn't need to. Your speech up there was so confusing, it almost went over my head. Yes, I did mean it by the way. '

Me: 'Sorry. There's no other way I can describe it.'

Olivia: 'What he means to say is that all you have to say is that you're transgender. You don't have to explain everything else, it's a normal thing.'

I don't know what's left me speechless more. Olivia's comment or Stuart's reaction. I've never actually been called normal before. Even when I was 'normal' before I realised I am trans.

Henry: 'So, what's the big news then? I've literally been online for hours just waiting for you to come online and tell us.'

Olivia: 'That was the news Henry. Time to wake up now!'

Henry: 'You have got to be joking?'

Stuart: 'Yeah, dude, to be fair you were quite dramatic with it this morning. I thought you were going to say something bad.'

They're not bothered by it in the slightest. Olivia said it was 'normal', are they all feeling okay? Not once have I felt normal. I've never even had a 'normal' conversation with people about it until just now. I thought Henry and Stuart would have ripped the crap out of me for it, but they're not bothered. Not bothered at all.

Me: 'Wow, guys. You have no idea what that means to me. I love you guys, you've got no idea, man.'

My phone vibrates from my pocket. It is the stranger again.

The stranger: 'What are you up to?'

Me: 'Erm, nothing interesting. What about you?'

Why I'm engaging in conversation with someone that is clearly playing games is beyond me, but something about the suspense of not knowing who she is has me slyly wanting the conversation to carry on the way it is.

The stranger: 'Same.'

Me: 'What exactly do you want?'

The stranger: 'Someone to talk to, I guess.'

Me: 'Well, what do you want to talk about?'

The stranger: 'I don't know. Life, I guess. I just feel so lonely.'

Me: 'Me too.'

Well I did up until I spoke to the guys online a few minutes ago.

The stranger: 'My parents hate me.'

Me: 'I'm sure they don't hate you.'

The stranger: 'They do'

She comes across as lost. Almost like she is so desperate for a friend that she'll open up to anyone that will listen. I feel bad for her, but whilst I do want to open up to her, how can I be certain that she is a genuine person, when she won't tell me who she is? I mean, she did say herself that I wouldn't want to talk to her if I knew who she was, so there must be something there.

Me: 'How long have you been feeling lonely?'

The stranger: 'A while. Too long. What about you?'

Me: 'A while too. It feels like it's been way too long.'

The stranger: 'I have to go, don't text back. I'll text you soon.'

Eleven

Unexpected

A thick, sheet of fog has covered the village and I can barely make out the street lights through it, let alone whether I'm walking in the right direction or not. Mum gave me a fog light to bring with me when I left this morning as she wasn't driving. She reckons it all will have cleared up way before midday.

Although it's difficult to tell whether I am in the middle of the road or on the pavement, there is something empowering about walking forwards without being able to see where you're going. I guess it's the thought of not knowing what is ahead of me that is weirdly encouraging me to keep going. I could be walking towards an axe murderer and be no wiser until I bump into them. A car could swerve off the road and squash me and I wouldn't be expecting it. I could even end up walking in the complete opposite direction to college and end up lost, forever. Although that last one is stupid as I know exactly where I'm going, I could do the journey blindfolded.

Today's weather closely resembles my life at the moment – forcing myself to walk forwards without a clue where I'm headed or what I'm going to run into on the way. It seems like every day is gloomy and funereal lately. I don't remember the last time there was a bit of long lasting sunshine in my life, both literally and psychologically. I fell asleep on my chat with the stranger, after spending hours re-reading the texts in the hope that I might be able to have read between the lines and figure out who she was. Still none-the-wiser, though. I feel slightly more powerful this morning. My online group of friends have given me a strength I never thought I had and they don't even know it. I've been waiting years for just one person to say, 'it's okay. You are normal' so to have all of them do so simultaneously has warmed my heart in unimaginable ways.

The bus stop is empty. Everyone is probably too nervous to walk through the fog not being able to see where they are going. The headlights of cars shine brightly as everyone drives cautiously to avoid a crash. The world has become slow, but for once it feels like I am a little bit further ahead.

As I sit at the bus stop and wait patiently for a bus that I have a strong feeling isn't going to arrive, I notice a skinny, dark figure walking towards me. The figure glides through the fog effortlessly, and doesn't seem to have noticed the way the world has slowed down. Whoever it is, is wearing a big, black, puffer jacket with the fur hood up and has their hands in their pocket. I'm too nervous to look directly at them as they approach, especially after making myself believe that they were looking at me. There's nothing worse than a stranger catching you staring, and having that awkward moment where you don't know whether you should smile or just look away. I feel a slight cramp on the back of my thigh as I focus on trying not to stand like an idiot. There's something about not making myself look stupid that makes me look stupid. If that makes any sense. I can't look at them. I'm too nervous.

Through the fog I can faintly see two, dull, yellow circles bobbing up and down as they get closer, meaning luckily for me, buses are working, and I don't have to stand here any longer. I've never focused on anything as much as I've focused myself on this bus coming, in my entire life. The figure hasn't moved an inch, from what I can see anyway. Not even to make their way towards the bus. I'm scared to turn my back on them, through fear that they're someone I would rather avoid. The bright red, double-decker bus finally emerges from the fog, although the driver is driving so slow, that I reckon it might just be quicker walking alongside it. I hold back as it pulls up beside me, so that I can allow the figure to walk in front, giving me the chance to run if they try and attack me from behind.

"Are you getting on buddy? You probably can't see it, but this bus is going into town," the driver yells across from his seat. His scarf tightly wrapped around his neck and hands warmly embedded in a pair of gloves. It must get cold opening the doors every few minutes.

With the driver here, and everyone on the bus as witnesses and potential life savers, I know that I can turn to face the figure behind me without fear of them being able to hurt me, much. My mouth dries up and the overwhelming, sudden need to pee, as well as the pulse in my ears, is the start of yet another anxiety attack. But I have to do this. For all I know, they could be a complete stranger that I'll never see again. I take one deep breath and quickly turn around.

Nothing.

They've gone. They've completely disappeared.

College

"Have you seen Tianna today, Wendy?" Miss Wortag asks in an unusually calm voice.

"No, Miss. I haven't." To be honest, I'd be happy if I didn't have to see her again, but that's never going to happen.

"Never mind. You'll just have to work independently when we do group exercises." She's adamant that I should only work with Tianna as it encourages me to work harder. Don't get me wrong, I am happy, as moving me away from Jessie came at the perfect time, but I don't work hard because Tianna makes me. I work hard because it's the only way to get the lesson to go quickly, and the quicker I am away from her, the better.

The class falls silent as we get on with independent study, when my phone vibrates again.

The stranger: 'What you doing?'

Me: 'Wondering whether it was you that I saw this morning and if so, why you didn't say hi.'

The stranger: 'This morning? Erm. I'm not sure. Did you?'

Me: 'I don't know. Did I?'

The stranger: 'Oh, yes. I think I remember now. You were standing at the bus stop, right?'

Me: 'You know I was.'

The stranger: 'Sorry.'

Me: 'Stop saying sorry.'

The stranger: 'What are you doing?'

Me: 'Nothing. Who are you?'

The stranger: 'I won't tell you over the phone, but I will show you if you like?'

Me: 'What does that mean?'

The stranger: 'Meet me in the park after college? By the playground.'

This is starting to sound familiar. What if the stranger is Helen? I mean, it makes sense that she would have just disappeared completely, as she goes to a posh college somewhere near Blackheath. If she were to get caught trespassing in our college, she would probably be banned from coming back again. It also makes sense that she thinks I won't want to talk to her, what with her and Jessie dating, but I do. I really, really, really do. I just don't know if I'm ready to go back to the playground just yet. I can forgive Helen for getting with Jessie, especially after what I've put her through. I won't be able to forgive Jessie, though. And I certainly won't be comfortable being around them both at the same time, but I reckon we stand a good chance of getting through this. As long as she is willing to stick with me until I have my surgery, that is.

Me: 'Can we go somewhere other than the park? I don't think I'm ready to go back to the playground.'

The stranger: 'Oh, well, we can meet somewhere else, but I thought the park would be a good place for us to talk properly.'

Me: 'Yeah, I guess you're right. Should I meet you there for around five o'clock?'

The stranger: 'Sounds good. What are you up to?'

Me: 'You've just asked me that. What are you up to?'

The stranger: 'Nothing much. Hiding. I didn't want to come into college today.'

Me: 'Welcome to my world.'

The stranger: 'My parents hate me.'

Yeah, probably because you threw away a good thing and got with a total idiot instead.

Me: 'I'm sorry to hear that, why do they hate you?'

The stranger: 'What are your parents like?'

She doesn't sound like the Helen I know. In fact, the reason I didn't realise it was her sooner, is because the tone of the conversation is depressing in comparison to the conversations we used to have. I guess she's kind of been through a lot, too.

Me: 'Annoying. I don't know. They hate what I am, but I don't think they hate me. It's probably the same for your parents.'

The stranger: 'Maybe.'

The peculiarity of these messages is somewhat exciting. Although I badly want to have it confirmed that I am talking to Helen, the idea of pretending that I don't know that it's her is the first bit of entertainment I've had in a long while. It reminds me of when I first met my online group of friends. On the other hand, it could be that she's so embarrassed to be seen making amends with me, that she has to meet me somewhere quiet and secluded, where no one will be able to see us together. It's a shame that no one is proud enough to say they are okay with me. No one except an online group of strangers that I'll never meet in real life. Don't get me wrong, I'm thrilled that they've been so supportive, in fact, I'll love them all forever for it, but social media and everyday life are two completely different worlds. All it will take is for my laptop to break and my parents to refuse to help me buy another one, and my whole online world is gone. Just like that. Whereas my real, dreaded identity stays the same and nothing changes.

Four O'clock

Nothing really happened during the rest of my short day at college. The only lesson I had today was English. The rest of the day was meant to be spent in the library, studying, but I'd rather be as far away from college as I can. Besides, I've agreed to meet the stranger now, I've got to stick with it. As the sky begins to darken, it's hard not to focus on the negatives of going to meet this stranger, who I now believe is Helen, in the park. The last time she asked me to meet her there, she wasn't alone, and it turned into one of the worst nights of my life. If this stranger really is Helen, I can't be certain that tonight won't be a re-run of what happened the last time I was here.

"Wendy!" mum yells from outside my bedroom door. She developed this new way of communicating when Max started screaming at everything. The only problem is that she now uses her new technique every time she calls me. I'm certain I'd be able to hear her properly if she just called my name normally. "Are you staying in tonight? I need you to babysit Max, if you are."

"No, I'm out, mum. Sorry," I yell back. I rarely turn down mum's request to babysit Max. Mainly because she gets really stroppy if I don't. She'll be annoyed that I'm not able to babysit, and when she comes snooping around my room, she'll be even more annoyed that I have left it in such a state. Meaning I've got a headache waiting for me over the weekend. Looking in the mirror, I begin to scrutinise myself from top to bottom. The random spots, dotted around my face, alongside my frizzy, afro hair kind of gives me the scruffy look that Cameron always goes for. I like it. I couldn't look more boyish if I tried.

Half past four

I've got a headache from the smell of dad's perfume after dousing myself in it. I think I might have sprayed way too much. I spent ages browsing through his wardrobe, in an effort to find something that looked half decent. After spending the best part of thirty minutes looking through shirts that all looked the same, I decided to go for one of his oldest shirts so that it would fit better. I tucked it into my skinny jeans and finished the look off with a tidy pair of boat shoes. If I'm going to try and win her back, the least I could do is look the part.

Four, Forty-Five

I decided to walk the long way around to the park, rather than take the short cut through the alley way near my house. The best part of my journey was spent analysing each and every single person I saw with a black, puffer jacket on. I saw one girl wearing the jacket. She was a lot skinner than Helen and was walking a dog, but for a split second, my heart went crazy at the thought of it being her. I haven't planned anything I want to say in particular, I just know that whatever I do say, will be the truth, the whole truth, and nothing but the damn truth. With her opening up to me so bravely, I reckon it's time I showed her the same respect and opened up to her too. I haven't gone all the way up to the playground, instead, I've sat myself behind one of the trees at the top of the hill, overlooking it. I figured it would have made me feel more confident in the situation if I was able to see for myself that she is completely alone.

Four, Fifty-Five

The park is dark and empty, and with the sudden drop in temperature, floods of memories from that night rush back through my mind. I don't think coming here was a good idea. I just knew it wouldn't have been. She won't be able to see me hidden up here, but even if she doesn't, someone else could. Who knows what hides in these bushes after dark.

I can't be here anymore. I can't do it. My head feels dizzy, hands hot and forehead damp with sweat as I look down at the playground. I can't stop staring at the little grassy bit where Helen and I had our passionate moment. I can still feel her heavy breathing and hear her quiet moaning. I remember the taste of her strawberry lip balm, and the way her soft hands stroked my hair. If I close my eyes and really focus, sometimes I can even smell her. My chest abruptly tightens as my thoughts move onto the night I was attacked, causing me to double over in pain. The thought of Jessie deliberately trying to hurt me, both physically and emotionally hurts way more than the chest pain itself. I clearly remember seeing Cameron's bloodshot eyes, as he openly mocked me, first in front of Helen, Mya and James, and then with Jessie at the hideout.

Five O'clock

Just as I begin to focus my mind on pulling myself together and leaving the park, I notice the dark figure walking towards the playground. Her long legs glide towards the gates as she looks around. I'm assuming she's looking for me. She's bang on time, but I hadn't noticed her walking through the rest of the park, it's almost as if she just popped up out of nowhere. She's wearing the puffer jacket, which is good, because it means I'd have been able to identify her if she was with other people. But she isn't.

She's alone.

She glides over to the swings and sits on the one she was on that night I met her. I can't really make out her face from up here, but there's no doubt in my mind that it's Helen.

Without giving it a second thought, I proudly stroll down the hill. Nervous. Definitely nervous, but also very excited. Her back is towards the gate as she swings on the swing, with a strong vanilla trail radiating from behind her.

"You got here bang on time," I say, raising my voice over the creaking of the swings. I stand behind them with my hands in my jacket pocket, back straight and head held high like a hunk. I want her to turn around and face me while I'm in my pose, and fall in love with me all over again.

"Oh, I'm very good when it comes to timing," she replies, jumping off the swing mid-air while turning to face me. She pulls off her hood and reveals a bush of fiery, red hair and looks directly at me with lime green eyes.

"You have got to be kidding!" I shriek in horror. It's Tianna. This has got to be some sort of wind up. "Where's Helen? What have you done with her?" I can't help but think the absolute worst in this situation. I hate to say it, but Tianna does come across as someone that would actually kidnap another person. "Please, don't tell me you are the person I've been talking to this whole time?" My disappointment is more than evident. "Can you say something?"

"Yeah, it's me." She giggles, completely oblivious to the fact that I am horrified. "I knew that if you knew who I was, you wouldn't want to talk to me." Well, she certainly got that right.

"So, you are the one from the toilets?" I'm clearly in denial.

"Yup!" she replies, grinning profusely. She looks so proud of herself.

"And you are going through a similar thing to me?" The thing is, if she *was* going through anything remotely similar to the situation that I'm in, I'm sure dad would have known about it. He'd have told mum, and mum would have told the world and it's wife. Me first, though.

"Yup!"

"How?" I reply through my teeth, smouldering with fury.

"What do you mean? Do you mean, what is going on with me? I told my parents and my friends that I am gay, and now my parents absolutely hate my guts, and my friends all think I fancy them," she replies, rather blasé about it if you ask me.

"Yeah, you said. This is weird."

"No, what you want to say is that you think I'm weird." She smiles, walking over towards the bench and gesturing with her head for me to follow her.

"I still don't believe you are the person I've been texting," I reply, standing still where I am and refusing to follow her. "Prove that you are, and I don't mean just show me the phone, because that could mean anything."

She slowly turns around, unzipping her jacket and holding the sides of it out to reveal a sequined jumper. "Smell."

"Pardon?"

That is why I will be gutted if the stranger really is her.

"My neck," she replies. Leaning her head over to one side. "Smell."

"No, thanks. Why don't you just tell me what it smells like?"

"Smell." She says again, this time louder and the tone of her voice suggests I don't want to say no again.

"Right." I sigh and walk towards her, taking one deep breath in as she forces my head towards her freckled neck. I can smell the strong, overbearing scent of vanilla, similar to that of the strangers.

"Dear God, you really are the stranger. I really wish you had told me this earlier." If I knew, I wouldn't have been so keen to meet her in person. Now, what am I supposed to do?

"Well, now you know, Mr."

"Why do you keep calling me that?" I reply, trying to stop myself from grinning. The word 'Mr' sends a wave of butterflies through my entire body every time she calls me it. She didn't really need to force me to smell her neck. That would have been enough.

"Because that is what you are, no?" She knows who I am. She knows my family very well, in fact. "Don't worry, it's not a trick question. I just think that everyone has the right to be whoever they want to be, without anyone getting in the way of that." Bizarrely, she reminds me of Olivia, even though I've never met Olivia in person. "It's okay, you can talk to me. I'm not going to run home and tell anyone." This is the most Tianna has said to me since I met her just over seven years ago. I didn't realise she was able to have an actual normal conversation. There were times I wondered if she even knew how to socialise properly at all.

"Yeah, I guess so," I reply back uncertainly. Dad does know about the situation, but with how he's reacted to it so far, he'd be mortified if Mr Robinson found out too.

"You never really gave me a chance, you know."

"Huh?"

"When we were eleven."

"Oh, yeah. I forgot about that." Please, let's not sit here and start trying to dig tunnels again. "What was that all about?"

"I was having a bad day and wanted to escape. That's all." She says self-assuredly.

"I can relate to that." Now more than ever.

"So, tell me about you then. What is your boy name?" She sits back down on the bench where she folds her legs and looks at me. Her eyes heavily focused on mine.

Oh, what the hell.

"If I had a pound for the amount of times I have tried to explain me to people so far, I'd be a millionaire by now," I reply. Slightly dramatic, as I'd most likely be the proud owner of a shiny £10 note at most. She's actually the first person to ever ask me that, and I like it. I walk over to join her on the bench, crossing one leg over the other like my dad does. "Basically, I was meant to be a twin. My mum miscarried my twin at sixteen weeks pregnant, a few weeks before she was due to find out what the gender was." I pause to make sure she's keeping up, as according to Stuart, I went overboard with my explanation last time. "I've always felt like I am a boy trapped inside a girls' body, and I think it might have had something to do with tha-"

"Well, I can tell you one thing for nothing," she interrupts. "It doesn't have anything to do with your mum. You are transgender."

"I know that I am transgender," I reply defensively, frustrated that everyone assumes that I don't know what I am. "I was just explaining the reason why I'm transgender."

"But, why?"

"Why what?"

"Well, if I'm honest, it looks like you are trying to make up excuses or reasons for why you are the way you are, and I think that's just plain old dumb." Her body twitches as she confronts me. "Look at it this way, you've described you being transgender, as if there is something wrong with you. When you talk of your twin dying, and something going *wrong* in your mother's womb, you use that wrong thing to explain what's 'wrong' with you, if that makes any sense?"

"Go on…" I'm interested to hear her theory.

"Everyone is different. Think about how many people are in the world and think about what our history was like. When Hitler killed all of those Jewish people, they were probably programmed into thinking there was something wrong with *them* and not him. When black people were used as slaves, they were probably programmed into thinking there was something wrong with *them* and not their masters. When someone is misunderstood for being who they are, they always tend to think there is something wrong with *them* and not the people misunderstanding them." She pauses and waits for me to catch up, her eyes widened and pupils dilated, almost like she is getting some sort of kick through talking about her theory.

"I don't get it." I mean, I do, but I don't. I can see where she is trying to go with this, but there is an actual reason why I am the way I am.

"What I'm saying is, you have thought of a negative reason for why you are the way you are, but have you ever just thought that you were meant to be born like that? Has it ever crossed your mind that you are not the product of something that went wrong? You are, in actual fact, just a normal, transgender person and whether your mother had a miscarriage or not, you would have been the same way anyway?" Well, no, actually. I haven't ever thought that. But why would I if there is a clear explanation? Don't get me wrong, she is making sense, but people like me aren't normal.

"I just think you should stop being so hard on yourself," she continues, her voice pleading with me, as if she has been able to read my mind. "It's confusing, I know, but don't look at yourself as if you are the product of something negative. Understand that you're unique and you may have been put on this Earth the way you are, so that you can make a difference to the world. Whether it is to educate those that don't understand, to support those that are going through a similar thing, or just to be you and put your stamp on the world." She reaches her hand over to mine and grabs hold of it firmly.

"It must be hard having homophobic parents. How did they find out?" I reply. My head hurts from talking about the same thing over and over again. I'd rather focus more on her. Don't get me wrong, I do want to thank her for being so understanding, but I don't really know how. The boys aren't really emotional, so having such a deep conversation with someone that isn't my parents is something I'm not used to. Behind Tianna's brave smile, anyone can see a lost and very lonely little girl. The faint bags under her eyes stand out against her pale skin and her sunken eyes just scream pain every time you look at them.

"I didn't know they were homophobic until I came out to them." She looks down and starts playing with a loose bit of fur on her jacket.

"That sucks. I'm sorry to hear that." I'm not really good at comforting people.

"Speaking of parents, we should really go." She stands up and waits for me to join her.

"What? How comes? We've only just got here?" For the first time since I've known her, I've found myself wanting to talk to her. The entire time we've been 'friends' she's hardly been able to construct a sentence that makes sense, let alone hold up an interesting conversation.

"I need to get home, I was only meant to be going to the shops to get bread and I've already been out for the best part of an hour," she replies, her eyes stray over to the gates, giving off the impression that she is desperate to get away from me. "I just came here to show you who I was. I'll text you, though."

Twelve

Wow

It was dark. All I could see was street lights in the distance, the smell of bonfire smoke slowly disappearing, as I found myself travelling further and further away from the woods.

"Paul," a soft voice whispered from ahead of me. I couldn't see who it was. All I could clearly make out, was the wild bush of red hair that belongs to Tianna. As I turned back, I saw Jessie. He was stood still with open eyes, watching me as I walked in Tianna's direction. I stopped and considered running towards him. My heart full of hope that we'd make up and become best friends again, but something was telling me not to be so hasty. I paused for a moment, torn between what direction I wanted to go down. Jessie still hadn't shaved his hair, and his heavy eyes were firmly fixed on mine. He had bruises. Two on his arm and one on the side of his face. I sussed him out as I tried to figure out whether it was safe to approach him, but just as I'd made up my mind and got ready to take the first step towards him, Helen appeared. I watched, heartbroken, as she wrapped her arms around his body and pulled him in for a long kiss.

I screamed in anger as they became engrossed in each other. Neither of them budged when I screamed. I watched

Jessie rub his hands around her waist and work his way up her top, towards her breasts, just like I did. My eyes wouldn't stop staring and the more I tried to focus on something else, the more my body forced me to watch. They were stinging and watering, but my eyelids remained glued wide open. I held my throat in an effort to push the choking lump down, and tried to slap myself awake. But I couldn't. The lump grew and my head began to feel like it was going to explode if I didn't take a breath imminently. As I grew weaker, my eyes remained fixed on Jessie and Helen kissing. Neither of them noticed that I needed them as I fell to the ground, holding onto my throat. Neither of them cared.

I woke up soaked with sweat. It took me a few minutes to get my head together and realise that it was just a dream, and I wasn't actually going to die with Jessie and Helen as my last thought.

Tianna didn't come into college the following day, or the day after that. Or even the day after that. I found myself feeling disappointed that I wasn't able to see her, but I figured that she was okay since dad hadn't mentioned anything about them. I checked my phone every few minutes and didn't hear anything, not even a response to my question asking how she was doing.

"Weddy," a husky little voice blubbers out from behind my door. Followed by the sound of something being slammed against it.

"Hey, buddy." My high-pitched, baby voice ringing through my own head, as I pick Max up and start bouncing him around on my hip. "Where's mumma?"

He has no idea what I'm talking about, but he smiles anyway. His mouth covered in dribble and his bib stained from the food he's just eaten. No wonder why he's in such a good mood.

"She's having a shower," Jake replies from his room. "She asked me to watch him, but I figured you could do it, seeing as you're in." There's no doubt that he's my mum's child with that attitude, but seeing as I'm in and I wasn't able to last time, I'll happily take care of my baby brother. Jake grew so quickly, I guess I need to make the most of Max's baby days, while we still have them.

"Well, okay then. It's me and you, Mr man," I say to Max with that cheesy voice I literally cannot stop doing. We head downstairs; Max on my bony hip, my phone in my mouth, my phone and laptop chargers wrapped around my arm, and my laptop. I most definitely can't let Max loose in my bedroom. Only God knows what he'll find in there.

My laptop fights for life as I settle Max into his Jumperoo and switch the TV on. Mum hates it when he's sat in front of the telly, but the little guy loves it so much. You've got to be evil to take away something that makes a baby happy. Besides, it gives me the chance to actually turn around for a second without turning back to find him choking on something he's picked up off the floor.

Me: 'I know I'm joining mid-convo, but just ignore me. I'll catch up.'

Olivia: 'Oh, hey. How's it going? I don't really think there's anything to catch up on. We're just having a debate on whether pineapple should be allowed on pizza or not. I vote yes, just in case you wanted to join in.'

Stuart: The normal people in the group have voted absolutely not.

Me: 'Ahh, sorry, Stuart. I love a ham and pineapple pizza, but we all know I'm not normal!'

Henry: 'No! You traitor.'

Me: 'What have you guys got planned for today? I wish we lived near each other'

Olivia: Just going to spend the day with family today, then might head out into town later on tonight. Drinks are half price on a Sunday.'

The thought of Olivia having a life outside of the group chat is weird. I'm so used to them being online when I come on, that I forget they also have a real life too.

Henry: I'm meant to be going to a barbeque later on, but my brother's really annoying me today, I might have to sit it out.

Stuart: I'm staying in, going to have a lazy day.

Mum's stomps as she rushes down the stairs, distract me from what was meant to be the first conversation with these guys in a while, where I don't have any distractions.

"Darling, can you go and have a shower and get yourself ready, please? Everyone will be here shortly," she says, taking off her shower cap, and brushing out her hair with her fingers.

"Who's going to be here shortly?" I ask, confused.

"The Robinsons?" she replies, waving her hands outwards, as if I was meant to be able to read her mind and just know that they're coming round today. "We did actually mention this to you last week, but you clearly weren't listening at all, and because you've been sleeping for half of the morning, you don't have long to get yourself dressed and presentable looking." She starts pacing around from one end of the room to another, something she does every single time she gets stressed out. I don't get it, just chill out and everything will be fine. "Can you bring your laptop and stuff upstairs, as I don't want any mess laying around. And also make yourself look presentable." She puffs up the cushions once I've stood up and brushes down the sofa, it's hardly as if I've dropped the lurgies on the sofa within such a short space of time. She doesn't have to worry about me looking presentable, that's for sure, because I want to impress Tianna. Despite the fact that she knows everything about me and I haven't seen her since we met in the park.

"Yes, mother, anything for you." My sarcastic tone earns me a very dirty look from mum. She'll lighten up once everyone has arrived.

I can't help but skip upstairs with excitement at the thought of Tianna coming over and us being able to continue on with our chat. I'm still taken aback by how mature she is. Some of the things she was saying, really made me feel like I can relate to her in so many ways. It's just weird as I've never known her to be so chatty. But then again, I've never seen her without one or both of her parents by her side. I wonder what she'll be like today.

The doorbell rings loudly as Mr Robinson holds his finger on it, almost deafening every person in the house.

"They're here!" Dad roars from downstairs. I can hear how stressed out he is just by the tone of his voice. He's just so hell bent on being better than Mr Robinson, sometimes it becomes cringing. "Wendy, can you come downstairs please?" His voice slightly higher pitched and more polite sounding, just in case the Robinsons hear.

I take a slow walk downstairs. I don't want to look too eager to see her. It's weird how I'd never really paid much attention to how I act around Tianna before, but now I'm fully conscious of it. My legs feel like jelly as I try and focus on walking properly and I've suddenly realised that I don't know where to look. Mr Robinson walks in first, followed by Mrs Robinson and then Tianna. They all walk single file through our narrow hallway. Mum's hidden Max's buggy in their bedroom so luckily for the Robinsons, they haven't had to climb over buggies, a handbag and shoes as soon as they walk in through the door. Mum guides them through the house and into her pride and joy that is the kitchen, while I trail behind slowly. Now, I'm the one being weird, but the more I focus on trying not to be, the more I feel like I am. They settle themselves down into the kitchen as mum takes their coats. Tianna hasn't looked at me once. In fact, she hasn't really looked at anyone. She's quiet again, and won't peel her eyes away from the floor.

"Can I get you a drink, Hazel?" mum asks Mrs Robinson. "Or you, Oliver?" She reaches for two glasses and starts pouring out some rum punch anyway. She's only doing that to show off the new crystal embedded water jug she just bought, which dad is furious about, by the way.

"Thanks, Nadia," Mrs Robinson replies. The room falls into an awkward silence with everyone sipping their drinks simultaneously. "Tianna, why don't you go and play with Wendy for a while so that we can catch up properly?" She pushes Tianna away from her and towards my direction, giving her no choice but to face me.

"I'm not a child," Tianna hisses back under her breath. I've never seen her brave enough to talk back to her parents before. She walks over to stand next to me, smiling at me briefly, before fixing her eyes back onto the floor.

"Should we chill out in my room?" I ask, uncertain on what her response will be. She nods back and follows me as I lead her back through the hallway and up the stairs. Her skinny hands grip onto the hand rail as she takes double steps, remaining right behind me. My room's not in the best of states, but as long as mum doesn't see it, I doubt Tianna will be too bothered. It's only a few plates anyway.

"Wow your room is really big, and tidy!" She says, running straight through the door as I open it; her mouth wide open in surprise, as if she expected it to resemble a squat. "You've got such a nice view outside as well." She stares out the window towards the row of shops.

"That's hardly a nice view, it's just shops and the street."

"Well, it might not be to you, but at least you have a view." She grips onto the window sill tightly with both hands.

"You don't have a window in your room?"

"Yeah, of course I do." She laughs. Her cheeks blush pink and she tucks her fingers into the sleeves of her hoodie. I don't understand the joke.

"So, what's the problem then?"

"It was a joke, stoopid!" She teases, pronouncing every syllable in the word with a deep voice and rolling her eyes back to pull a funny face.

"Okay. Now I do feel stupid."

"Ha!"

Her face drops a little when she notices a photograph of the whole family with me centred right in the middle of it, hung up on my wall.

"Your family really love you, huh? You're a really lucky guy." She gently moves her finger across my face in the photo, causing my stomach to flutter. Her effortless ability to refer to me as a guy, when she's known me as a girl for the past seven years, is fiercely attractive and I've found myself really enjoying her company. She dashes over to a photograph that I'd have hidden if I had notice that she was going to come into my room. It's mum's pride and joy – an utterly embarrassing photo of me wearing a bright pink tutu at a children's party when I was four. I was holding onto a pair of yellow pom poms and beaming from ear to ear.

Mum loves it so much, because she reckons I was at my happiest before I became a teenager.

"Oh, my, God. That is so cute! How old were you here?" Her over excited expression at the sight of me dressed like a girl is concerning.

"I'm not sure, probably like four or something." I definitely know that I was four years old, but I don't want her to think I'm as proud of it as mum is. I'd much rather not relive my past, and be reminded of the days my mother used to dress me up like a walking joke. Tianna looks over at me with concerning eyes, before carefully putting the photo back where she found it. I must be making it pretty darn obvious that I hate that photo if she's been able to get the hint that quickly.

"So, should we talk then? I haven't spoken to you at all since we met at the park." I feel a little rude being so direct, but I've been itching to talk to her. I had so many questions, most of which I can't remember, but I've still wanted to talk to her anyway.

"Well, what do you want to talk about?" her blasé attitude is a little difficult to work with. I guess I don't know what I want to talk about, but I feel like our conversation the other day was cut short and would have gotten a lot deeper if she didn't have to go.

"This isn't what I wanted to talk to you about, but what is it with you and your parents? You're so weird around them." Weird is probably a very insensitive word to use in this situation, but there really is no other word more suited to it than that. Her body tenses up and her jaw tightens, causing me to feel a little uneasy sitting next to her.

"I hate them. I already told you what's going on."

"Jeez, I didn't know it was that serious. There is some real tension between you guys," I reply sympathetically. I wouldn't normally care before, but right now I do.

The awkward silence in the room is suddenly interrupted by the loud, boom of thunder, making my body itch with adrenaline at the thought of heading out in the rain.

"Hey, do you like the rain?"

"I beg your pardon?" She replies, confused. I mean, it's not every day someone asks if you like the rain; people normally complain about it.

"So, basically. My dad used to take me and Jake out in the rain every time there was a thunder storm, and I still do it now. Sometimes" My voice trembles as I feel nervous asking if she wants to do something with me. It feels no different to asking her out on a date. "I was just wondering if you wanted to come out in it, now?"

A large grin shoots across her face, as she immediately starts making her way towards the door. "I'd love to, let's go."

The rain pours down in bucket loads the second we leave the house, just how I like it. In fact, if I could have planned the perfect date, a simple walk in the pouring rain would be perfect. She's not fazed by the weather in the slightest. In fact, she's more of a child than Jake is, and to think, all this time I had no idea. I regret thinking anything negative of her, without having given myself the chance to get to know her properly. She's not bad, but the impression I've had of her for the past seven years, has been the total opposite.

"What?" Tianna asks suspiciously, after catching me smiling to myself.

"I don't know, I just can't believe you're not the hermit I thought you were!" There's really no other way to put it.

"Wow, you really know how to flatter a girl," she replies, brushing her hair behind her ear as she does. It feels like it's been so long since I had a real life friend and not just an internet one.

"How comes you're so quiet in college? Actually, how comes you're so quiet in general? I've never even seen you talk around your friends."

"Because, everyone is so childish. I made one, stupid joke with Alice, and she's now got it into her head that I fancy her." She rolls her eyes as if to give off the impression that she's been here before. "All I said was that if I was a guy I'd give it to her. I meant it in a friendly way and would have said it if I was gay or straight, but she's gone and told everyone I tried it on with her. Which has just made things really awkward. Anyway, what's your favourite food?"

"Don't you try and change the subject, missy! I think I'm finally starting to figure you out a little," I reply. She's not running away from the conversation that easily, especially seeing as she knows so much about me already. "So, Alice went and told everyone that you tried it on with her, and then what happened?"

"Nothing actually came of it, they just all started to be really funny with me. They stopped inviting me to sleepovers and nights out. I could just tell that they were being off, you know?" Her sorrowful eyes scan the room as she tries to put on a brave front. It's not hard to see that she isn't comfortable with talking about the subject. And once again, I regret even saying anything. "I've made up with them, but I've since resorted to muting myself at college, just in case I manage to incriminate myself for making a joke or speaking my mind."

"Yeah, that makes sense. I guess, if you can't even make a joke with your friends, you can hardly be comfortable being yourself," I reply, trying to continue the conversation on a little.

We take a slow stroll through the alley way that leads to the park, but turn off through one of the estates instead. I'm not really planning on taking her anywhere special, I just thought it would be nice to have a wander around. Especially since she hasn't had a tour around Hither Green yet. The rain begins to slow down a little and find its pace, while the smell of wet soil flows through the air. The silence doesn't feel awkward, or unnatural, it feels weirdly comforting just having someone by my side again. As we walk through the estate, a recognisable black BMW X5 drives past, windows down and music blaring out loud for everyone to hear. I stop as I watch the car pull up outside the house that I've just realised I must have subconsciously walked towards. Cameron's. I watch on as his dad switches off the engine and makes his way over to the boot of the car, before letting Cameron's younger siblings out.

"Let's go," Tianna says quietly, tugging onto the side of my t-shirt. "You're only going to hurt yourself. Let it go." I don't know what she thinks I'm going to do, but I don't want to go anywhere. I want him to see me and feel scared that I'm going to tell his dad about his behaviour.

Cameron jumps out of the car and scans the estate around him, locking his eyes onto mine the minute he notices me. I should have known that by standing so obviously, and right next to his house, he would be able to see me.

"Let's go, Mr. I don't want any trouble." Tianna tugs at my t-shirt a little harder as he walks over to us, making me lose balance. I'm not budging.

"Well, well, well," Cameron teases. "I see you've moved on. I'll pass the message onto Helen." He's trying to get a reaction from me in front of his dad. Well, I won't give it to him. "It's a good thing she's already in a happy relationship with Jessie. Or she'd have been pretty upset, don't you think, Wendy?"

"Oh, leave him alone, you bully!" Tianna hisses at him, moving to stand in front of me protectively.

"Your girlfriend is touchy," he replies, completely ignoring her request for him to leave me alone. "What rattled her cage? Did she have to find the truth out the hard way as well?"

"Shut up," she says. While I stand here, pathetically frozen, but so grateful she is here. "Now go away, before I do something you will regret."

Cameron glares at me with dark, squinted eyes; his nostrils flared and fists clenched. He turns back and walks towards his dad without saying another word. Tianna made standing up to him look so straightforward, even though she knows that she'll see him again at college.

"We're going. Please, just listen to me the next time we are in a situation like that."

"Sorry," I reply with my head hung low, like a child.

"Don't apologise," she replies comfortingly. "I just don't want you to get hurt. I don't like the thought of you being unhappy, Paul."

The walk back home was quiet. All I was listening to, was the sound of car tyres, splashing through the wet road as they drove. Tianna didn't look unhappy, but then again, I've never been able to read her before I *really* met her. I've learnt that she is outspoken, smart and kind. My conversations with her flow effortlessly and I feel like her wisdom far exceeds mine. After speaking to her about my 'theory' on my mum's miscarriage, I've realised that she is incredibly smart in the majority of what she says.

Thirteen
Crush

Tianna: 'Are you awake?'

Me: 'Well, I wasn't, but I am now. Are you okay?'

Tianna: 'I had a blazing argument with mum. I can't sleep. Would it be bad if I woke her up to talk it out?'

Me: 'Oh, I'm sorry hon. Yes, I think it would be bad to wake her up at 4am to apologise. It might make matters worse. Leave it until a more suitable time. Like the morning.'

Tianna: 'But, I won't be able to sleep until I do : ('

Me: 'Try not to worry. You'll be able to sort things out, you two always do.'

Tianna: 'I've got to do it.'

Me: 'Oh, boy. Don't say I didn't warn you. Let me know how it goes in the morning, goodnight again. X'

I can't believe I'm about to say this, but I think I fancy Tianna. I keep trying to make up excuses, such as my desperation for someone to love me or be my friend. But they don't really seem to be sticking. I've found myself leaving my phone on loud, directly under my head below my pillow, just in case she calls me, or sends a text when I'm sleeping. As well as the fact that I get way too excited every time she does contact me. I reckon a lot of people would get quite frustrated with her, with the way she carelessly calls in the middle of the night, but I quite like it. It's nice to be needed. Just as I finally begin to fall asleep again, my alarm goes off. Waking me up for the new day. I must have been in and out of sleep, as it literally felt like a split second had passed.

As I rush out the door, down the hill and towards the bus stop, with a slice of toast hanging out of my mouth, I notice her bright coloured hair from what feels like miles away. She smiles as she spots me walking up to greet her.

"Well, hello there, stranger," I say with a big grin on my face. I can't hide my excitement at her being here. "What brings you around here, then?" She never comes this way. She doesn't need to. In fact, I think by her coming this way, she would have had to go in the opposite direction to the one she would have, to get to college. She lives closer to it than I do.

"Hey, you," she smiles back cheekily. "I was just coming to say hi to a special young man that I know. Definitely not you, though, don't worry." She winks and bites her bottom lip. "I just thought I'd come and surprise you, that's all." Okay, I definitely fancy Tianna.

"Well, this is a very lovely surprise." I can't wink and make it look sexy like she does, but I do have a pretty cute smile. It's a little cheesy, but I've always been told that it's cute.

The bus driver takes one look at me with my tracksuit and hood up, and shakes his head at me as other people tap their oyster cards and find seats.

"Sorry, no free rides," he yells from his seat, closing the door before I'm able to respond.

"What the hell?" Tianna yells towards the bus driver as he begins to put the bus in gear. "It's probably because you look like you've been sleeping rough for ages," she grunts at me A strong look of disgust over her face.

"Do I?"

"Yeah, you do. Come on, we're going back to yours to get you cleaned up." She pulls on my arm and starts walking back towards the hill. "We'll have you looking like a well-respected young man, rather than a homeless one, in no time. Just you wait." It's actually quite mortifying that no one has told me I've looked homeless this whole time. I thought mum's moaning was just her moaning. The majority of the time, It's hard to tell whether she is making a valid point, or just moaning for the sake of it. Everyone on the bus looks at me with revulsion as it speeds off towards the high street, and I can feel that awful sinking feeling in my stomach again.

"Mine? We can't go to mine. What about college?"

"What about it? You need a lesson in fashion. Trust me, it will be the most educational day you could have had out of the two. Besides, you said your parents are both at work now that Max is in nursery." It's not the fact that no one will be there, it's mum. She can find evidence of anything, anywhere. I'm certain that she will take one step into the house and just be able to tell that I've bunked college, she won't even need to see me to figure it out.

"Fine, fine. You spoilt princess," I tease back playfully, following her lead as we both bounce back towards mine. We won't be getting inside if mum is there, but it's still nice to have her company anyway.

"That's my boy." She winks again. It feels like every time I look into her eyes, they stand out more. Her confidence in doing whatever she wants is a characteristic I've longed for, and I can already tell that she's going to be around for a while.

I follow her as she boldly leads me back to my house. The warm heat from the sun made it more difficult to walk up the hill, and embarrassingly, I found myself panting a little while I caught my breath. Of course, it came as no surprise that Tianna was able to walk up the hill effortlessly. As we approach my house. I gesture for her to hide behind the wall while I go inside and quickly check that no one is in. The bottom bolt is locked, meaning mum has either locked herself in (which she just wouldn't do) or she's definitely out of the house.

"It's safe!" I whisper shout, holding the front door open with my foot; my head in the doorway, scanning the immediate area for anything embarrassing. Now I see why mum panics so much when people come over.

She pops her head over the wall and snorts a goofy giggle. "I'm going to nip across the road to the shop. Do you want anything?"

"No, thanks. Ring the bell when you're back outside."

The house is still warm from where the heating was on this morning and I can still smell Jake's golden syrup flavoured porridge. There is something really calming about being at home alone, especially knowing I'm not meant to be here. I don't think I've ever been home alone before, and if I have, I've been stuck in my bedroom without a care in the world, completely oblivious to everything going on in the rest of the house.

I quickly puff up the cushions on the sofa, pick up Max's sippy cup and run it to the kitchen, while looking around for anything that might embarrass me when she gets back. Jake's pants that he always seems to leave laying around, for example. I sprint over to the fireplace and put a towel over a hideous photo of me in a Big Bird costume when I was seven, as well as another one of me in a neon green dress with pig tails in my hair. Why mum still has them up, I will never know. The funny thing is, Tianna would have seen them a thousand times before. That's if she's ever peeled her eyes off the floor. I don't know why I still feel like in order to impress her, I need to hide who I am, when she's made it very clear that I shouldn't feel that way. Nevertheless, I continue to anxiously scan the room, for anything else that has the potential to embarrass the life out of me and find nothing. Everything is hidden.

The doorbell rings.

"It's open!" I shout towards the door, holding the remote in my hand and quickly throwing myself on the sofa, trying to act cool. I'm also trying not to make it obvious that I really care about her opinion on my embarrassing childhood photos.

She squeezes through the door holding a plastic bag that looks like it is full of goodies. "I bought us some bits to munch on. Should we watch a film?" She asks, as she pulls out a big bag of cheese and onion crisps, alongside sour cream and chive sauce, and lays them out on the table in front of us. "It's weird, I've been to your house so many times, but I've never sat down and watched TV here. Just sitting here, like this, feels weird." I guess she makes a good point, it's all very formal when her family come over.

"So much for our fashion show, but yes, I'd love that," I reply a bit too enthusiastically. "I've never really noticed that before you mentioned it." I pick up the remote and begin flicking through the channels, reading the information on each channel before moving onto the next one. Tianna gently takes the the remote from my hand, brushing over my fingers with hers. She begins to scroll through the TV guide, crunching on some crisps.

"Have you seen this?" she asks, stopping at something that I've never seen before in my life. "It's hilarious. If you haven't, it will definitely put a smile on your face." She puts it on without waiting for my answer. Little does she know, *she's* already put the biggest smile on my face that I've worn in a while.

"Nope, but it looks like you've already made your mind up!"

She carefully moves the crisps and dip over to mum's brand new, glass, coffee table and cuddles into me as I put my arm around her, without having given it a second thought. With how pleasantly surprised I've been at my friendship with Tianna, I hadn't noticed that I also feel more confident than I have done in a long while. Her hair smells like coconut and her skin smells like shea butter. Two of my most favourite smells. Her skin is hot and makes her feel like a hot water bottle with her body pressed against mine.

As the movie plays on, I can feel my attention span wear off. This always happens when I can't relax properly. I do feel comfortable around Tianna, but where I'm trying to impress her so much, I can't totally relax. My cling film has shrivelled up into an awkward line of plastic, stretched across my chest, causing me to wince in pain.

"What's up?" Tianna asks, moving away from me, thinking she is the cause of my pain.

"Oh, it's nothing," I reply reservedly, trying to pull her back towards me, but she refuses to move.

"No, tell me. Please don't keep anything from me. It sounded like you were in pain," she begs. Something in me feels comfortable talking to her about it, but the other part is way too nervous about revealing my darkest secrets. "You can tell me anything, Paul." Her green eyes penetrate mine. It's like she's speaking to me through them.

"Honestly, it's nothing."

"Please?"

"Okay." I sigh. "I wear cling film." My whole body instantly heats up and begins to sweat, as I realise what I've just done. She doesn't move an inch, her eyes still fixated on mine. "I wear cling film to make my breasts appear smaller. There. Are you happy now?" God, it's so hot in here. I'm sure the radiators were cooling down as I got in, not heating up.

"Yes, actually. As a matter of fact, I am. Thank you, for being honest. I can see that was very hard for you, but it wasn't that difficult, now, was it?" I can't tell whether she is patronising me or genuinely being nice. "Now, show me," she continues with a warm smile.

"Absolutely not."

"Oh, Paul, stop being so ridiculous," she mocks. "I'm not going to let you sit here in pain. If you don't show me, I'll just have to look myself." Her threat sends a few chills down my spine, as I remember seeing her floating around the toilets. I quickly lift my top up without hesitation; using one arm to cover my breasts and the other to pull the string of cling film down towards my stomach. "What is it with you and your insecurities, eh?" She leans down towards my stomach and gently brushes across it with her lips, before biting the cling film off. Her warm hands are pressed against my cold body. She scrunches the cling film up and puts it into her pocket, and then begins to stroke over the painful indents in my skin with her fingernails. Her rainbow coloured acrylics stroke each sore line, back and forth. "One, two, three, four, five, and we'll count this faint looking one as number six," she whispers, counting the amount of painful lines I have across my chest, from where the cling film has moved around. She moves herself in closer to me and holds her lips close to mine. I can feel her every breath and begin to want her, badly. "Do you know what that means, Mr?" She looks up at me and holds my gaze as she waits for my response, making me feel shy and a little perturbed.

"No, what?" I reply shyly, quietly clearing my throat.

"It means six kisses for you," she whispers, leaning in, pressing her warm, soft lips against mine. She holds onto the side of my face as she kisses me vehemently, making my heart race with emotion and driving my hormones insane. I can't focus on anything but her, and that feeling like no one else in the world exists has come back, reminding me a little of Helen. Her kisses are different to Helen's, though. She isn't as passionately aggressive as Helen was, she is softer and gentler with her approach. Her warm, delicate hand on the side of my face has me leaning into it as I crave her touch even more, without her having done a single thing. I feel greedy for her, and that uncontrollable desire to touch has come back to test me again. As I gently stroke her back from under her hoodie, I realise just how warm her skin is. Warmer than anything I've ever felt before.

She pulls away, keeping her eyes closed and breathing heavy, while her face sits close to mine. Her eyelashes are short and curly, and her button nose is cute. She teases me by keeping her lips close to mine, causing me to breathe a little heavier. Neither of us saying a word. I can't stop looking at her as she pouts her lips outwards towards me, but still maintains her distance. She wants me to man up and make the next move. I slowly adjust my head to a different angle as I lean in hungrily and kiss her again. The feeling of wanting to grab her is uncontrollable, and I find myself doing so without feeling uneasy or awkward in any way. This kiss feels different to the one we just had. It is faster and deeper. Her hips move around and my hands rub against her waist as we long for each other. I tightly squeeze onto her back as she leans against my stinging chest, but something about the pain makes me want her even more. I can't help but move my hands closer to her breasts. My desire to want to explore a female body that isn't mine is overbearing and it seems like when I am in a situation like this, I can't fight it. The urge to explore and take things to the next level is overpowering as my hands wander around her body. I work my way over to her breasts and run my hands around her bra strap as we continue to kiss each other heavily. I feel brave and daring, confident that I can explore her body without needing to overthink anything or feel nervous. I cautiously move my hands behind her back and begin to undo her bra so that my next meal dangles in my face once they have been freed. The thought of it makes us both kiss each other deeper.

"Oh my god, stop!" I screech, as I hear a pair of keys drop outside the doorway. "I think it's my mum! What time is it?" I whisper/yell at the same time, throwing Tianna off me, fixing my clothes and quickly picking the crisps up from mum's coffee table as she begins to open the door. Tianna picks herself up from the floor, fixes her bra and looks at me blankly. Maybe I shouldn't have thrown her off me like that. "I'm going to get in so much trouble. Don't say a word. Let me do all the talking," I say quietly, looking her dead in the eye to make sure she understands that mum is not someone you want to mess around with when it comes to bunking college.

As the door opens, I quickly stand to attention to greet mum, smiling awkwardly as I do. She walks in with a few bags of shopping, while Tianna and I both race towards her to offer a helping hand.

Mum stops and looks at me. She then looks at Tianna, and back to me again.

"You got home quickly. Did you get let off early or something?" She asks with a frown on her face, confused.

The clock behind her reads 13:30, which works for me.

"Yeah, lunch started at quarter past today and it's so cold I just thought it would be easier to come back here," I reply, trying not to act suspicious at all.

"Oh, really?" Something tells me she doesn't believe me. "Number one, today's been a very lovely day, weather wise, so that's a lie," she says proudly, giving me that look that just says 'wait until your friend has left'. "Tianna sweetie, I think you'd better get back to college. I need to speak to my daughter." Her confrontational eyes stare deep into mine as she probably tries to figure out whether she wants to embarrass me now, or wait until Tianna is out of view.

Tianna's face drops and my heart sinks at the thought of her having to leave me. "Sure. It was good to see you, Mrs Samuels." She smiles at mum.

"See you at college," she says to me as she squeezes past mum and the shopping. She wouldn't dare call me Mr in front of my mum. I wave back at her and wait for her to get off the driveway before grabbing the rest of the bags indoors and bringing them into the kitchen. Mum follows me in, carrying two bags. I almost bump into her as I turn around and attempt to disappear out the door after Tianna.

"Stop," she says, hands on her hips and staring deep into my soul. "Do you think I was born yesterday?" Mum is scary when she is in this mood. She asks me trick questions and knows instantly when I am lying.

"What do you mean?" I ask innocently.

"I said. Do. YOU. Think. I. Was. Born. Yesterday?"

"Well, clearly not, because you're twenty-six years older than I am so you can't have been." I joke, trying to make light of the situation.

"Why are you bunking college, again?" How does she know this time! I don't reply. "You do realise that this is your future and no one else's, don't you?" She moans, slamming both hands on the kitchen island as she opens another bill. "I will not see my child throw their life away, so they can sit at home and do nothing, while your father and I work to earn enough money. Money that makes sure *that* child has everything *they* need. Why did you not go in today?" Her quiet, calm, but aggressive tone is intimidating.

"Because I didn't feel well. I was actually going to tell you this morning, but you were too busy with Max, so I left and then came back." I most definitely cannot admit to her that I realised I looked a mess the minute Tianna said it, despite the amount of times mum has moaned about it. Besides, the only thing we did with my appearance was add a gigantic smile to it. We didn't get round to doing anything else.

"Oh, you didn't feel well, did you? Now answer this; do I look stupid to you?"

"Mum. No, you don't look stupid. I didn't go in because I didn't feel well, You're not a doctor, so you can't tell me when I am well enough to go in." I'm so sick and tired of hearing her complain about college. There are problems in the world that are far greater than me missing a few hours of education.

"Okay. You want to be a big woman? Give me your phone," she demands, hand held outwards.

"What?! I'm not ten years old." I can't give her my phone. I might die if I don't hear from Tianna within the next five minutes, there is no way I can give this woman my phone.

"Give me your phone," she demands. "I have tried to reason with you, understand you and support you. The only thing I ask you to do in return, is respect me. If you want to behave like an adult, you can be an adult and pay for you own phone. You are an adult now, after all." I stare at her in disbelief, she's never confiscated my phone from me before "Give it to me now, or I will simply get it disconnected and you won't be able to use it anymore. Your call." She walks away and begins to unpack the bags. I hate it when she is like this. Every time she is in a bad mood, the whole house gets left in a bad mood too.

I throw the phone on the kitchen side and storm upstairs into my room, yelling "I'm not going anywhere until you give it back. YOUR CALL!" Before slamming the door and running over to the window. It isn't the phone I am worried about. She can have the phone and do what she wants with it. It is the thought of not hearing from Tianna while she has it, that hurts. I scan the street up and down, searching for her, to see if she is waiting for me and can faintly make out her slim frame sitting at the bus stop down the road. I run down the stairs, sliding my hands down the bannisters, using it to take giant leaps down multiple steps as I go running out the door.

"Bye, mum. Love you!" I shout with excitement, so she doesn't try and use me not saying bye as an excuse to keep my phone any longer.

Nothing seems to bother me when Tianna is around, despite the short time that I've known her properly. I couldn't care less that mum has my phone. As long as I can be with her, nothing else really matters. As I sprint through the driveway and across the road towards her, I notice a fancy looking Mercedes pull up next to her. I stop in my tracks as I watch her look at the car pull up in horror. A man gets out, grabs hold of her arm and drags her into the back of the car. My instant reaction is to protect her, and I've found myself running, as fast I can in the direction of the car. Managing to reach it and bang on the windows at the back, where she is seated. I can't see who's driving it.

"Tianna!" I shout, as I look through the window. She refuses to look at me. Instead, she keeps her head focused towards the front of the car, back straight and hands rested on her thighs.

"Wendy," a deep, vibrational voice says as tall, muscular man gets out of the driver's side door. It is Mr Robinson. I should have known it would have been him, really. "I heard about your unfortunate situation, and whilst I sympathise, I don't want you to talk to my daughter again." He folds his arms to assert more authority. That might work with my dad, but it won't work with me. I won't have him come in between what could potentially be the best friendship of my life.

"Mr Robinson, please don't stop me from seeing Tianna." I figured it would be best to at least try and reason with him before I flat out tell him that there is no way in hell I am going to leave her alone. "She is my best friend." I look over at Tianna, but she still isn't looking.

Mr Robinson bursts out into a fit of laughter. "She's not your best friend, you two barely know each other. Look how many years you two were forced to talk to each other. But now that you have something in common, you think you are soul sisters? You are probably the reason why Tianna is the way she is." So cruel. I can't get my head around how he can be so horrible with such ease and contentment.

"No, I am not the reason why she is the way she is; she is who she is, because she was born that way. No one can change her, and do you know what? I won't leave her alone." I'm trying to ignore the tremble in my voice as I stand up to someone that could potentially snap me if he wanted to. Tianna doesn't look impressed at all, though. Her sad eyes focused on the road ahead, but she clearly knows full well what is going on. With the window a little open, she'll definitely be able to hear everything too. She shakes her head in disapproval, and I can't help but panic at the thought of making things worse for either of us.

Mr Robinson moves in a little closer to me, staring at me intimidatingly.

"You will not speak to my daughter again," he repeats, before walking away, getting back into his car and hastily driving off. I feel helpless as I watch the car drive off with Tianna in it, unable to help her in any way. I'm disappointed in myself, for not being able to stick up for her the way she has me, and scared about whether he really meant that he will stop me from seeing her again.

Fourteen

Lost

With mum having confiscated my phone for the weekend, I was unable to contact Tianna at all. I did try and send her a message on her Facebook and Twitter pages, but she hasn't been online. If she had, she'd have replied to me by now. Surely, she can't be mad at me? I feel slightly mortified that she saw me try and fail to stand up for her, and by now, she'll be more than aware that I am most definitely not her knight in shining armour. Dad didn't really say much to me over the weekend, so I'm assuming he's spoken to Mr Robinson. Mum wouldn't tell me what he said, if he has said anything at all. All they have told me is that they're dealing with it. Mum doesn't seem angry at me, but dad. Dad's furious, and it's hard to tell whether he's angry at me or Mr Robinson. One of them disabled the WIFI when they noticed me using my laptop, which I thought was a real crappy move on their part. At one point, it felt like the weekend was never going to end, it was the most boring two days I've had in my entire life.

"I don't think she did anything wrong, I mean, he didn't mention that she actually said anything rude, did he?" mum whispers to dad at the bottom of the stairs, as I walk down them. She takes one look at me, moves in closer to dad and continues whispering. "He was the one made out like our daughter was the problem, when his problem is with his own daughter."

"Yes, I didn't even do anything wrong," I interrupt, directing my comment at dad who clearly needs convincing that I am not the cause of all of this.

"This is an adult conversation, Wendy," dad replies. "Go back upstairs until we're finished."

"Well, seeing as I'm eighteen, I'm officially an adult," I tease back. He doesn't find it funny. Neither of them do. "Look, dad. I admit, we were both bunking college, but that's all I did wrong. Tianna's dad said that he doesn't want me to have anything to do with her anymore." I sound like a whining child. "I did try and stand up for myself and Tianna, but he basically stuck by what he said."

"But, why would he say that for no reason?" he replies, turning to face me with one hand making gestures as he talks. "That's what I don't understand. We've spent years trying to get you two to become friends. Why would he randomly just stop you from talking to her?" He scratches his chin and scrutinises me. Dad has always done this thing where he stares at me until I feel uncomfortable and tell him the truth, he's done it since I was a child, but I'm not lying, and besides, that doesn't work on me anymore.

"Honestly, dad?" He won't want to hear it, but I will tell him if he does want to know. He nods, still scratching his chin. "Because she is gay and I am trans. He must think that me being transgender, has caused her to be gay." It's kind of hard to get the words out. Every time I mention the word transgender he winces as if I've poked a finger through his side.

"So, let me get this straight. Mr Robinson thinks you've passed what you have onto her?" I'm not really sure how I feel about that comment, but if he is just using it as a way to clear things up then, sure, fine.

"Well, yeah, basically." I reply, trying not to sound too eager just in case he was trying to offend me. Without saying another word, he yanks his jacket off the bannister and storms off outside, slamming the door behind him. My heart sinks as I watch my own father slam the door on me, his body tense, face angry and his manner disgusted. At me.

"Get ready for college, Wendy. We'll talk later," mum says, walking back through to the kitchen as if none of that just happened.

"What is going on, mum?" I ask, following closely behind her. I hate it when they get secretive, I need to know what is going through dad's mind. "Have I made dad mad?"

"Nothing, Wendy. It's adult stuff."

"Stop treating me like I'm a child!" I yell back, I wouldn't dare get this brave in front of dad with the mood he is in.

"Don't talk to me like that, you're lucky I even stuck up for you-" She stops herself from carrying on with that sentence and takes a deep, quiet breath. "You shouldn't have been bunking college. He thinks you are a bad influence on Tianna, that is all. Go and get ready for college, don't make me tell you again." She turns away and switches the kettle on, standing there awkwardly as she waits for it to boil. Both of them were so strict with secrets when I was growing up. They said that no one should be making me keep secrets from my parents, and that I should feel comfortable talking to them about anything. They instilled it into my brain that I should always be honest, and it's now that I'm realising where the problem is. I don't know how to be upfront and honest, because my own parents don't know how to either.

"Hey, mum?" My voice softens to sound a little more childlike. She looks at me with confused eyes and then briefly scans the room. Almost as if she was wondering where that sweet voice just came from. "Can I talk to you about something?"

"Yes, of course," she replies suspiciously. Her mood lightens up as she heads over to the table and plumps up a cushion on one of the chairs, holding it out for me to sit down. "Do you want a hot chocolate?"

"No, thanks."

I hadn't really thought about this before I just went and did it, so I don't know exactly what I'm going to say or how I'm going to word any of it. I feel like I've tried to get through to her so many times that there really is no point in wasting my breath, but every time I have tried, she's been with dad. He's made his feelings very clear, but mum hasn't really said anything. Well, she hasn't voiced her opinion on it yet, anyway

"What do you want to talk about, darling?" She makes herself comfortable on the chair opposite me, placing her coffee in the middle of the table. The strong, overpowering smell off coffee beans, next to today's fresh flowers, isn't really a nice mix. I hate coffee; it stinks. She looks pleased that I've decided to open up to her. She used to love our girly days and would always try and get me to open up and talk about things during them. When that failed, she resorted to gossip, thinking it would excite me, but I have a strong dislike towards repeating and creating rumours.

"So, I don't really know where to start, if I'm honest. We've had the trans talk, so I'm not going to go on about that at the moment. I just wanted some advice." My head drops and body begins to heat up and sweat instantaneously. "You might not like it, but can you just hear me out?" My hands are shoved as far under the table as they will go, so that I conceal the fact that I am a shaking mess.

"Yes." Her voice is unexpectedly warm and inviting. "I can give you my expert advice. It's going to cost you, though," she teases, gently punching me on my arm. I don't know where she's learnt that, but she had better not try and do it to me in public.

"I think I'm in love with Tianna and I don't know what to do," I whisper. Strangely enough, saying the words out loud only made me feel more certain that my feelings are real. I look up to see mum's unreadable expression, staring at her for a few minutes to try and make sense of it. Nothing. "And, I don't want Mr Robinson to stop us from talking to each other. I'm sorry for bunking college and for being rude, but can I please, please have my phone back so that I can put this right?"

"And how do you plan on putting things right?" she asks inquisitively. She doesn't look impressed at all. "You do know that Mr Robinson is homophobic, don't you"

"Yes, I do know that bit. I just don't know how I'm going to put things right, but I really need to speak to Tianna. I haven't spoken to her since, and for all I know, they could be shipping her out as far away from me as possible." I feel a sharp pain in my chest at the thought of never being able to see her again.

Mum stands up and walks back over to the kettle, despite the fact that she hasn't even touched her coffee. "What makes you think you love her?" Her patronising tone of voice should have been enough for me to just give up, but I really need my phone. I'd be brave enough to go and get it myself, if I knew where she'd hidden it.

"I don't know, mum. She's supported me in ways I didn't even think were possible. She stood up for me, and she is the only person that treats me like I'm a real person, with real feelings. Also, it's definitely not a crush as I've never felt this way about her before." I feel slightly bad admitting I have no idea why I love Tianna, and it's difficult finding the words to explain exactly how I feel.

"I treat you like a real person with real feelings," she replies defensively, scrunching her face inwards and holding her hand out like a Diva. It wasn't meant to be a dig at her. I wouldn't have said anything if I had realised how it sounded. "It's a tricky one," she continues, crossing her arms and changing her facial expression to her thinking face. "I think first of all, you need to tell Tianna how you feel. I wouldn't go anywhere near Mr Robinson just yet." She walks back over to the table and sits in her chair. "Actually, I wouldn't go near him at all. I think you should just focus on things between you and Tianna. All we can do then, is hope that things don't turn sour between him and your dad." She picks up her now cold coffee and begins swirling it around in her mug – something she always tells me off for doing.

"So, let me just get this straight. You think I should tell Tianna that I'm in love with her? What if she doesn't feel the same way?" I reply nervously. Still can't believe I'm concerned about the way Tianna feels about me. I don't want to cross the line and rub things into her face too much, but I need her advice more than anything right now.

"Darling, I think you would know if she didn't feel the same way. If you love someone, the worst thing you can do is not say anything and live life regretting it. If she really doesn't feel the same way, you can remain as friends. No biggie." Why does she keep making such an effort to be cool? It's not cool at all, she's my mum! She walks over to the fridge, dragging a chair with her. "Here, hold onto the back of this, will you? I don't want to fall." She's scared of heights, bless her. She reaches up to grab my phone from on top of the fridge. What a clever hiding space, I could have torn the house apart and wouldn't have thought to look there. "So, if you two do get together, will that make you a lesbian then?" she asks with a cheesy grin on her face, handing me my phone.

"No, mum. I'm still transgender and still want to be a man." The smile slowly fades from her face. "I don't know what I will be, but I love her. I guess they do say all you need is love." I was hoping she wouldn't try and go there with the topic, but I guess I do owe her some clarity as, thinking about it, it does look a bit contradictory. I never thought I'd ever be asking my mother for advice about a girl and most certainly not Tianna. Saying that, though, I never thought my mum would happily offer me advice about a girl, knowing full well that it means I'm definitely not a straight girl at the least. "Should I do it now? Or wait until I see her?"

"Well, when are you going to see her?"

"We've got English today for second period. I'll do it today!" I jump up with excitement, wobbling the table and almost knocking her coffee out of her hands as I do. "Thanks, mum." I walk round the table and kiss her on the back of her head, before sprinting upstairs to go and make myself look my best. I don't think I've ever been so sure on something in my whole life.

Me: 'Hey, I've finally got my phone back. I'll get to the bus stop early today so we can have a cuddle and catch up before college? Let me know if that suits you. X'

I don't have any lessons for first period, it's just English and science today. Meaning, I've got plenty of time to browse the internet and look for tips on how to tell someone that you love them. Not being able to speak to her while mum had my phone, made me realise that my attraction to Helen was completely different to the one I have with Tianna. With Helen, I had a crush on her the moment I saw her, and couldn't stop myself from wanting to be around her all the time. I found myself constantly husting and longing for her every time she crossed my mind. When she stopped talking to me, and started dating Jessie I was more furious at Jessie for doing that to me. Don't get me wrong, I was and still feel humiliated and heartbroken by it all, but I feel like if that happened with Tianna, I will be devastated. My feelings for Tianna sort of popped up out of nowhere. I don't feel like I have any control over them, but I don't think of her and automatically feel aroused at the thought of us getting close. What I do think of, is her just being around.

Me: Guys, I've got news. I'm in love again.

Henry: It's just me online, dude. The others are at work. But, did I just read that correctly?

Me: You most certainly did. Did I ever tell you about that girl, Tianna Robinson?

Henry: I can't remember. Describe her to me so that I can try and think.

Me: Her dad works with my dad. I met her when I was eleven.

Henry: Nah, still not coming to me

Me: Ginger hair?

Henry: Nope, nothing.

Me: I expressed a strong dislike towards her?

Henry: The one you said looks like a cross between Peppa Pig and Voldemort?

Me: Yes. I didn't mean that by the way.

Henry: The one that's so weird, you're surprised her parents let her out?

Me: Yes. I didn't mean that either.

I guess I won't be introducing her to anyone anytime soon, because if any of that gets out, Tianna will probably never say another word to me again. And I can already see what that feels like.

Henry: Okay, I remember. So, who are you in love with, then?

Me: Her. Doofus!

Henry: What? How does that even happen? It's way too early for these mind games, ha!

Me: If I tried to explain it all to you, I'd probably sound like a lunatic, but I've recently taken the time out to get to know her, and she's perfect. She's so lovely! And she actually talks. Dude, the girl speaks English.

Henry: Ha! Love that. I'm sure she's been able to speak English her entire life, Paul. So, does she know how you feel about her?

Me: Nope, not yet. I'm going to tell her today. I thought about making it all special and doing something romantic, but then I thought it might actually be nice to just whisper it in her ear during English. What do you think?

Henry: I'm no good at this, but I do think whispering it in English sounds cute. Very good plan.

Me: I've sent her a text, but she hasn't replied. Should I call her?

Henry: Absolutely not. Just because you're in love, doesn't mean you should let your guard down. You should still play it cool, for now anyway.

Me: Yeah, I guess you're right. I've been lazing around for a while now anyway, I've got to go and get ready for college. I'll come back online later and update you on it all.

I ended up leaving myself thirty minutes to get showered, dressed, put my lady parts away and my boy parts on. I got dressed so fast, I wasn't able to put my cling film on properly, and there are little bits of it lightly brushing against my skin like a feather, making me feel really itchy. The cool breeze from the wind cools my face down, as I feel myself becoming anxious at the thought of telling her how I feel. I kind of regret bringing my biggest jacket out with me, as the warm sun makes my body feel like it's melting inside it. Saying that though, I can't be sure whether my overheated body is a result of my anxiety playing up, or the weather.

It's 09:57 and she isn't at the bus stop. English doesn't start until 11:00, surely she would have waited for me if she was here. I can't imagine she'd have come out of her way to get here, and then leave without contacting me if I'm not on time. Besides, we still have loads of time to get to college. It only takes twenty-five minutes from my house, there's no way she would have left that early. I can feel myself begin to panic slightly, as I fear the worst – Mr Robinson moving her as far away from me as he possibly can. Just before I've been able to tell her how I feel. Something like that would be just my luck. Finally lucky enough to find someone that is so perfectly suited to me, and has been for years, and they end up moving away just to avoid me. Typical.

"Hey," a recognisable, half broken voice says from ahead of me as I storm through the college gates. I was so focused on staring at the ground and avoiding everyone, I hadn't realised I was walking right towards James.

"Leave me alone, James," I reply back coldly, brushing past him. I don't really know what his part to play in everything is, but still, I'd rather not talk to him just in case he does have anything to do with it all. Even if he hasn't actually done anything, I haven't seen him stick up for me once. Not the way Tianna so easily did. Besides, what is it with him and Jessie trying to talk to me lately? If they've just realised that they made a huge mistake in doing what they did, it's way too late for that. The boys did always say that me and Jessie together were what made our group an enjoyable one, so I guess I'm not the only one to have lost out. "Actually." I stop and turn back. "Have you seen Tianna?" Normally I would have been embarrassed saying those words out loud, especially to someone like James, but I don't care. I need to tell her how I feel, before it's too late.

"Who?"

"Tianna, ginger hair. The one that used to always try and talk to me."

"Oh, you mean, the one you said was a freak and won't leave you alone?"

"Yes."

"The one that made your skin crawl every time you saw her?"

"Um. Yes"

"The one that you said you wouldn't be seen dead with?"

For crying out loud. "Yes."

"Nah, sorry, dude."

I expected to see Jessie, Josh and Cameron emerge from behind James when I was talking to him, but they didn't.

They did come to English, though. I made sure I arrived there in good time so that I could have a moment to talk with Tianna before we went into Miss Wortag's lesson and get forced to remain silent for two hours. But she didn't come. In fact, she didn't come to English at all, and she wasn't in the toilets when I scanned them before Science.

Me: 'Hey, I don't know what's going on at the moment, with your parents that is. I just really hope you're okay. If I've made you angry, in any way, please, just let me know so that I can put things right.'

No reply.

"Hello," Jessie says sarcastically, as I walk up towards our desk in Science. "I heard you've got a new girlfriend?" His face seething with fury, he looks jealous. "When did that happen then?"

"What is it with you guys, today? I told James not to talk to me. The same applies to you," I snap back. I can't control my short fuse.

"Sorry," he replies. "James doesn't talk to us anymore. I thought you would have known that." He grits his teeth. His eyes peering up at me while his head remains facing downwards.

"Why would I have known that? And did you just say sorry?"

"Because I thought you two were best buddies. Seeing as he thought the way I behaved was so wrong that is." Jessie's eyes narrow and nostrils flare. He looks at me, waiting for some sort of reaction, but I have no idea what he's going on about.

"Whatever you're talking about has nothing to do with me. I don't want anything to do with any of you."

"Fine." He huffs, turning to face the opposite way, almost as if to punish me.

Fifteen

Heartbreak

James sits next to me in science as opposed to Jessie. Odd, but I couldn't care less what they are up to. All I'm focused on is seeing if Tianna is in during break. He looks over at me every so often, thinks I haven't noticed and then looks away. I can tell that he wants to say something, but I can't forgive any of them. If Josh wasn't even there, and I won't forgive him for not talking to me since, James doesn't stand a chance. My body twitches, as I watch the clock ticking and wait for the bell to go, so that I can race to the toilets and search the lunch hall.

"Hi." James says quietly, looking over at Jessie and Josh to make sure they aren't listening.

"Hi?"

"You do know that I have never had anything to do with any part of what has been going on, don't you?" His eyes gaze into mine reassuringly. "I hope you know that I never would. I don't want to be involved in anything they are doing," he says under his breath, facing forward so as not to let Mr Ringer know that he is talking. To be fair on James, he has always been a good guy. He never gets in trouble or does anything out of line. Now that he has mentioned it, I haven't seen him do anything, but I didn't actually see who beat me up that night. All I know is that he was there, and he didn't try and stop it.

"Why are you telling me this now?" It's a little too late for him to try and be on my side now.

"Because I don't want you to think I am involved, and I wanted you to know that I don't have a problem with who you are. Every child, is a child of God." He smiles. It's hard to tell whether he is being sarcastic or serious, but his parents are very religious. Still though, the way that I am goes against everything that he believes in, so how can he be accepting of it? I don't trust him.

"I don't know what to say, James. I can't trust anyone." I feel sad pushing him away. Out of everyone he is normally the fair, opened minded and reasonable one. He doesn't like confrontation and keeps his distance when everyone starts messing around, although unlike Tianna, he's never stuck up for me.

"That's understandable." He looks disheartened. "I just wanted you to know that I don't care who you are. You're a good person, that's all that matters." His weak smile seems genuine. "I've stopped talking to them lot anyway, and no, before you think they kicked me out of the group, or whatever. I made a decision to stand up for you, eventually."

"What?" I whisper loudly, trying not to make anything obvious to the two out of three musketeers that are sitting at the front.

"Yeah. Cameron's become really nasty and has started calling the shots with everyone. They've turned into a group of pretty toxic people, and I don't want to be known as one of them," he replies. His facial expression scream out sincerity, but I'm still reluctant to trust him. I'm not really sure what to reply back to that, as there is a lot I would love to say about Cameron right now. I won't, though. For all I know, Jessie and Cameron could have set this up as a master plan to humiliate me even more. I mean, I have no idea how they will be able to do that as they've already done the most, but you can never really tell with them two.

Lunch

I've searched all of the toilets in the building, including the hidden staff ones in between the S and N wing. I've searched through all of the empty music rooms that I've seen Tianna bunking in previously. I've wondered up and down the corridors and looked in through the gap in the library door. I can't find her in the lunch hall or behind the curtains on the drama stage. Alice and Katie are sitting by the entrance and I overhear them arguing about whether the chicken or the egg came first, but no sign of Tiana. She isn't in.

"Have either of you seen Tianna today?" I ask them, instantly wishing I hadn't started a conversation with them in the first place. I do regret seeing Tianna as weird before I got to know her, but these two are a different kind of weird that I have no intention of spending any of my time with. If Tianna and I do progress to the next stage, there will be no double dates or mixing of our friendship groups. That's for sure.

"No, she hasn't been in today, but when you speak to her, can you get her to give me a call?" Katie replies warmly.

"Oh, just quickly!" Alice interrupts, "What do *you* think came first, the chicken or the egg?"

Christ almighty. "I have no idea, Alice."

As I scan the room again, I notice James sitting in the far right on a table on his own. He looks content eating by himself. Jessie, Cameron, Josh and their new team of bullies gather around a table at the back, far away from James. None of them paying any attention to him whatsoever. It's hard to tell whether this is a set up or whether James has genuinely stopped talking to them, but he doesn't seem to have noticed me in the hall, none of them have.

The next day

It is raining outside. The dark, gloomy looking clouds fill the sky with grey and the rain is smashing against my window. Children are jumping around in puddles for once, with their colourful wellies on with adults holding umbrellas up over their heads. The weather depicts the exact way my mind feels at the moment and it feels like the rain has purposely come out to play on the one day in ages that I feel this lonely. I was awake last night, looking at my phone and praying that I heard some word from Tianna. I scrolled through social media to find nothing. It's almost like she never existed. Her social media accounts have miraculously disappeared, her phone has been disconnected and she hasn't been at college. If she was bunking, I like to think I would be the first she would have told. Her parents wouldn't have banned her from going to college in a bid to keep her away from me, but there is a chance she could have been moved to a different one. Would they really do that just to stop her from seeing me? Surely not, when they were itching for us to be friends in the first place.

   The idea to go around to her house hits me like a light bulb and I quickly put my shoes back on, after falling asleep in my clothes in the early hours of this morning. I run straight out of the door, bringing my keys, phone and charger with me.

The world becomes a blur as I find myself running as fast as I can, ignoring everyone and everything around me. I'm not worried about what anyone may think of me running like an idiot through the rain, nor am I worried about accidentally bumping into anyone or having someone trip me up. My mind is focused. If Tianna's dad won't let me see her, I will simply go there myself. Nothing and no one will break us apart. I can feel my chest become tight and my legs ache with exhaustion, as I struggle to carry on running. It might have been a better idea to have brought my oyster card with me and jumped on one of the many buses that have driven past me in the time that it's taken me to get here.

Tianna's dad is outside their family home, sorting through boxes and dumping them into his car. They look like moving boxes. He walks into the house and comes back out with another two, piles them on top of each other on the passenger seat and then drives away. No sign of Tianna. The car drives off into the distance, turns right down Island Row and then disappears out of view, making it safe to go over there. I don't know what I am going to do when I see her. What can I do? I guess just knowing that she is okay will be enough for me. I just want to have a cuddle and hear her tell me that she isn't ashamed of me for the way I behaved. If her dad is moving them away, I won't let her go. I can't. I'll run away with her if I have to, or beg my parents to let her move in with us. I'll hide in her cupboard if her dad comes home and stay until her parents go to bed, so that we can pack her bags and leave. I'll do anything just to be able to spend the rest of my life with her. The saying 'you never know what you've got until it's gone' reigns true here. The past few days without her, have made me realise that I have somehow managed to fall madly in love with every single part of her. I cannot and will not live without her. Not without a very big fight anyway.

Blood rushes through my body as I pluck up the courage to knock on the door assertively. I am a man and I will be treated like one. If her mother is behind the door, I would like her to treat me like the respectable young man that I am, and hear me out as I beg her not to take her daughter away from me.

No answer from the door.

The curtains from the room on the bottom right twitch as someone quickly pulls away from the window. It must be Tianna. She has got to be in there. There is no way she could be anywhere else, unless they have managed to get her into another college so soon. Why didn't the window twitcher just open the door? My knocks become louder as begin to panic that I'll never be able to see her again.

No one answers.

"Tianna!" I shout through the letterbox, not caring who might be in there, or what they will do to me if they know it's me. "It's Paul, come to the door I have something for you." If she won't answer because her parents are stopping her, she can at least let me know that she is okay. If she won't talk to me because she is upset with me, hopefully me turning up will let her know that I am not giving up that easily. I let Helen go without a fight and I *thought* I loved her. I *know* full well that I am in love with Tianna. I'll never forgive myself if I let go, like I did with Helen.

She doesn't come to the door.

"Tianna. I'm sorry for what happened," I plead through the letterbox. Every word echoing through the empty hallway. "I wanted to protect you, but I wasn't brave enough to stand up to your dad. I've learnt my lesson and I won't ever let anything happen to you again. Please, please come to the door." My head hurts as I find myself praying that she opens the door. The thought of her not letting me in causes me to well up. "I don't know if it's that you don't want to talk to me, or if you can't, but if you don't have a phone at the moment, I just wanted to give you mine. I've got it here with the charger and I've recently put some credit onto it. I'll top it up however often you need me to, and I'll ask my dad to buy me a new one so that we can talk. Will you at least take the phone, please?" I don't want to risk putting it through the letterbox in case someone else picks it up and throws it in the bin knowing it's from me.

Still no answer and no signs of movement from within the house.

Why is it that whenever something goes right for me, life has to come and make things ten times worse? It feels like every time I manage to take one step forward, life pushes me at least two steps back. Except the only difference is that every time I am pushed backwards, there is a new kind of heartache waiting for me. After everything Tianna has taught me, I refuse to believe that she is purposely ignoring me.

Heavy rain starts to fall again, soaking me in ice-cold water, sending shivers through my body. The hairs on my arms stand to attention as I try and rub them warm. "Listen. It's starting to rain, but I don't want to leave. I saw your dad packing boxes into the car and I've got this burning feeling that he might be moving you away. Tianna, I can't let you move away. I can't lose you. Not after everything we've been through together. Please let me help you," I sob, sniffing back snot as I try and stop it from running out of my nose. "My mum is good at talking to people, if you don't want to let *me* help, at least let me talk to her. She will be able to get through to your parents. I know she will." My fingers are beginning to ache from holding the letterbox open.

Three hours pass and no one opens the door. The wind makes my body feel wet from where I've been drenched in the rain. This is the first time in a while that I've been frustrated that it's raining. Now I know how normal people feel. My charger is soaked, and my hands are white and wrinkled with how wet they are. My clothes are sticking to me and as I try to stand up; it feels like they are weighing me back down again. The thought of having to leave without having seen her or being able to have given her my phone is agonising. I've come this far and although I know that someone is in there, I can't understand why they won't open the door.

"You alright there?" A friendly voice says from behind me. It's the postman. He has a small, funny looking umbrella hat tied around his bald head, and a bunch of letters in his hand. He probably either thinks that I am a thug trying to burgle the place, or a complete joke of a human being in general.

"Sorry. I'm just looking for my friend," I reply, moving out of the way to let him gain access to the door.

"The young girl?" He knows her!

"Yeah, Tianna?"

"She left this morning with her mum. I live across the road. Do you want me to let her know you're looking for her when she comes back?"

"No, it's okay, thanks. I'll see her tomorrow at college. Do you know if they are moving out? I saw her dad packing boxes into his car when I got here." Just the thought that she is coming back is enough for me. Besides, I don't want her dad to know that I have been sniffing around again.

"I have no idea, lad. They're a very private family. Keep themselves to themselves. The parents were very angry at her when they left, though." He looks over his shoulder and then leans in towards me, lowering his voice. "You probably haven't seen her because she is grounded or something. They're very strict on the poor lass. They're always arguing over the fact that she isn't allowed to do anything, sometimes their arguments go out into the street and the whole neighbourhood can hear." He softly smiles before posting the bundle of letters through the letterbox and making his way off the driveway.

My efforts to get her to open the door were wasted as she wasn't even inside in the first place. Typical. It's a good thing I didn't end up putting my phone through the letterbox. Tianna taught me to trust my instincts, that was one of the moments she would have been proud of.

The walk back home is painful. Hail stones smash into my face and bounce off my skin, making my arms sting badly. It doesn't compare to how hurt my heart is, at the thought of not hearing from the only person that has ever made me feel safe in who I am. Nothing seems to matter now that Tianna isn't around. In the short time that I've known her properly, I've become so fond of her that I'm really disappointed I hadn't given our friendship a chance all those years ago.

Thinking back to everything that has happened, this is the lowest I have ever felt. All I seem to do is let people down, cause problems for those I love and hurt everyone with my cowardly behaviour. My inability to stand up for something I strongly believe in has managed to ruin everything I have with everyone that I love, especially with Tianna. I had the option of pulling her out of the car and carrying her away somewhere safe. After everything she has told me about her parents, I should have known that was the right thing to do, but once again, my fear left me numb and unable to do anything other than freeze in the moment.

I didn't hear anything from Tianna the next day, or the day after that. Or even the day after that. It's been just over a week, and it's like she has disappeared from the face of the Earth. She hasn't been in college and not a single person has asked where she is. I feel like someone knows something, but no one wants to tell me what it is. Probably because no one seems to even care that she is missing, not even Alice or Katie. I keep having to remind myself that she is a strong woman who knows her own mind. The conversation with the postman made me feel slightly at ease knowing that they argue. Arguing means she tries to stand up for herself. Arguing means not backing down and not being able to see eye to eye with the other person. It means that regardless of what is going on, she isn't going to give up on making her parents accept that she is the way she is.

"Can everyone hurry up and take a seat please." Miss Wortag demands as she bursts through the door and dumps her bags on her desk. She's in a worse mood than she normally is. That can only mean trouble. No one listens to her, except me, but I was already sitting so it doesn't count. Tianna's empty seat next to mine kind of makes me feel cold, but I'm slowly beginning to accept that she won't be coming back and has really moved away. I miss her, more than she'll ever know. "Everyone, sit down, now!" The warthog screams at the top of her lungs causing everyone to suddenly jump into their seats and fall into a dead silence. I've never heard her shout o loudly before. She's never really had to. Every time she opens her mouth the class get scared and stop talking. Maybe she's losing her touch.

She takes one long look at me. Her sorrowful eyes staring at me the way she did when she was 'trying to get through to me'. She closes her eyes, her wrinkled eyelids squeeze shut, before taking one deep breath and opening them to face the class. "There is no easy way to say this, so I am just going to come out and say it. Tianna Robinson committed suicide last night. Now, I know all of you know who she is, and that this will come as a huge shock to all of you." Her voice wobbless as she fights on through her sentence. "In a few minutes, we will all go into the hall where we will have a minutes silence for her and her family. If anyone would like to talk to myself or any of the other teachers about what happened, we are always here to support you."

"Wait." I yell loudly without putting my hand up to ask for permission to talk first, and without even feeling bad about it. "What did you just say?" Surely, I misheard, that can't be true.

"Wendy, Tianna has committed suicide."

"You mean, she's dead?"

"Yes," Miss Wortag replies. "She sadly passed away last night."

Sixteen
Grief

Floods of people begin to flow into the dining hall, all tiptoeing past me, whispering and staring at me as they do. One boy points in my direction causing a group from Tianna's music class to look back at me, while another group continue to whisper, making it obvious that they are whispering about me. Everyone in the hall sits down on the cold floor like we did in school. Line by line and row by row, everyone files in next to each other, filling the empty spaces and squeezing as close to the person next to them as they can, to allow more room for everyone else.

The hall is packed with people; some are crying, others look numb, but none of them actually knew Tianna. For the first time in history, the entire building has become silent, without anyone being asked to do so. Miss Wortag is holding a bunch of tissues up to her eyes, using it to wipe the tears away before they've had a chance to drop. The headteacher, Mr Hannaball stands still, with his hands down by his side and both of his fists tightly clenched from under his blazer sleeves. His undeniable angry expression makes it obvious that this has hurt him, just as much as it has the rest of us. He begins to make his way over to the front of the hall. His face numb and lifeless, but his head held high. He reaches the front and turns to face the main hall, coughing loudly to get everyone's attention, before tapping the microphone to make sure it is working. Everyone stops whispering and looks up at him.

"Okay, guys. By now I am assuming that a lot, if not all, of you have been told the news about Tianna." He quickly scans the room for reactions, to make sure that the majority of us had been told. "I am very sorry to confirm that she committed suicide last night." He drops his head and holds his hands together. "Now, I know I speak for everyone when I say that we are all shocked and heartbroken after hearing the news. I have asked everyone to come into the hall, to ask you all to refrain from posting about it on social media, but I am confident that you will all respect that anyway." He makes a swift glance over at Cameron. "The family are going through a very difficult time, and have asked us to support them by ensuring that it does not circulate on social media. Katie and Alice have arranged a memorial service for her at the end of the day tomorrow in this hall. If you would like to come and pay your respects, you are all more than welcome to join us. Thanks, guys."

"Sir, are we going to be allowed to go to her funeral?" someone interrupts, before he's been able to make his way back out of the spotlight.

"I don't know anything about the funeral at the moment, Alex. With everything that has gone on, it is fair to assume that the family will let us know the details of the funeral arrangements when they are ready to do so. I will, of course, let you all know, but in the meantime, it does not mean that we cannot honour her memory here, internally." None of this feels real at all. I have a gut feeling that this is all a hoax, and I'm expecting Tianna to text me tonight and tell me that she is alive and fine. She'll probably tell me she is planning on running away, and may have tried to fake her death or something. You know, so that her family wouldn't come looking for her. I don't know, but she wouldn't just kill herself and leave me, surely. I don't believe a word of it. I've come to know her so well. There's just no way she would do anything like that, she's a fighter.

As everyone in the hall begin to get up and leave, they all start whispering again, with eyes twitching back at me and then back towards the group they are with. Almost as if they know that she is really alive and think that I am in on it too.

"Are you okay, Wendy?" Miss Wortag gently holds onto my shoulder, looking at me as if she wants to give me a big hug. "Would you like to say a few words at the memorial? You don't have to give me an answer now, but have a think about it. I think it would have meant a lot to her." Her eyes glossy, sad almost. As if she has any right to feel sad. Out of everyone, she was the worst, and if she could completely brush me off the way she did, imagine what she could have done to Tianna. It's only now that someone has 'killed themselves' that she has learnt how to be compassionate. How convenient. I can't talk to her. I can't talk to anyone. I push her arm off me and storm out of the hall, towards the exit gates of the building. I can feel my eyes burn and begin to swim with tears at the thought that there is a possibility it might actually be true. I storm straight out of the school gates and begin to make my way home. I want to be alone and wait for Tianna to come and find me. Failing that, I want to get into bed, curl up into a ball and stay there until she comes back.

She's not dead. She can't be.

And, what does Miss Wortag expect me to say? I can't stand up there and pretend that I'm happy that she's gone. Everyone usually always says 'they're in a happier place now', but she isn't. She would have been in a happier place with me, I would have made sure of it. I don't want to say a stupid speech for her. I don't even have anything I'd like to say on the subject for that matter.

The walk home is lonely and empty, and I can't help but look at my phone every two minutes, waiting for her to text me. It doesn't feel real. It just can't be real and I refuse to believe it. Tianna used to make stupid jokes, tease me and wind me up about silly things. She found it hilarious when I would walk into the room thinking no one is there to have her jump out at me causing me to scream for my life. She loved tripping me up when we were walking and burst into tears of laughter when I walked into a lamppost one day.

She is the kind of person that would do something to make you worry and then say 'JOKING!' knowing full well that I was not impressed, but still finding it funny anyway. I'm expecting her to come back and tell me this was all just a joke that went too far. I need her to tell me that everything will be okay. I don't feel sad that she is gone because I don't believe that she is.

I've found myself standing still in the middle of the street, unable to think of what direction to take next and literally feeling like my whole life has come to a standstill.

A little boy comes up to me and stares at me for a moment. I smile at him awkwardly in an attempt to not look like a complete creep, without realising that by standing here alone, smiling at a child, I've probably gone and done just that.

"What are you doing?" he asks curiously.

"Um. Nothing? What are you doing," I reply, looking for his apparently non-existent parents. He's a lot younger than Jake is, but kind of reminds me of him in some ways. It's the chubby little cheeks and dimples on either side of his mouth.

"Why do you look sad?"

"Sad? I'm not sad."

"You are a big boy," he says proudly. "Sad spelt backwards is das, and das not good. That's what my mummy says." There is something about the innocence of children that warms my heart a little. Their little faces as they try to figure the world out, and their brutal honesty, no matter the situation. If I looked like a girl, he'd definitely have called me one.

A car horn sounds from behind me, causing me to jump around hoping that it might be Tianna with our getaway car.

"Bye," the little boy says as his mum pulls him away, while giving me a dirty look and eyeing up the car.

"Get in," dad says, leaning over to the open passenger's side window. My head hurts from the thought of what happened to Tianna, I don't want any more grief and I certainly don't want to be left alone in a car with someone that hates what I am. "Wendy, please get in," dad pleads when he sees me remain where I am, his facial expression looks worried. Fearful, in fact.

"What's wrong, dad?" Although I feel numb and unable to care about anything other than Tianna, the sight of my dad feeling sad instantly makes me feel protective. I get into the car and slouch down on the seat, avoiding eye contact so that he doesn't realise what is going on. He switches the engine off and pulls me in for a long, warm and comforting hug, making me feel weak in his embrace.

"It's okay, honey. Let it out. I'm here," he whispers, holding onto me tightly.

The warmness of his hug causes me to burst uncontrollably into tears and I feel myself hyperventilating. My hysterical crying soaks dad's shirt in tears as I cling onto him tightly. It has all started to hit me all at once and as much as I have tried to be strong, the way Tianna would have wanted me to without her, I no longer feel like I can. It hurts so bad, I feel like I can literally feel every part of my heart tearing apart. The thought of her feeling so lonely that she felt like that was her only way out, feels no different to a knife, slowly being pulled through my chest. The agony is unbearable, and I can't get the thought of her hurting herself out of my mind, although I am fully aware that she wouldn't want me to be thinking like that.

"I don't think I can do this, dad," I sob, holding onto him so tight that I'm unsure if he is even able to breathe. "I'm scared. I'm not strong enough." The lump in my throat feels suffocating, except this time, I don't mind if it does suffocate me.

"I know, I know." He isn't saying much, but his words are comforting. I pull away and wipe the tears away from under my eyes, trying to catch my breath as I continue to hyperventilate.

"Five things you can see?" he says calmly.

"N-N-Not now," I blurt out, unable to catch my breath.

"Five things you can see," he repeats, asserting his authority.

"A- A- I can't"

"Yes, you can," he replies, his voice low, quiet and still very calm. "Take one look around you and tell me five things you can see."

"A shop, a car, you, a cat, a tree," I reluctantly reply.

"Four things you can hear?"

"Traffic, the radio, you and people talking."

"Three things you can smell?"

"A barbecue, petrol. I don't know, dad."

"Okay. Two things you can feel?"

"I don't feel anything, dad."

"How do you feel?"

"Empty."

"One thing you can say?"

"She's gone." The words feel like they are cutting me into pieces, and I'm still struggling to get my head around the thought of her no longer being here. I don't think I can.

Home

My room feels cold and empty. Nothing has changed apart from my bedding, which mum must have done when I left this morning, yet everything feels so different. The remote has been placed neatly by my bedside cabinet and my laundry basket is empty. My eyes are stinging from all of the crying which is making me feel tired, although I know I won't be able to sleep and if I do, all I will see is Tiana hurting herself. I can't help but keep my phone in my hand just in case she does text me, telling me that everything was a joke and that she really is fine. At this stage, I can't imagine being angry at her for it. In fact, I will probably be the happiest I've ever been, just knowing that she is alive and okay. I'll obviously make it very clear that she can't pull a stunt like that again, though.

Dad knocks on my door before letting himself in. "I ran you a bath," he says quietly, standing by the door with both of his hands locked together respectfully. "I know you probably won't want to eat, but I will order you a pizza too. You can eat it tonight or tomorrow, it's up to you. Can I come in?" I nod, yes, although I'd much rather be left alone. He comes over to sit next to me on the bed. I can sense how awkward he feels at not knowing what to do, but his company will suffice. "Mum knows and is on her way back from work, but I've told her to leave you alone for tonight. You know how she is." His words are like music to my ears. The last thing I want is mum asking me a million questions about it. She means well, and I know she is probably desperate to support me, but I need to be alone – Dad understands that.

"Thank you," I whisper back, unable to get my words out properly.

"Wendy, there is something I feel like you need to see," he replies, pulling a neatly sealed envelope out of his back pocket and handing it to me. "Tianna's mother came over this afternoon and dropped this off for you."

"What is it?" I ask, knowing full well that if it's from Tianna's mother, it's probably a letter blaming me for it all. I'm not strong enough to take the blame for this, not yet.

"I think you had better read it. Do you want me to stay with you while you do?"

"No, it's okay." My voice trembles. "Dad?" I feel weak.

"Yes?" His eyes light up a little.

"Miss Wortag asked me if I wanted to say something at Tianna's memorial in college, but I don't know what to say." I don't even know if I want to say anything at all.

Dad smiles sympathetically and tucks loose bits of hair behind my ear. "I had to do a speech at Granny Daphne's funeral. You probably don't remember that because you were so young. I spent ages thinking about what I was going to say and ended up so stressed that I gave up, but on the day it all just came to me." He rests his large hand on my back comfortingly. "If you can't think of what to say, talk about how she made you feel and then say goodbye to her." He swallows and looks up at the ceiling as tears fill his eyes. "It'll come from the heart, that's all that matters. I'll be downstairs if you need me, I love you."

As he leaves the room, I turn the envelope upside down and carefully place it in my bedside drawer, in exchange for my laptop. There's no way I'll be strong enough to read that anytime soon.

Paul

Me: 'Is anyone there?'

No reply. Not from a single person. They've all probably washed their hands of me for not speaking to any of them for a while.

Olivia: 'Welcome back. How are you?'

Me: 'I don't know.'

I don't even know why I've started a conversation knowing that I don't know what to say. I guess I just want the comfort of knowing that someone *is* still there.

Henry: 'What's up buddy? You can talk to me. I take it you spoke to her then?'

Me: 'I don't know where to start.'

Olivia: 'From the beginning, I've got all evening.'

Drops of tears make it hard to type on my laptop properly, and difficult to see if what I am saying makes any sense. My hands automatically stop typing as I figure out how to word what I am trying to say, without making it sound like I am talking gibberish

Me: 'She committed suicide last night. She is... was one of the kindest people I've met. I don't know what to do.'

Henry starts typing and then stops. Starts typing and then stops. Starts typing again and stops, before starting again.

Henry: 'Ah, man. I'm so sorry to hear that. I wish I had all the right words to say now but, I don't. Do you know why she did it?'

Me: 'No. Well, I mean I do have an idea. She is a lesbian and her parents are homophobic. She lost all of her friends when she came out and her family tried to force her to be someone she isn't. She's had a pretty hard time of it all lately.'

Henry: 'Ah, that's awful.'

Me: 'The thing is, though, I don't know how I feel. Is it so wrong that I feel so, so, so angry at her? Because I do. I'm furious that she's left me. We'd just found something special and now it's gone, forever. I'm so angry at myself too, because I always thought that my problems were far worse than hers, and I hadn't noticed how much she was suffering. I didn't really pay much attention to her skinny hands, or the way she behaved around her parents, compared to how she was with me. I just thought it was normal, because she hated them. I saw her loneliness as weird and said some really horrible things about her. Honestly, I don't think I'll be able to get over this.

Henry: 'You know, sometimes people feel like that is their only option. They don't realise how much pain they're leaving behind, because the only thing that is going through their mind is how much pain they are suffering at the time. I understand you're hurting, I don't even want to begin to imagine how I would feel, but I refuse to allow you to blame yourself for any of this. If you knew that she was planning on ending her life, you would have dropped everything to help her. That's what makes you a good person. What you aren't, and will never be, is a mind reader. You probably won't believe it now, but she is in a much better place.'

Me: 'If there is such thing as an afterlife, I'll never forgive her for it. Ever.'

In order to avoid the whole 'being in a better place' crap that's about to come, I log off. I want to talk to someone to understand my pain and not just say that they do, because it's the right thing to say. He doesn't get it, and whilst I know that he has all the right intentions, the thought of her being in a 'better place' doesn't help at all. I could have made the world a better place for her. If I wasn't so cowardly in front of her father, maybe she would have realised that. I would have grown stronger and more confident in time, though. Especially after that incident. I would have protected her against anyone that doesn't accept her for her, and fought with tooth and nail for her. I knew I shouldn't have given up when I went to her house, something deep down was telling me to go back every day until I saw her, but I was scared that it would have made her dad even more angry. Now, look. I'm furious at me, her, her parents, the teachers in college. I'm so sick of it all. When will my nightmare of a life just end?!

The rest of the day went by too quickly. Dad left a giant pizza on the floor outside my bedroom that I haven't touched, and no one has bothered me. The heartache is numbing, but the burning desire to read the letter from Tianna's mum is overpowering, even though I know full well that it is going to hurt like hell. It might provide me with some answers regarding what happened.

The envelope has 'Mr' written on the front of it in messy handwriting. It's actually from Tianna.

'Mr,

You are strong, kind and caring. You are beautiful in every, single way. You are funny. You are smart. You are you. I want you to go out there and not be afraid to show everyone who you are and what you are made of. I want you to celebrate my life with your head held high, knowing that I am in a much happier place. The times I had with you were the best times of my life. You saved me. You made my last few months on this Earth worth it. You made me laugh and feel something that I have never felt before. You are special. Don't be sad or angry. Don't feel lonely without me and don't blame anyone for what happened. I have always said that you ALWAYS have a choice. I had a choice and I made one that would have made everything go away.

I am sorry that I have let you down and left you feeling like you are on your own, but the truth is you are not and you never will be. You have parents that adore you. They might not understand you right now, but they love every inch of you. Your job is to make them understand. You have two little brothers that sit at home waiting for you to come through the door so that you can play with them. You have your nanny Shelby who, in her eyes, can do no wrong (She clearly has no idea what we used to get up to, ha!). You have your uncle Toby who adores you and will support you in everything that you do, and auntie Trina who will always welcome you with open arms.

You also have me. You might not be able to see me or hear me, but I will always be there. When you stub your toe on something, that is me reminding you that I am there. When you walk into a lamppost, I will be there laughing at you. When you drop your phone and curse the way you do, I will be there chuckling. When you are crying, I will be crying with you. When you are lonely, I will be walking next to you. Every time you see a robin – it is me. Every time a wasp follows you around a room, don't run from it – it is me chasing you for attention the way I do. Every time the sun shines brightly in your room, waking you up and making you face another day – it is me.

I want you to stand up for who you are. I want you to face people and tell them that if they don't like it, they can do one. Hold your middle finger up high, and be so unapologetically you that everyone has no choice, but to accept it.

The difference between me and you is that although you couldn't see it – you have always been a lot stronger than I was. You were put on this earth to make a difference.

You are so special and so unique, but you are not alone. There are thousands, if not millions of people in your shoes. They are confused and lost in who they are. They have no one to talk to that will really understand, and for some of them, standing up and telling the world who they are is a task that has proved to be too difficult. Your task is to go out there and help as many of them as you can. Be their strength and show the world that transgender is just as normal as everyone else.

I love you – I always have and I always, always will.

T x'

Seventeen
Moving On

It has been exactly fifteen days, twenty-two hours and thirty-six minutes since Miss Wortag told us about Tianna. The time went by in a blur and it's hard to remember much of it. Mum spent a lot of time trying to force me to eat, which made her and dad argue as he became protective. I've found myself unknowingly looking at my phone every so often, in the hope that she would have gotten in touch. But she didn't. Alice and Katie postponed the memorial service while the family waited for the post-mortem results, while Mr Hannaball spent the time educating everyone on the LGBT+ community. As if no one knew about it already. The extra time gave me enough time to write down some sort of speech, although I still haven't decided whether I'll be reading it or not. I haven't really spoken about her much since, so I don't know if I'm strong enough yet. I've spent the last two weeks staring into space, feeling hopeless, numb and cold.

    Tianna would have expected me to read her letter and go back out into the world feeling confident, but it has had the complete opposite effect to that and didn't help in any way. I keep it under my pillow and sleep next to it, inhaling the scent of her perfume from the bottle that she gave me, in an effort to convince myself that she is still here. I've gone from feeling totally lost and confused to angry and cold. I hate every, single person that has now decided to care, when it's too late. I hate the teachers for failing to notice that something was going on with her and for proving it, by turning a blind eye to everything that has been going on with me. Miss Wortag especially. But most of all, I hate myself for letting her down. I will never be able to forgive myself for not being someone she could call when she needed to talk. It would have taken just one person to support her, and she didn't even have that. I wish I could take back every negative thing I ever thought or said about her, because she was perfect. I'm still seething that she acknowledged I would have felt alone in her letter, but still decided to leave me anyway. I mean, she definitely wrote the letter before she died, so why, after writing it, did she go ahead and kill herself? I feel like I am not good enough for anyone to stick around and despite how strong our brief relationship was, I just wasn't enough.

Alice and Katie have decorated the main hall of college with candles and flowers. Instead of making everyone sit on the cold floor, chairs have been laid out in rows across the hall, with benches on the sides for those that do not have enough space in the centre. There are more people here than there were two weeks ago, the majority of them sobbing and talking amongst themselves as they look around at the effort the girls have gone through. I feel more nervous than anything. I've got to get up in front of all of these people and read a speech I've written, about the death of someone I love. I've never had to do anything like this before, and it's now that I've realised I am in no state to stand up and read anything about Tianna.

A large photograph of her pops up, projected onto the wall using the halls projector. She looks young. Her hair almost bigger than her petite little body. Her smile looks as if she doesn't have a care in the world. She is holding a certificate in the photo that reads, 'World's most caring person', which just sums her up completely. Even before she knew what love was and realised that she was gay, the world knew that she was a kind person. The photograph turns into a slideshow of different snaps of her growing up. One with her winning a swimming competition in primary school, a maths competition in holiday camp and getting her college acceptance letter. There is one of her at her sister's wedding in a stunning bridesmaid dress and another of her and her parents. They all look so happy in that photo. You wouldn't believe that anything was going on with her parents if she hadn't mentioned it. This was obviously taken before she came out to them.

"Thank you all for coming," Mr Hannaball begins. His attitude a lot more positive than it was two weeks ago. "I'm sure Tianna would have been happy to know that so many of you care about her and want to show your support." He slows his voice down as he scans the room. I think he's looking for me, but I'd rather he didn't see me, assumes I haven't come and then make someone else read a speech. "Wendy is going to read a few words and then we will follow that on with a moment's silence." His eyes pace back and forth, row by row, as he frantically searches for me. "We will then lay a wreath that Katie and Alice have made, down in the garden area for her. Wendy?" He announces, finally finding me and signalling for me to join him on the stage next to the pretty wreath.

My hands are sticky, and the sound of my heart blocks out any other sound in the hall. I can feel loads of beady eyes watching me as I quickly walk up onto the stage, knowing full well that Tianna would be encouraging me to be brave and do this. My head feels a little light headed as I look down at my feet and focus hard on not falling over in front of everyone, but I'm secretly hoping I do faint. As I get to the stage, my face begins to feel hot and oily, and my neck sweaty. If my fingers don't stop rattling against each other, I won't be able to read anything. The firm grip on the crumpled piece of paper loosens as I slowly peel my hands open and turn to face the hall full of pupils. The hall has fallen in silence as the college waits for me to read out my speech. I can't look up through fear of seeing Jessie, Cameron or Josh mocking me. I don't know how I'd cope if they were to make light of a situation like this.

"Tianna." I take one deep breath in and focus on the task at hand, my hands shaking so much that I can barely read my own writing. "Tianna was a good girl, and she didn't deserve to go the way she did." My throat feels dry, making it difficult to get my words out. "When I first met her, I made the mistake that everyone else did and just assumed she was weird. I didn't want to talk to her or give her the time of day. I didn't want to be in the same room as her. It creeped me out when she tri-" The thought of me being so cold towards her has me blubbering up like a baby, unable to get any more my words out, crying frantically in front of everyone. My speech is two pages long and I've already lost myself after reading out the first few lines. The hall remains silent, but beyond my sobbing and through my tears I can't hear or see anyone mocking me.

A soft hand rests on my shoulder. It is James, smiling at me reservedly. He takes the paper from my hands and shuffles up next to me by the microphone, making me move out the way to give him space. My heart warms a little at his support.

"It creeped me out when she tried to talk to me." He stops to clear his throat, before straightening up his back, pulling the paper in closer to his eyes and squinting as he tries to read it. My handwriting isn't the easiest to thing to read. "I remember watching her dissect her burger, just to put it back in the bun again and eat it, and I remember clearly thinking that she was a freak. I remember seeing her in the toilets and sitting there worried that she was going to jump over the cubicle and kill me." He stops at that bit as his lips begin to twitch. It would have been funny if she was here, I guess. "I remember how annoyed I was that she wanted to be my friend, and my reluctance to give her a chance. It was only when I stopped behaving like the sun shined out of my backside, that I realised she was one of the most beautiful people I had ever met in my life. She was brave, strong and fearless. She went above and beyond for the people she cared about and did so, so bravely. She stood by me and taught me how to love myself again."

James pauses for a moment and holds his hands over his mouth before taking a deep breath to continue. "She was the only person that gave me a chance. I loved her, with all of my heart and I will love her until the day I die. But now, I guess I have to say goodbye." He hands back the paper and spuds my shoulder before walking back off stage to sit back down. The hall begins to fill with sounds of whispering, making my head spin and hands tingle. They're talking about me. They probably think I'm pathetic seeing as I wasn't able to read out a simple speech, especially after letting Tianna down the way I did. Rather than stand here knowing full well that everyone probably blames me for it, I begin to hastily make my way out of the hall. Pupils begin to get up and make their way towards the exit, making me feel claustrophobic and unable to escape. The tingle in my hands get a little more intense and the spinning room is making me feel like I'm about to faint, but that doesn't stop me from trying to get away. My feet almost trip up over themselves, as I speed through gaps in between people and head towards my safe space. In through the creaky door and slamming the cubicle door behind me.

I can't breathe.

The floor feels like it is going to cave in and swallow me up, and the loud monotone, ringing noise in my ear is deafening. I feel like I'm going to die, I can't breathe. *'Five things you can see'* I try and tell myself, as I struggle to control my breathing. The quick, sharp breaths aren't allowing enough oxygen into my lungs, but I don't even know how to breathe normally anymore, I can't think straight.

The door creaks loudly as it opens and quietly as it closes. Someone has just walked in. I quietly take one deep breath in, and allow my trembling body to exhale slowly as I listen out for signs of life behind the door. Is it Tianna?

"Wendy," a stern, recognisable voice says from behind my cubicle. "This is Miss Wortag." Her voice serious and unsympathetic. "I've just been informed that you were seen speed walking into the toilets and looked like you were about to cry. Can you open the door please? I would rather speak to you, as opposed to a door." She sounds frustrated. Well, if she doesn't want to be here, she doesn't have to, because I don't want her here either. There is no way I am opening the door to her. The last face I want to see is hers, especially when I'm already in a rubbish mood. "Open the door now, Wendy!" She raises her voice, which I'm assuming is her attempt at getting me to do what she says. It's not going to work.

"Okay." She lets out her usual sigh of annoyance. "Please forgive me for failing to listen you when you needed it the most. You looked at me to support you and I brushed it off as nothing. After seeing what happened to Tianna, I don't want you to go down that route either." She still sounds annoyed, but I guess she's done it now; said something nice and cleared her guilty conscience. She moves around the room for a while. Her shadow follows her back and forth as she does.

"Wendy," she starts again. The tone of her voice tired, but gentle. "I lost my son eleven years ago. He was fourteen years old and he took his own life because he was being bullied." She stops, and for a second, I can feel her pain without her having said another word. "I ignored what was going on with you, because I thought that it was nothing in comparison to what he was going through, and I was so wrong. I have been struggling to come to terms with it. As much as I love my job, seeing happy kids walk around college without a care in the world kills me a little bit more inside every day. I put on a hard front, Wendy, because it felt like the easiest thing to do, but now I don't know how to be happy. I've tried to ignore my grief for so long, that I haven't yet grieved for him at all and I've had the worst life ever since. I don't want you to do the same thing. You deserve to be happy and live a life full of enjoyment from here onwards."

"But I'm scared," I sob. I had no idea that Miss Wortag had a son. I feel bad that I've been so harsh towards her, but grateful that she has opened up to tell me that.

"I know you are, but me and all the other teachers are here to give you the support you need. Now, will you open the door so that I can see you are okay?" she asks lovingly. Her voice still monotone, but slightly higher pitched. It seems she really has blocked out all emotion since her son died.

Miss Wortag walks slowly towards me as I open the door, holding her arms out wide and pulling me in for a warm embrace. Her clothes smell of a mixture of fresh linen and dead cigarettes, and her breath smells of stale coffee but despite that, I still let out a massive cry and allow her to comfort me.

Home

"Wendy. Can I come in?" Mum asks from behind my bedroom door, which I've accidentally left slightly ajar. She's already opened the door fully before I've had a chance to reply. She stands in the doorway. Dark bags weigh her sunken eyes down as she struggles to make eye contact with me. She looks exhausted. Her once average sized figure has become skinny unhealthy looking. I've never seen her like this before, in fact, I'd never even noticed she was losing weight. "Jake has been scouted by Hither Green football club. He wanted to tell you yesterday, but he wasn't able to," she says quietly with tears in her eyes.

"Oh, wow that's amazing! When did that happen?" Jake is crazy about football and they've been trying to get him signed up to a team for some time now. He really deserves it, he's worked so hard for it and there's no doubt that he's a professional football player in the making.

"Two weeks ago," she replies proudly, smiling as she thinks of it. "You were actually the first person he wanted to tell, but with everything going on, we thought it was best he didn't mention anything yet. He was going to tell you yesterday in the hope that it cheered you up a little but when he heard you crying in your room, he came back downstairs. He really misses you. We all really miss you." She wraps her arms around my shoulder and pulls me in for an awkward half hug. Two weeks is a long time for a little boy to be waiting to tell his big sister something important. Two weeks is too long. The thought of his disappointed face, watching me walk straight into my room and slam the door is heart breaking, and I can't help but feel remorseful. "I love you, darling." She bursts into a silent cry, covering her face and holding her finger up, doing the 'one minute' sign. I can't bear the sight of my mother crying. Out of everything that has happened to me recently this is up there, not far behind from the thought of Tianna hurting herself. I slide my arms in around her chest like I used to when I was little, lean in and hug her tightly as we both cry silently. What a mess I have made of my whole life so far and look at how much I've let her down. We've done nothing but fight over the past year, but at the end of all of it, all she really wanted was to be there for me. In her own, weird and confusing way.

"Love you too, mum."

Another knock at the door makes us both stop and stare at it. Mum clearly didn't know anyone was in either.

"Come in," mum brazenly says towards the door. Isn't it meant to be me that gives people permission to come into my room?

Dad pops his head around the door. "Can I come in?" I love how he just completely ignores my mum and actually respects my privacy. Dad's not bad when he wants to be. He walks in carrying bags of shopping as I nod in response to his question. It's lovely to see that he has treated himself to some retail therapy during this difficult time. It must be so hard on him. I mean, he did just lose someone he loves and can't seem to get his head around it, so why not. He drops the bags by the bed and walks straight over to me, embracing me in another one of his warm cuddles. It feels good to have my parents back again, whether they are ready to accept me for me or not. "I bought you something. It's only little, but it's the little thing that counts, eh?" He smiles shyly, pointing towards two posh looking paper bags.

"What is it?"

"Have a look." He reaches over to the bags and hands one to me, keeping one for himself. Inside the bag is a long, black box with fancy writing on the front. It doesn't sound like there is anything solid in there. It doesn't feel like there is anything in it at all. "Don't just play with it, open it, then!" he teases, guiding my hands over to the edge of the box in an effort to help me open it. Another thing he used to do when I was a child. He gets excited when he buys me things and it's normally hard for him not to rip them open himself, even though he knows full well what's in there, seeing as he was the one that bought it. I slowly lift the lid and slam it back on again as I notice what looks like patterned clothing. Something is telling me he's bought me a dress and I don't know if I'll be able to pretend that I like it. Not today, anyway.

"Open it, sweetie." Mum interrupts, looking at me with trustful eyes. She must have been able to read what I was thinking just by looking at my facial expression. I take one deep breath in, close my eyes and prepare myself to pretend that I'm really happy about the dress, as I slowly open the lid.

It is a pair of boxers. Designer boxers.

Boxers?

My first ever pair of boxers. From my dad. Did he accidentally give me the wrong bag?

"Dad?" I don't know what to say.

"We love you, darling, and we just want you to be happy no matter how that might be. I think it is safe to say that Tianna's death has taught us all a lesson. I don't know what I would do without you, Wendy." Tears roll down his face, mine and mum's as we all lean in for a hug. I don't remember the last time I felt this close to my parents.

"Does this mean I officially have a big brother?!" Jake yells excitedly, as he bursts through the door and bundles himself onto my lap, sending all three of us into a akward, hysterical laugh at the thought of it.

Eighteen

Looking Back

I have very few memories from my childhood. I remember when my granny Daphne died, and dad broke down telling us at the breakfast table. I also remember when mum's water broke when she was pregnant with Jake, and I shouted loudly, "Mum you've wet yourself," confused as to why she told me off every time I did it, but then went ahead and did it herself. I remember dad rushing around the house, packing random things into a bag and on the phone to Uncle Toby, asking him to hurry up and come over. The next memory I have from that moment was mum coming home with Jake!

My great grandad died when I was around four years old and mum was heartbroken. It was the first time I had seen her cry. It broke my heart and has stuck with me ever since. She flew out to Ireland to go to his funeral and came back three days later, still very sad.

One memory that will always stick with me is Christmas thirteen years ago, when I was five years old. The months running up to Christmas were the most magical times of my life each and every, single year. I would count down the days until Santa paid me a visit, and the closer I got to opening all of the windows on my advent calendar, the more excited I would get. I would lay awake for hours every night, praying that, that year I would be lucky enough to meet him. Christmas eve was the best, I would leave out a minced pie and some milk for Santa, a carrot for Rudolph and a little card saying '*Thank you*' handwritten by mum and sealed with a kiss by me. Mum and dad would tuck me into bed where I would wait and wait and wait. The waiting never really worked out, as I would wake up bright and early on Christmas day wondering what the hell happened.

Unlike most children, my favourite part of Christmas wasn't just the presents. I loved having my family over; everyone was just so happy on Christmas day. There was something magical in the air that made families get together, and made that one day of the year the best out of all of the other 364 days that we had.

That Christmas was the first day that I realised that I was different, though. I remember creeping into mum and dad's room at 5am, asking them if it was morning yet and being yelled at to go back to bed. Eventually, they came to get me and I went running into the living room so fast, they barely had a chance to blink before I was there. I stopped as I got to the doorway of the living room, analysing all of my presents that had been neatly organised in descending order. I scanned them all, looking for the one that looked like the best one and stopped at a large, square shaped item. It was wrapped in red paper that read 'Ho! Ho! Ho!' all over it, sealed with a pretty gold ribbon that was sellotaped to a name tag with my name on it. I dived towards it and started ripping it open, trying to guess what could have been inside – the remote-control car that I had asked for? Or maybe that robot dog that ate *real* food and made *real* dog noises? I remember thinking it could have been the telescope that I begged dad for months prior to that, but the box was a little too large for something that small.

When I unwrapped the present and looked at the box, my heart sank with disappointment as my eyes focused on a big, fat, pink buggy with a baby and bottle attached to its hand. I sat there with the box on my lap and five other unwrapped presents around me and sobbed; ungrateful for the fact that I had been lucky enough to even get presents in the first place, and so unhappy that Santa had made me the complete opposite to what I had wished for. Mum asked me what was wrong and why I wasn't pleased with what I got and I remember sobbing "I didn't want a buggy, mummy, I really wanted a Robo dog or a remote-control car."

She wasn't pleased and neither was dad. They both looked at each other with guilty eyes before mum reminded me that the particular buggy Santa had made me, was the newest one that everyone wanted. She told me that Santa went through a lot of effort to make me those and reminded me that he was still watching my reactions. She then went on to say that the baby looked just like me with the brown skin and bushy hair. She seemed more excited than she expected me to be when she told me that we would be twins; while she pushed Jake around in his buggy all day, I would push my baby, reminding her of what it was like to push me. The buggy really should have been gifted to her. The rest of my presents were so disappointing that all I can remember from them is seeing them all neatly lined up in front of the fireplace. I have no recollection of what was behind the wrapping paper and none of playing with any of them afterwards.

Mum used to invite the whole family around and would make a huge roast with all the trimmings. We would pull the crackers open after dinner and read out the not so funny jokes that came inside them. The adults would reminisce on funny childhood stories, and we would all raise our glasses (or sippy cups) in a toast to 'family.' Everyone was just genuinely, happy. Aunt Trina made us watch hour long soaps back to back and Granny Daphne would always buy me these giant, life sized dolls that were almost the same height as me. Every year, I was given a new one from a different part of the world; that year I had been given a Vietnamese doll. She came with a diary that told me a bit about her country and I loved it. I was so intrigued to find out about different parts of the world, how far they were from me, the time distance and most of all, how different all of the dolls looked. My cousin, Sharina, would bring her dolls and play with me for hours while the adults drank mulled wine. Sharina is a lot older than I am and I could see the dolls she brought over were old and hadn't been played with in months but she would always make the effort.

Whilst we all sat down to have dinner, all the adults would talk about whatever it is adults talk about. Sharina would generally get involved in the adult conversations and I would sit there, interrupting mum every two minutes with something random that popped into my mind. After dinner, we would exchange gifts and I, as the only baby in the family that was old enough to open presents, would always be given my gifts first. Uncle Toby made me a mini wishing well. He used to make these awesome toys in his garage and would always create something that had an amazing story behind it. The wishing well was painted Yellow and had 'Wendy' written on the top and a wheel that I had to turn in order to make a wish.

"Once you've made your wish, turn the wheel three times and really feel in your heart that your wish will come true. Go on, give it a go, put your hand on the wheel, close your eyes and make a wish." He pointed towards the well. I picked it up with big, beady eyes, excited to make my wish knowing that one day I would have it.

I closed my eyes and thought long and hard about the one thing I wanted more than anything in the world while everyone in the room went quiet. Then I whispered, "I wish I was a boy," with a big smile on my face. Proud that I had put the only wish I wanted out into the universe and that if I really believed it, it would happen. I turned the wheel three times and really felt in my heart that my wish was going to come true. I was so excited. I opened my eyes to find everyone looking at me with blank expressions on their faces. They were so quiet you could have heard a pin drop and none of them really seemed to know where to look.

"Well, at least she didn't wish for anything expensive!" Dad jokes, breaking the silence and making the whole family burst into tears of laughter.

Aunt Trina grabbed hold of my hand and managed to get out: "You are a funny little character, Wendy. You never fail to make us laugh! Don't you ever change," as she carried on laughing with the rest of the table. I couldn't understand why everyone found it so funny and I could feel my face blushing with embarrassment. It's only now when I look back on it, that I realise how utterly pathetic they must have thought I was; so much so, that they all thought I was purposely trying to make them laugh!

Confident

Confidence. What does it mean to be confident? Does it mean certainty? Full of conviction in what you do? Brave? It's a word that I have always struggled with, but determined to be. I've never fully figured out how to be truly confident in myself, in my body and everything that I do. I'm not the type that is brave enough to go out without worrying about what other people think. I've always been scared to speak up in front of a crowd full of people, or explain something that someone doesn't understand. I've never really been able to stand up for myself or ignore negative comments. I have been confident enough to know that I am transgender, but not confident enough to say it proudly. I've been confident enough to face my parents with it, but not confident enough to *make* them understand.

I'm confident that I want to change the way the world looks at those that don't fit into the 'norm', but not confident enough to be the face of it all. My experiences in life have taught me a lot, but the most valuable lesson I have learned is that you will never be happy until you are able to find true happiness within yourself. I have spent years fighting myself and not knowing how to behave. I lived two lives just so that I didn't upset those that would have been offended by Wendy saying she wanted to be Paul. I hid the best parts of me from the people that I was closest with, in an effort to protect *them.* I wasn't confident in how I looked, the things that I did and the things that I said. I was a coward in thinking that someone or something would fix everything when it all laid within *me*. I blamed myself for everything going wrong, without realising that the reason it all *was* going wrong, was because I was attracting the worst into my life, just by refusing to be grateful for what I already had.

Gratitude

Apparently, in order to feel real happiness, you must express gratitude for everything that you have in your life and you have to *really* mean it. But how do you express gratitude when everything seems to be going the wrong way? What is there to be grateful about when life is so hard sometimes?

I haven't once been grateful that I have always had a family that loves me unconditionally. When Helen left me, I wasn't grateful that she had made me realise my worth. When Jessie, Josh and Cameron turned against me, I wasn't grateful that if it wasn't for them, I would probably still be hiding my true identity now, and would have been struggling to come out with it all. If it wasn't for everyone ignoring me and brushing it off, I wouldn't be so determined to make the world see us. I didn't express gratitude that Tianna came into my life and changed my whole world around. I didn't once show gratitude for my group of online friends that despite knowing the truth, stood by me and supported me throughout it all. Sometimes, they didn't even realise they were being as supportive as they were.

I was angry and resentful at everything. I hated everyone including myself. It is only now, when I look back on it that I realise that I am the product of my own feelings. Whatever negative feeling I had, resulted in negative things happening. I have spent the past two years practising how to be happy and express gratitude for every, single thing in my life and I have noticed a significant change in my experiences. I am shy but fiercely emotive. I love hard and hurt even harder. I have fought depression, anxiety and bullying. I feel powerful, strong and unstoppable.

Looking back on everything that I went through in college, I guess Tianna was right when she said that I would have been okay. There is not a day that goes by that I don't think of her, though. Every decision I make and every emotion I feel makes me think, 'What would Tianna do?' Her logical look on life is the one that I have adopted for me, and has seen me through some difficult times since.

My parents, despite everything, have tried their hardest to support me. It's easier for mum to call me Paul than it is dad, but he is getting there. Max has taken to my new identity easily, but still calls me 'Weddy' every now and then. The one person that has surprised me the most is Jake. He is everything I could ask for in a brother and more. The minute my parents accepted me, he went straight out into the world and told everyone proudly that his big sister has now been replaced by his brother. He is so proud of me it makes my heart melt. When I go to his football matches, he proudly tells all of his friends that I am there. It's made our bond so unbreakable that I can't imagine my life without him. His favourite part of me being his big brother, is when mum gives us money to go shopping. He loves buying matching outfits and having me go into the men's toilets with him. Despite the fact that I still have to go into the cubicle and close the door behind me. He just proudly does the same, even though he could easily use one of the urinals.

"Paul, thank you for coming," the doctor greets me at the door, shaking my hand and then my parents' as we walk through and take a seat. The leaflets about fighting cancer, having sexual health screenings and information for new parents always seem so interesting when I'm at the doctors. He rushes over to a window and pops it open, before taking a seat and loading something up on his computer. "So, following on from our last appointment. Did you think of any questions you wanted to ask?" I was completely speechless the last time we were there. The big words he was using went over my head and when I got home, I had completely forgotten what everything was called. Luckily, mum's embarrassing notepad and pen came in handy, as she was able to remember everything and research it all, so that she could dumb it down and explain it to me differently.

"I have a few questions actually, doctor," mum interrupts politely. She reaches for her bag that she had placed on the floor, and takes her glasses out, fixing them onto her nose before flicking through her notepad. "The bilateral mastectomy that you spoke about. What will happen to Wendy's nipple? Paul, sorry." She blushes with embarrassment as she gets my name wrong again. She is trying, that's all I can ask.

"The nipple won't be removed. The mastectomy is just to remove the breast itself. The skin, nipple and everything else will remain the same. It should take around four to six weeks to recover." He is looking at me, but directing his answer to mum. Which is why I didn't really want to bring her in the first place.

"And how long after that will the bottom surgery be?" she pushes. I know she is anxious about losing her little girl.

"The bottom surgery is done in different parts," he replies, rubbing his hands together on the desk in front of him. "The hysterectomy will remove the uterus and may include the removal of the cervix, ovaries and fallopian tubes. The metoidioplasty is what will move the clitoral tissue forward so that it is in the approximate position of a penis." Mum scribbles away frantically as he repeats the long words that he used the last time we were here. I have no idea what any of it means, and if I'm honest, I don't really care. I just want my boobs removed and a willy. "The testosterone injections will have enlarged the clitoris. The phalloplasty is the surgery that constructs the penis. Skin will either be taken from the forearm or the thigh. It is a very complex procedure and will be completed in a few surgeries as opposed to the one." So, he's basically saying I'm going to be in and out of hospital a few times with the amount of long words and surgeries he's just mentioned. I'll never understand how someone is able to learn such big words, without their heads exploding, but each to their own.

Mum and dad hold onto each other's hands tightly as I cringe at the thought of the surgeon talking to them about my clitoris and new penis. I think this is something I probably should have done alone.

"Paul." He looks at me with concerned eyes. "There is just one thing we need to discuss before we go ahead with any surgery." This doesn't sound good.

"Go on."

"Have you ever thought about having children of your own?"

"Yes," I reply back nervously, avoiding eye contact with my mother. "Why?"

"Well." He cuts a quick glance at mum, who is leaning in closely. "Once we begin lower surgery, there is no going back." He pauses dramatically, as if that was meant to have a negative effect on me. That's exactly what I want, I don't want to go back. "At the moment, you are in a perfectly healthy state and will be able to have a baby of your own. By that I mean carry a baby of your own. Once you have surgery you will never have the chance to experience that again." He briefly looks at my parents and then back to me as mum straightens up and pushes her glasses back up the bridge of her nose. I think it's just hit her that once I have my surgery, it means she won't ever get those precious pregnant moment with her only daughter.

"What do you mean?"

"What I'm trying to say, is that we can remove your eggs, freeze them and when you decide you want children, you can have IVF treatment with your eggs." He stops and waits for mum to catch up with her scribbling. "Or, you can have children yourself and then choose to have surgery at a later time." His words hit me a little as I had never thought about how I would go about having children. I always just thought it would happen.

"But, what if I don't ever meet anyone that wants to have IVF with me?"

"Well, then you won't be able to carry children as you won't have any of the body parts you'll need to carry one. There is always the option of a surrogate, though. I strongly suggest you go away and think about it. Take as much time as you need."

A baby.

A baby changes everything.

With the way my past two relationships went, there is a high chance that I won't be able to find anyone to have children with. Not everyone will be as accepting and want to have IVF treatment with me, knowing full well that they can get sperm from a real man that produces millions every time he lets one out.

"How do you feel, sweetie?" mum asks excitedly as we head back to the car.

"I don't know, mum."

"Well, do you think you could carry a baby of your own?" She's trying not to sound keen, but she's so excited at the thought of me having a baby. I feel really bad for putting her through all of this. "I mean, I'll be here to support you all the way. You won't even have to leave the house while you're pregnant if you don't want anyone to see you like that." Yeah, there's no doubting that she won't be there to support me.

"Yeah, I guess I could just stay inside. I mean, how hard can it be. It's only nine months, right?"

"Exactly, pumpkin. So, do you think it's something you could do?" She pushes, she just doesn't give up.

I don't know how I feel about having a baby of my own. I hate my body enough as it is, but with everything that's gone on, can another nine months of being stuck in it be that bad? If it means that I will be able to have a baby that is biologically mine without having to wait for someone to carry one for me, how hard can it be?

To be continued.

Printed in Poland
by Amazon Fulfillment
Poland Sp. z o.o., Wrocław